Fascinating Book p.H.

THE LANDING PLACE

A NOVEL

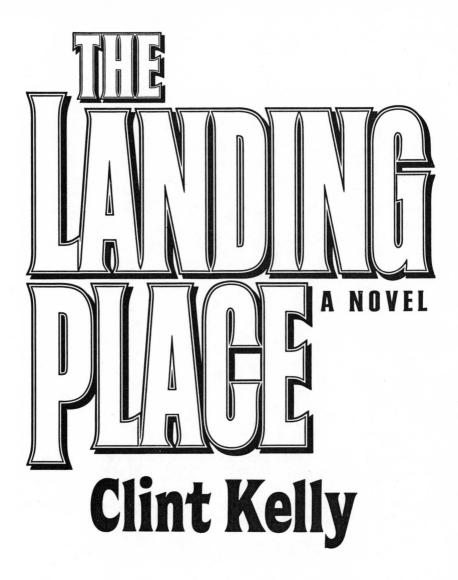

THE LANDING PLACE

A NOVEL

Clint Kelly

A JANET THOMA BOOK

THOMAS NELSON PUBLISHERS
NASHVILLE

Published in Nashville, Tennessee, by Thomas Nelson, Inc., and distributed in Canada by Lawson Falle, Ltd., Cambridge, Ontario.

Scripture quotations are from the NEW KING JAMES VERSION of the Bible. Copyright © 1979, 1980, 1982, Thomas Nelson, Inc., Publishers.

Library of Congress Cataloging-in-Publication Data

Kelly, Clint.
    The landing place / by Clint Kelly.
      p.   cm.
    ISBN 0-8407-3463-8 :
    I. Title.
    PS3561.E3929L36   1993
    813'.54—dc20   92–23307
                                               CIP

For Cheryll, the love of my life.
You have made for me a safe landing place,
where in life's adventures I may go
for rest and restoration.
Thank you, cheri.

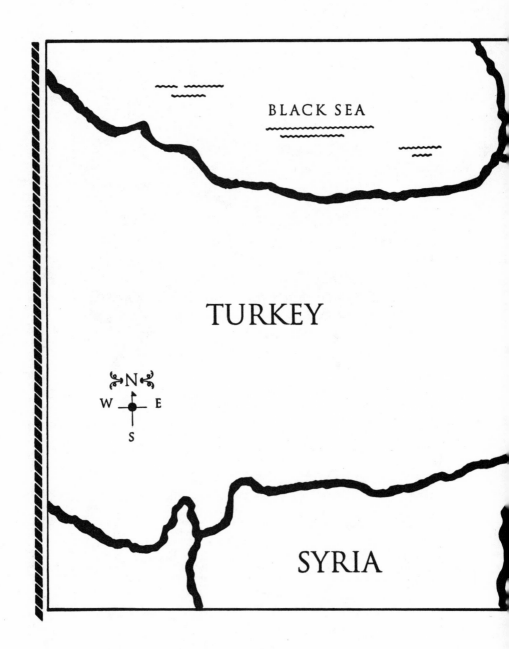

THE LANDING PLACE

A NOVEL

CHAPTER

1

THE GULLS WHEELED and cried, forming a feathered phalanx about the rented Plymouth sedan that wound its way over the rutted track. In the distance was a stark white cottage hugging the sea cliff and looking for all the world like an enormous mound of gull guano.

Reg Danson smiled. *So that's the home of the godfather,* he thought. The left wheel fell into a rut, and the steering wheel fought to follow suit. The car bucked down and up. Danson checked the rearview mirror, half expecting to see a tailgating gull plastered against the back window.

His lean, tanned face broke into a grin. *Yeeha! Ride 'em, Reggie!*

Is this any way for a prematurely gray, thirty-nine-year-old cryptoanalyst to act? he chided himself. He relished his job as agent and project coordinator for the Enigma Society, a private foundation based in Phoenix and dedicated to unraveling mysteries of hidden significance. People looked at him funny when he tried to explain. Sometimes it was simply easier to say he was a plumber. No one had to ask what a plumber did.

Except the lady at church who asked him to fix her shower drain. She was a bit miffed to find he was a plumber of mysteries. He wasn't trying to mislead anyone. Besides, he was a pipe and wrench man of sorts. A cryptoanalyst ranged the world over banging on the pipes of human understanding. A planet gone mad with crime and corruption needed a tantalizing mystery or two, a biological bagatelle or an archaeological whodunit now and then to keep it on track, to keep people humble yet ever searching with their God-given curiosity.

And if he had to plunge a commode now and then in the line of duty, what of it?

The society of enigmatists for which he worked was headed by Richard Bascomb, founder and president of one of the largest heavy equipment manufacturers in the business. International clientele. Money to spend on pet projects. So far, just a voice at the end of the phone, but a generous one.

Danson carefully negotiated the fringes of a mud puddle that had all the appearances of bottomlessness. *I wonder if the godfather's even home.*

The job meant the freedom to play sleuth and attempt to solve the confounding enigmas of the world. Bankrolled by a man of wealth and principle, a man he never saw and who seldom meddled, Reg was content. Mercifully rare were those times of nagging doubt, of a disquieting sense that it was all too neat, that one day the job description would expand to include something beyond his ability.

Lately, he'd been assigned to a zoological trust in Chicago that wanted to establish a breeding bank for endangered species. He inventoried existing rare species and had spent the better part of a year along the Rio Negro in Brazil tallying the astonishing varieties of life in the Amazon rain forest. A particularly controversial part of the study included attempts to clone already extinct species—such as the woolly mammoth—by removing the DNA from preserved remains.

But without warning he had been pulled from the project and sent to the Oregon coast to see Arthur Bryce, a renowned mountaineer considered to be the godfather of a special band of treasure hunters. Among their ranks were businessmen, evangelists, princes, soldiers, scientists, and even an American astronaut. Their quest: to find Noah's Ark in the mountains of Ararat in eastern Turkey.

Bryce was in his early seventies and had climbed Mount Ararat twenty-one times. Although others purported to have photographs and actual pieces of the Ark, Bryce had been denied so much as a sliver of proof he could call his own. Ever the pragmatist—the curmudgeon, some huffed—he said it only proved how many opportunists lived in the world.

Bryce claimed to hate the rivalry between search expeditions, believing that in the end it was to every child of God's advantage that the Ark be found. And yet he rarely gave interviews and often denied access to the research. No one but Bryce could get at hundreds of files and miles of video and audio tape comprising the world's most extensive research on the hunt for the massive wooden boat. According to the ancient Hebrew texts, eight righteous people and breeding pairs of every kind of land animal rode to safety on the back of a global flood divinely designed to wipe out wicked mankind. The Ark's final mooring place was sworn by many to be fourteen thousand feet above sea level in the bosom of Ağri Dağh (pronounced *a-ru' da-u*), the Turkish name of Ararat.

Ağri Dağh was known to the fearful peasant farmers at its feet as the Mountain of Agony.

Reg laughed as a leaden oaf of a gull slid down his windshield, stumbled forward, and formed a portly hood ornament. It tottered there, facing into the wind. When the car at last braked to a stop in the yard, the gull pitched forward and with a lumbering flap of its wings barely cleared the roof of the cottage. "It's the seabird fat farm for you, Gus!" Reg called after it. He checked the hood. At least Gus had been polite.

It was at times like this when he missed Barbara the most. She had loved accompanying him on these junkets into the sometimes strange workings of God. They had spent a Christmas in Texas studying the overlapping footprints of humans and a three-toed dinosaur on the Paluxy River. They had explored three continents in search of the elusive apeman creatures known as *yeti*, and they had sipped lemonade together in the ancient excavations of Tel Jemmeh in the Negev.

On their first expedition to Loch Ness together, he'd lost her. Two glass-bottom exploration boats hunting "Nessie," the supposed sea serpent, had collided in dense fog, and Barbara was thrown into the lake. Reg nearly drowned himself in a frantic but fruitless search of the murky depths. He knew she was safe with God, but the lonely ache of her death, though lessened in the two years that followed, haunted him still.

No one appeared to be home in the cottage. Reg knocked loudly several times. No answer. The cottage was an ill-kept affair perched dizzyingly close to a hundred-foot drop and the surf-pounded rocks below. Bryce was a recluse—as the song goes, no phone, no pool, no pets. And no patience whatsoever for the tabloids and fortune hunters who had hounded him since his sensational discovery of a Sumerian shrine in the shadow of Ararat, a shrine engraved with cuneiform inscriptions. A competing search team beaten to the site had screamed fraud, and a disgusted Turkish government had canceled all exploration permits for two years. No one knew what had become of the cuneiform inscriptions, and Arthur Bryce wasn't talking.

But "Bombastic" Bascomb had financed more than a few of Bryce's expeditions, and apparently the two of them were tight.

If Barbara had come, she would have poked him playfully in the ribs and started a game of ring around the cottage. From the day he left the Smithsonian, their love had been given a chance to grow, and they had regained a sense of fun and romance buried in his five years as curator of cryptoantiquities, or mysteries of ancient times. A scientific bureaucracy within a governmental bureaucracy within a city oozing bureaucracy was tough on the nerves—and on a marriage. In light of their shared commitment to God, it was at times intolerable.

The crunch came when Reg protested a proposed pseudoscientific display in the National Museum of Natural History, an exhibit flagrantly prejudicial against the creation theory. Called "Dynamics of Evolution," it filled the entire main exhibit hall, outlining the evolutionary process in the latest electronic razzle-dazzle. But nowhere among the museum's four million specimens out front or under lock and key was there the remotest mention of divine creation—not even as a quaint belief held by a religiously fanatical few.

He went to the press with his resignation, and on page one he was quoted quoting the Duke of Wellington: "Divorce religion from education and all you will produce will be a race of clever devils."

Their church rallied around and the mail was three to one in support of Reg's stand. Yes, he'd done the right thing, but a loss far greater than the job was the estrangement of their only child. Tony was fifteen then and bent on a career in archaeology. But unlike that of his parents, his search did not turn up evidence of a divine hand in history, but rather a raft of unanswered questions. He was fascinated with theories of lost links in the evolutionary chain and ancient astronauts said to have been sent from the gods. He was rapidly developing a passion for an eventual superhuman evolution and a radical hatred against defense programs whose nuclear arsenals threatened that very evolution.

When his father made headlines by questioning the integrity of the Smithsonian Institution, Tony began to view his parents as themselves an increasing threat.

Still, the summer following the Smithsonian affair began beautifully with a promise of reconciliation. Reg invited Barbara and Tony to help him assemble a wonderfully intact six-thousand-pound blue whale skeleton for a small scientific research institute in New England. They literally whistled while they worked, so thrilled to be a family again, facing a tough challenge together. It was like an enormous jigsaw puzzle with thousands of interlocking pieces, an animal wonder so exciting that even Tony lustily joined in the work party hymn sings, tussled playfully with his dad, and actually seemed for a time to shed his resentment.

"Hello? Mr. Bryce? Hello!" Reg shouted about the yard, but he was only one against the cries of the gulls and the crashing of the surf. Then he saw, far below on the beach, a tousled, snowy-haired figure in faded white shirt and ragged Robinson Crusoe pants kneeling in the sand and praying against a great twisted stump of driftwood. Head bowed, back erect, skin weathered a rich chestnut brown, the man was a natural extension of the wood and wind. For just a moment, it seemed to Reg the man had been there on the beach praying for years, rubbed and shaped by the tides.

Reg picked up a stone to throw near the praying man, then thought better of it. He could wait.

The explosive argument had come midway

through the whale skeleton project when Tony wondered aloud why when some sea life had abandoned the depths to evolve a life on land, whales had remained water dwellers. Could their occasional beachings be ongoing displays of a primordial urge to evolve into land creatures?

Reg instantly bristled at so preposterous a theory. He prayed for strength to control his anger and use the question as an opportunity for teaching about creation. He spoke of "leviathan," how the psalmist made mention of the leviathans God had made to play in the sea.

Tony snorted with all the swagger of a fifteen-year-old and said, "Geez, Dad, I'm a little old for a Sunday school lesson. Why don't you level with me? All the evidence you've got to go on is in your guts. Science has the fossil record."

It was all Reg could do to keep from striking his son with a three-foot section of whalebone. How many hours had they spent arguing over the flaws and gaps and inconsistencies in the fossil record? Could Mr. Tony Smart Guy Danson dig up a ten-thousand-year-old eyewitness who had actually observed the transformation of one species into another? It hurt to be challenged and doubted by his own son. Reg had to admit he didn't know which disappointed him more, to have his parental authority and understanding questioned or to hear God's master plan dismissed as religious myth.

Pride was a many-headed monster.

The man on the beach rose suddenly, bowed to the air, and strode from sight beneath the cliff face at Reg's feet. In a remarkably short time he emerged fifty feet south of Reg's position as if he had risen on an elevator of air. He wasn't even breathing hard.

He stopped and looked at his visitor with all the warmth of an ocean gale. He strode to a side door in the cottage, calling out in a husky baritone, "Five minutes to straighten up."

Him or me? Reg wondered wryly. He was vaguely uneasy with this tall explorer whose carriage and hoary mane were reminiscent of a beachcombing Moses. Imagine investing your life in the search for Noah's Ark! What strange wonders and exotic intrigues were locked in the godfather's head and heart? Had he brushed within yards of the Ark without knowing it? Why did he live in seclusion when he must be fairly bursting with knowledge and spiritual insight?

Bascomb had been unusually vague, although his tone seemed barely able to contain something. What? "Drop everything and get out to the coast, Reggie, my boy. See Arthur Bryce. He has something for you. Can't say too much about it. Suffice it to say neither you nor I, nor most of mankind for that matter, will be the same again. This is big, Reggie. Very big indeed. The biggest. Can't say too much though. Said too much already."

Well, they didn't call Bascomb bombastic for nothing. Everything was the end of the world to Rich Bascomb. Everything.

"And Reg, son, listen. Be careful. Be very, very careful. What Bryce has for you is wonderful and deadly. Handle it right, and there'll be healing for us all. Make a false move, and you'll be dancing with the angels. I wish I could say more but this is not a

secure line. You can't find a truly secure line anywhere anymore. Nor a good cup of coffee, for that
matter."

Did Bryce know more than he let on to the
world? What was waiting inside that dumpy little
cottage that could rattle nations and kingdoms?

Reg walked over to the spot where Bryce had
emerged from below. A narrow path clung to the cliff,
so faint a trail that a week's erosion could scour it
from sight. It was the way the godfather of
"ark" aeologists moved over the face of the earth—
with little trace.

*Barbara, Barbara. You would adore this craggy
master of conundrums, himself a puzzle.* Life after
the whale skeleton blowup had been no mystery.
Tony was allowed to work at a small boat rental
nearby. Time for them both to cool off. Reg and Barbara finished the project with the help of three local
college students. The day the Dansons packed the
wagon for the trip home and said their good-byes, the
call came.

The phone was ringing at midnight when they
dragged road-wearily into the house. An officious
secretary quite used to placing calls for her employer
at all hours informed Reg that Richard Bascomb and
a highly select group of enigmatists from around the
globe admired Mr. Danson's courage in taking on
"the plunderers of spirituality." They wished to hire
his services—at twice the salary the government had
paid plus a travel stipend. Bascomb Earth Movers,
Inc.—"If you felt the earth move, Bascomb was on
the job!"—had the highest credit rating from Standard & Poors, employed more minorities, sponsored

more youth sports teams, gave a higher percentage to charity . . . just ask the Phoenix Chamber of Commerce.

Reg did and discovered Bascomb was a corporation more secure than Fort Knox. As a private foundation, however, Bascomb was difficult to trace. Enigmatists didn't take out newspaper ads. But then, neither did cryptoanalysts. Both were as rare as brain transplants.

Reg and Barbara prayed. It felt right and they took the risk. He liked that about faith. It was like putting a foot in the Red Sea and expecting the waters to part.

The sea did part, and for two glorious years Reg and Barbara tramped in seven-league boots and swung from the vines of adventure. Only Tony rained on their parade by stoutly refusing to join them on what they said would be the grandest education any boy ever knew. It pained them to leave him behind with grandparents, but he seemed to settle into school and not suffer a great deal from their prolonged absences.

For their last wedding anniversary together they secretively dashed about finding the perfect gifts to express the amazing grace that had entered their lives. They opened their eyes to discover that each had given the other a David Livingstone jungle helmet. They laughed for days.

Then Tony went to college and Barbara drowned. For three months Reg suffered an icy loneliness before grace took root. Late one night researching prehistoric animal annihilation theories, he felt a trace of the old contentment well up as if Barbara were again by his side and God was again eager to share His marvels with them. The sense of purpose and divine support grew, and before long he was again investigating with gusto what the earth and its inhabitants had to say about their Maker.

He often spoke aloud to the Lord about the work and hoped that Barbara, too, was getting the message. Maybe even Tony would one day understand.

"So you're the guy who turned the Smithsonian on its collective ear."

Startled, Reg whirled to face Arthur Bryce. "I'm Reg Danson," he said nervously.

Bryce shook hands. "Still prefer creation by a loving father figure to random reality brought to you by a tall, cool glass of swirling gases?" Bryce had yet to smile.

"Why, yes, as a matter of fact," said Reg, fascinated by vast tracks of character lines in Bryce's face. Charlton Heston could play this man. "When the church decreed the world flat, Galileo said round. When the church branded him a heretic, Galileo said as you will. I'm as big a fan of truth."

Bryce eyed him thoughtfully. "Are you as big a fan of expediency?" the godfather asked.

"What do you mean?" Reg was growing decidedly uncomfortable. Were they ever going to get around to the purpose of the visit?

Bryce exhaled noisily and looked off to the horizon. "You work for a profit for a man who works for a profit. I work for no one."

Reg flushed. "Oh, then you must live off the sea—and all the money Bascomb offered your Ararat expeditions went to the orphans of Turkestan."

Bryce gave a dry and mirthless laugh. "The money was Bascomb's idea and every penny went to pay off the permit clerks and security gendarmes. Turkey's crawling with them. It saved time, to be sure, but he needn't have bothered. I have my contacts. You'd be surprised what transformations can be wrought by growing a beard and wearing a peasant's tunic.

"No, my food and drink, this cottage, all supplied by a handful of churches whose priorities do not include potluck socials and name speakers. I travel light. I leave the scientific gadgetry, the expeditionary tonnage to others. Noah's Ark will not be found by machine. It will be located by the most sensitive tracking device ever made—the human heart."

He jerked his head toward the cottage door, and Reg followed the great man inside. The dimly lit interior was crammed floor to ceiling with metal filing cabinets, racks of recorded tapes, piles of books, and cardboard boxes and wooden orange crates overflowing with papers, news clippings, and oddments of a life spent collecting.

The only artificial light in the room came from a swing-arm lamp over a worn rolltop desk, which itself spilled papers and envelopes from every drawer and cubbyhole.

"Touch nothing," Bryce ordered, deftly negotiating the piles and files by way of a narrow rabbit run down one side on his way to the desk. "There's no time to take you on a tour of two hundred years of findings and losings and more findings. Wouldn't think you could lose a monster craft like that but it seems to jump around the mountain with the freedom of a checkers king."

Reg didn't know whether to sit, follow, or reply, so he stood and said nothing. Bryce seemed to be poring over some photos on the desk. Once or twice he started to pick them up, and then he'd put them down as if struggling with a decision. His breathing became more labored, and once he half staggered against the desk. When Reg started forward, he received a sharp rebuke. "No! Stay there."

Bryce fumbled with a bottle, shook two pills free, and took them dry. "Too much time at high altitudes for the old ticker. Ararat's free of me. But you—" He stopped, gripped the desk with two burly hands, then recovered. "You're young, but once you get in the pull of that mother mountain, your insides will grow old first, then your outsides. Maybe you should ask for your job back at the Smithsonian."

He paused a moment, took another long look at the photos in his hands, then turned slowly to face Danson. His voice broke. "Who am I kidding? Just as Moses was denied the Promised Land, I've been denied the Ark. I broke faith with God. I hoarded the evidence all to myself, took every twist in the trail to heart, squandered my vitality to be the first. I forfeited romance, children, service to others, all for the sake of laying hold of Noah's Ark." He snorted derisively. "I even began to believe my own press. I was the godfather of Ark hunters. I hunted alone and cooperated with no one. I looked more times, spent more resources, dreamed more dreams of success than anyone else. I diverted the offerings of those church people away from mercy and missions to finance my personal dream. But for my sins of selfishness and arrogance I have been denied the prize, and now the mantle must pass to you."

Reg started. "What's that?"

Bryce held out the photos. "Do you know what these are?"

Reg shook his head.

"Look at them. They are photographs of me standing beside the cuneiform writings and pictorials I found in the foothills of Ararat."

"Yes, I remember," Reg replied. "They made the headlines for a time but I never heard what became of them or if they were ever deciphered."

"They were deciphered all right, by Professor Murad, Ankara University, foremost expert of Sumerian origins. They speak of the Flood, of the Ark, of Noah the patriarch and his family. And I believe they give the reason the Ark has remained hidden, why eyewitnesses die before they can be interviewed, why actual photographs disappear, why the weather conditions are so monstrous, why the upper terrain keeps shifting like the desert sands and the location of the Ark has been 'pinpointed' in a dozen different locales."

Reg waited, heart racing. The ancients had spoken. What had they said?

Bryce resumed. "I will read from Professor Murad's translation: 'God planted a garden in the east, in Eden, close by the mountain not far from here at the source of the Pishon, Gihon, and Euphrates rivers. It was a good land, but evil was committed there by the man and the woman God made. The man and the woman were banished from the good land and God placed at the entrance heavenly beings with a flaming sword that flashed to and fro to guard the way to the tree of life.'"

"The Genesis account," said Reg.

Bryce nodded. "The Flood undoubtedly played havoc with those riverbeds and erased or altered the sources. But I believe the gate to Adam's Eden is somewhere near Ararat. Doesn't it make sense that the new Eden of Noah would spring from near the same spot? The incredible troubles on the mountain, the negative forces pulling every expedition apart, are the work of the warrior guardians of the Tree of Life. The savage lightning bolts that hammer the peak are from the flaming sword of the Lord. The Bible gives no indication the warriors have ever been recalled from guard duty, so you heard it from Arthur Bryce that they are still on the job!"

He'd recovered his composure and now glared at Reg, square jaw jutting defiantly, daring the upstart to question his conclusions.

Time passed while neither man said anything. Eventually, Reg cleared his throat and placed a business card on a paper-strewn table hunched under an already impossible load of data. "Why I've come, Mr. Bryce—"

"I know only too well why you've come, Reg Danson. You are the one to whom I must pass the torch." Suddenly all the starch left the godfather. The shoulders sagged, the zealous light went out of the eyes, the gruff baritone softened.

"Don't worry," he said with a dispirited sweep of his hand about the room. "You won't be needing all this."

Reg did not trust himself to speak. *Dear Lord,*
what is this man saying? Reg cleared his throat a second time. "I- I don't—"

"Noah's Ark has been found, Mr. Danson. Your
job is to get it off Mount Ararat."

Reg gripped the back of a kitchen chair and
steadied himself. "But you just said it was unap-
proachable."

"Oh, I never said I thought you'd succeed. In
fact, I'm fairly certain you'll die in the attempt. But
when the Ark is sitting there exposed as a yacht in
dry-dock, you have to try, man. My heart won't toler-
ate high altitudes again. You must do it. Not for yourself. That was the mistake I made. Do it for the
world's sake.

"Bascomb's got the ear of the president on this
one. Why doesn't that surprise me? Uncle Sam's footing the bill, anything you need. There's what I say
take and there's all the newfangled gear Uncle's going
to throw at you, so you're going to have to pick and
choose carefully. One item you mustn't leave home
without, and that's the superchoppers they've lined
up to pick the plum. Incredible lift capacity. The
president wants the Ark safe and sound in the U.S.,
not in the hands of some religious terrorist group out
to make a name for itself. What's the matter with
you? You look as green as moldy seaweed!"

"It's all so overwhelming," Reg said faintly. Bryce
gave him a long appraising look. Understanding of
the enormity of the task showed in his eyes.

"You said a mouthful there, Danson," he agreed,
a light quiver in his words. "In all the days of sweat
and blood I've spent on that mountain, I never once

thought about what I'd do if I did find the Ark. Plant a flag and head back down? Stay with it for fear I'd lose it again?" He laughed bitterly. "Patch up the holes and pray for rain?"

The godfather's eyes were moist, the defeat of a life's dream enveloping him like a body bag. The cottage and its contents no longer held meaning. His life was bereft of purpose.

"Arthur. Mr. Bryce . . ." Reg hesitated, pity for this great man and all he had invested in the search putting a lump in his own throat. "We'll need your expertise at base camp. You could teach us, give us a kind of crash course in mountain survival and what we're likely to find once we've—"

Bryce held up a hand to silence Danson. "No!" he cried, turning his face away. "God has denied me, but He loves me nonetheless. Moses lived to 120, and by faith he received a place in heaven—but no Promised Land on earth. God will receive me to Himself also. Until then I will continue to lecture. I will give all my research to the church—" He paused, a trace of a smile crinkling his face. "—or the Smithsonian!"

Reg liked the man's spunk. But it felt all wrong to be taking from him the thing for which he had worked so hard. Plus the thought that he, Reg Danson, had been given the nod was both wonderful and terrifying. Noah's Ark! There was no artifact of more enormous significance. Found after eight to ten thousand years! To think that he would soon place a hand on the very ship that saved mankind from annihilation—it was the most stunning turn of events.

But before Reg could speak again, Bryce blew his nose loudly and said, "Truth is, Mr. Danson, I don't think I ever really wanted the Ark to be found . . . something about blessed are those who don't see and yet believe.

"There's something quite sad about solving a mystery."

Reg nodded. He liked this mystery man and wished they had known one another long before the end of a dream. "Mr. Bryce—"

"Call me Art."

"Art, I couldn't help but notice you on the beach on your knees. I need guidance. Would you pray with me now? Would you give me your blessing?"

Both men sank to their knees in the cottage by the sea. Outside, the timeless waves crashed, and the gulls uttered the same hoarse cries gulls had been making since creation. Inside, the tough old Ark hunter placed his great hands on Danson's head and looked at the ceiling. "O God of the impossible, hear my prayer . . ."

FAR to the north and east of Ankara and Istanbul is the harsh region known as Turkish Siberia. It is there that Mount Ararat has stood sentinel over centuries of death by sword, earthquake, and famine. The mountain is said to hold glorious hope and terrible judgment in an icy grip. The secret of a mighty wooden vessel long buried in its glacial rib cage might offer eternal life for millions or turn to ashes in their mouths. It is whispered in the myriad hovels and villages in the mountain's shadow that whoever would brave the devils of Ararat and find the Ark of Noah unlocks the secret of the mountain and discovers the power to coax humanity back from the ledge—or to push it over.

In the year of the Great Melt, half a world away, there was such a man. When Reg Danson rose from his knees in the cottage by the sea, the road ahead lay dark and treacherous.

2

O N THIS DAY, death was everywhere apparent in Istanbul. Coups and countercoups had reduced General Kemal Ataturk's plan for secular salvation from Islamic domination to little more than religious rubble. His stirring admonition to "Rise, Turk. There is no boundary to your loftiness!" rang hollow in the ancient land of King Midas where in 1979, eight politicians a day were assassinated for a variety of real and imagined transgressions. To walk the streets of the capital was to invite machine gun fire. To be the pope was to be the target of a Turkish terrorist.

Now lightning flickered as delicately as a snake's tongue across the grieving faces of the throngs gathered in Beyazit Square. The heavens stuttered thunder that caromed off the surrounding hills. Even at this early hour, torrid heat rose in shimmering waves. The rain did not come. The air hung motionless and malignant.

It was first light, that twilight time when the

carpet weavers, those who had not yet gone blind, could distinguish white thread from black at arm's length. This morning their nimble fingers and flying needles were stilled. The greatest among them lay dying, and the business of death must of necessity be conducted before the business of commerce could commence.

At the home of Cemal Erdemir, sultan of all Turkish *wallahs* or rug merchants, preparation for burial had been taking place since midnight when the *hoca*, or holy man, had been summoned from the mosque. In tones funereal, he had recited the Koran over the rapidly expiring body of Zamira, Cemal's soul companion and his country's premier weaver of Oriental masterpieces for more than six decades. At age seventy-six, she had defied the life expectancy of that demanding land for twenty-two years.

Accepting now her extinction as graciously and with as much dignity as she had her existence, Zamira Erdemir received the final droplets of water from the trembling hand of Schzette, dear friend and cocreator of a magnificent goat's-down Isfahan hanging still in the presidential palace. Zamira smiled thinly in remembrance of the long-ago summer Cemal had been crowned champion of *yaḡli güreş* (grease wrestling), the national sport.

The water eased the ache in her parched throat. And it applied a ceremonial balm to the anguish of the living, she knew, a liquid assurance of eternal bliss. It was commonly thought that Satan tortured his dying victims with a glass of water held just beyond reach. Should they denounce Allah before death, they would be granted a swallow from Satan's glass but in so doing forfeit their souls. A glass of water now could prevent a fatal yielding to temptation later. Zamira benignly observed the ritual but, ever fiercely practical, she refused to place any credence in it.

She felt herself slipping irrecoverably toward departure. For that is what it was to her, a passage to an uncertain life. Hers was such a militant and violent faith that it gave little more comfort in death than it had in life. Faintly, through tear-clotted eyes, she perceived the preparation for the washing of the body. *Mine,* she mused half-consciously, a tendril of fear penetrating the numbness in her spine. *Must death be so solitary?*

But unknown to her, her body would not exit alone. Another, bearing a message of monumental significance, would also occupy the coffin of Zamira Erdemir.

Muslim belief prohibits embalming, for God created the human body from earth and to earth it must be returned as quickly as possible. But it must return cleansed of all human corruption. Relatives placed a bench near the front door of the house, and beside it on a small stand were set a rope, a basin of warm pure water—compliments of Hamed the water merchant—and newly purchased soap, and a length of snow-white cloth. Assorted sponges and bottles were arranged alongside.

An involuntary shudder passed through Zamira as she observed the readying of ablutions. As long as she remained on the bed, she was someone. Once transferred to the bench, Zamira Erdemir, weaver of carpets, ceased to exist.

From near the ceiling came a pinprick of immaculate light, then as suddenly a gathering gloom. She did not struggle against the fear; she did not resist the coming night. Without a sound she was dead.

Cemal's brother glanced up from washing the bench and laid a gentle hand on the stout rug merchant's arm. The husband looked to his wife and the vacant coal-black eyes that had once gazed upon him in compassion, love, bemusement, admiration, and, on rare occasion, anger. Twenty-two grandchildren had called her blessed.

Cemal crossed the room to the portable bed and touched the fine old leather of his wife's arm. Her hands, their long, slender fingers callus-tipped from guiding countless needles, were folded in gentle supplication. His body felt rubbery with remorse for not having provided her an easier life. Sorrow threatened to swallow him, but he denied it with a shout: *"Evet!* (Yes!)," he cried fiercely, *"Evet! Evet!"* Though he willed it, no life pulsed beneath his touch, and tears of regret and longing fell onto the venerable worn hands that would never again touch his face in tenderness.

Gently, the sobbing carpet merchant was led from the room. All was now studied efficiency. The dead did not keep at such temperatures. Schzette tied a strip of fine batiste under Zamira's chin and knotted it at the top of the head to prevent the jaw from dropping open. Mouth and eyes must remain closed in death to keep insects and snakes from entering the body and devouring the dead from within. Schzette threw off the bedclothes and drew the feet together and tied them in place by binding the big toes as one.

Six of the grandsons positioned themselves, three on either side of the bed. The sheet upon which their grandmother lay was rolled up close to her body. Lifting in unison, they carried the body to the bench and set it carefully down, allowing the sheet to fall to the floor. Then they took leave of the house to wait in the courtyard as did all others except Schzette and one other young female friend of the deceased.

Schzette began to cut away the death dress and underclothes of her dear friend with scissors. Turks believe the corpse is easily bruised, and therefore all burial preparations must be conducted with utmost caution. When Zamira's aged but not uncomely nakedness was exposed, the younger woman poured warm water over the body while Schzette carefully sponged with soap. The first general washing completed, Schzette stepped to the door and called softly to the Muslim *hoca*, who immediately resumed the Koranic singsong. Then began the second washing.

As prescribed by Muslim custom, the holy sponging began at the nose, three times. The strident tones of the Koranic incantations swelled voluminously through the closed door almost as if the *hoca* were chanting through the keyhole. Next came the sponging of the mouth, three times; the entire face, three; the neck, once; each forearm, three, with the left following the right and likewise the feet, three times, identical order. The body was then dried with towels. Schzette picked up a little pile of cotton plugs and used them to seal off all bodily orifices to prevent the escape of gases.

A commotion at the door caused the women to

pause in their work. Schzette opened the door a crack and then wider to allow the family physician to enter. Sadly, he examined his former patient. Satisfied that death was the result of natural causes, he signed a certificate of burial and rejoined the swelling crowd outside.

The women carefully unfurled a rectangular piece of cloth with a hole in the middle, cut sufficiently large for the head to pass through. The shroud. Lovingly, Schzette inserted Zamira's head through the opening and then folded the cloth to overlap the two narrow sides. Deftly the women sewed the long sides of the shroud shut, then drew up the loose ends extending below the feet and tied them with the rope. Finally, they placed leaves of thyme on the shroud and sprinkled it with spirits of camphor to discourage insects and with rose water to mask the odors of death.

Their duties done, the women each touched the flaxen cheeks of the one who had taught them much. Tenderly they traced the high cheekbones, the delicate jaw, the tiny mouth that had spoken so sweetly. Then they departed, wanting to cry but prevented by a hollow longing more terrible than either of them had ever known. Soft little yelps of agony were all they would permit themselves. Before the door, they stopped to regain composure. To join the others they must appear to be at peace. Allah had claimed one of his own. It was a time for bravery.

Outside, the crowd ceased its murmuring, and every eye turned to the opening door. Schzette nodded once to the six grandsons who moved as one to a plain, unadorned coffin, hefted it to their shoulders, and, followed by the *hoca,* reentered the house. A wave of ritual wailing surged over the mourners as they extended their hands in grief toward the home of the fallen one.

It seemed as if all of Istanbul had risen at four in the morning to bid farewell to Zamira. In many ways she had been a mother to not a few of them, and for all, especially the women, she had been a symbol of strength and undeniable proof that a peasant, a female peasant at that, could rise to a position of authority and respect. A messenger had already been dispatched to deliver the news of her death to the dusty obscure little village of her birth known as Nerede, meaning "Where is it?" The villagers would offer prayer for her.

Scores more arrived in a steady, perspiring stream, filling the wide boulevard that led to the Erdemir home. Most were strangers, believing it their sacred duty to join the funeral party, a deed of goodness that Allah would see and Allah would reward.

UNKNOWN to the throngs, a man with a folded piece of paper was most anxious to reach Zamira Erdemir's coffin. Though the paper contained a message of the greatest value to the American detective of ancient mysteries, its courier was dead to the fact. Being under the condemnation of Allah, the man had more pressing matters to attend to.

He had been told to wait for the American and to deliver the message personally. He could not do that now. Life no longer held meaning. The last significant thing left was to take his sorrow—and the message—and place them both in the coffin. Then—and only then—he would be free of all responsibility and could disappear from Allah's sight forever.

Ahmet Erkmen shifted the package from under his right arm to under his left. Sweating excessively, he fought the press of the crowd, working his way steadily toward the back door of Cemal Erdemir's house. Though his heart was thudding dully in his chest, constricted by a viselike dread, Erkmen did not fail to note the four black hearses parting the dark masses.

But they were not his concern. The two men behind and closing fast were. They had dogged his every step since he'd left the shanty. He knew what they were after, and he was suddenly very determined they should not have it. He clutched the parcel more tightly and patted his coat pocket. The message was still there. Reassured, he glanced behind. The two made no attempt at concealment. Boldly they stood on the fringe of the clamoring crowd, black-suited, hulking, dark glasses glinting sunlight, picking their teeth in feigned disinterest. *Who are they?* he wondered. *They must not have it!*

Then he was alone, the macabre babble behind him. He hurried to the rear entrance. On the stoop he paused, drawing in a painfully deep breath that was held for a moment and then expelled in a raspy sigh. He held the rumpled parcel before him and looked upon it with yearning. The contents were crudely wrapped in the front page of yesterday's *Hurriyet* daily and tied with string. A large coffee stain encircled the photograph of President Suleyman Koraltan addressing the Grand National Assembly on a matter of grave importance. Erkmen smiled weakly at the irony in those words.

The package was no longer than a man's forearm. *Nor much wider*, he thought woefully. A rather insignificant bundle for all that it embodied—everything he had worked for, hoped for, dreamed of. It could just as well have been a fish or a loaf of bread for all its worth now.

He was a simple man. A coffee vendor. A man who made little and laughed even less. He had once enjoyed frequenting the tiny folk bars on the back streets of his beloved Stamboul, fancying himself to be something of an *askilar* or troubadour. His first son came stillborn as his father downed an eighth glass of *raki*, the national beverage, a highly intoxicating mix of raisin juice flavored with anise. A neighbor rushed into the Olimpia Cabaret with the news, and Erkmen sat the remainder of the evening beating out a disjointed tattoo on the bongo drums, drained of his former mirth.

Son number two came and died of umbilical strangulation between acts at the Sanzelize where Erkmen was performing as a singing musician. He liked to divert the drunken crowd from his amateurish sleight of hand by serenading them with ribald mountain ditties. He could not, however, divert his mind from the naked truth: Allah did not want him to have a son. He was spiritually impotent. The shame he bore knew no relief. He stopped going to the bars, trudging home from his coffee rounds at the Grand Bazaar each evening at seven-thirty to a shabby hovel and a wife who could give him no living sons.

He began to supplement the five daily prayers all Muslims must say with private devotions of passionate intensity. He took to playing a battered old sas, a traditional instrument resembling a Russian balalaika. The songs he composed were forlorn and anguished, and his wife would not tell him she was pregnant a third time. When he noticed at last, he took to praying by her bedside, grasping her taut belly in his hands, willing the child within to live and be male. The only thing more cruel than a dead son would be a living daughter. To nurture a female as his only child would mock his manhood beyond his ability to endure.

Erkmen's bushy black eyebrows dipped down in a frown. He squared his shoulders, tucked the parcel back under his left arm, smoothed the frayed lapels of his vintage suit, and opened the back door.

Inside, a long dim hallway stretched straight ahead to the main living area of the home. It was cooler here. Erkmen walked slowly over the hand-polished flooring, passing several doors that opened into the sleeping and dining areas. One door stood slightly ajar, and through it he glimpsed a coral pink *tuvalet* or toilet, Cemal's one concession to Western decadence. As he approached the portal to the living room, Erkmen stopped to remove his ragged shoes. Though holes gaped at toes and heels, he felt no embarrassment, only profound weariness.

He paused in the doorway to the splendid room where the Erdemirs had hosted heads of state and international rug merchants. *What two eyes can absorb such grandeur!* Everywhere, covering floor, walls, ceiling, so that not so much as a square inch remained bare, were the most intricately conceived and masterfully woven prayer rugs, carpets, wall-hangings, and decorative pieces of craftsmanship the poor seller of coffee had ever seen. To his untrained eye they were fabulous enough, but to a practiced rug merchant they amounted to the most priceless privately owned collection of Persian and Oriental coverings west of Tehran. Magenta and maroon, indigo and cobalt, cadmium and cinnabar, emerald, gamboge, and jet—a rich blend of tint and hue hung not in a riot of discordant colors but in harmony with the trained eye of the expert. Here were Bokharas, Joshgans and Afghans, Royal Kermans, Imperial Tabriz, Belouche, Birjands, and Ferdoos. An entire wall was one hundred percent Silk Qum. The ceiling of the thirty-by-fifty-foot room was bordered in a checkerboard of 160-foot-square goat's-down panels dyed heady, vivid shades.

The complex patterns and colors served only to heighten the starkness of the coffin in the center of the room. It had been placed on a narrow table, and against the iridescent backdrop, the marbled corpse of Zamira Erdemir shone silver pale with an unearthly sheen all its own. The *hoca* ceased his chanting as Erkmen approached the bier.

The holy one knew Ahmet Erkmen well, having offered prayers for him that Allah, blessed be his name, might see fit to bring forth a son from the womb of the young man's wife. But that had been two dead infants ago. Secretly, he did not now believe the couple's *kismet* would permit it and had therefore prayed for Allah to make this third dead child of Erkmen's a girl. If it were female, and dead, it would at least indicate that Allah was not totally indifferent to the couple's plight. *Insallah*, he had concluded, if God wills it.

Erkmen tried not to see the corpse's ghastly pallor. There was so much death in Istanbul these days. He began to pant, partly from fear, partly from the heat, partly from a nausea induced by the florid room, the glowing cadaver, and the knowledge of the contents of the package in his hands. Erkmen stared imploringly at the *hoca*. The holy one nodded. Erkmen placed the bundle, hands trembling, atop the half lid that covered the body from feet to waist. He'd promised his wife no pauper's grave for this one. A final dignity was all he desired.

The coffee vendor fumbled with the knotted string, fingers clumsy, useless. He fought the string like a madman, the panting now become sobs.

When he thought he must rip the wrapping to shreds, he felt the *hoca's* sure grip on his wrists, staying the frenzied struggle. The holy man worked the knots patiently. "Six Executed for Plotting to Overthrow Koraltan"; "Bomb Diffused in Cafe Dishroom": the headlines screamed their ill from the stained newspaper. The string fell away at last. The *hoca* parted the paper and stared, heartsick, at the foul contents.

It had been dead for little more than two hours, but decay had already begun. A naked boy fetus, lying on a filthy towel, eight weeks before its time. Tendrils of damp hair clung to the miniature human head. Milky flakes of amniotic fluid mottled the purplish-blue skin. The eyes were closed, the cheeks sallow, the nose as small and delicate as a newly formed bud. The scrawny limbs were straight, toes and fingers uncurled. There had been no struggle for life, no will to live. Only death. A womb of death.

The *hoca*, his knees weakening, gripped the side of the coffin and laid a shaky hand over the thin doll chest. The palm covered it completely while the fingers draped limply over the tiny shoulder. He tried to speak some hallowed words, some blessing of comfort. He had rehearsed a speech about the inevitability of this death, and even that would have sufficed to fill the awful void, the crushing hush that settled upon the room. The keening of the crowd outside seemed a wail from hell. The words would not come. For the first time in his life, the holy man was dumb before Allah and man.

How could this be? It was to have been a female, a female, a female! His mind screamed the truth to him over and over. He, Ibrahim Hasan, seventh-generation *imam* never once guilty of *bidah* or deviation from the teachings of the Prophet Mohammed, had willed the death of this boy child. He had committed intercessory murder.

"Please, oh most holy one of Allah," pleaded Erkmen, shattering the awful moment, "please, I beg of you, do not allow this, the last of my attempts to present Allah with a son, to be placed in a beggar's mound. Let him be buried in this coffin with this woman of substance. As she is honored with the acclaim of thousands, so let him be borne above the heads of the crowds; then he, too, will receive some small measure of the respect and admiration he would surely have earned as a man."

Erkmen swallowed hard, fearing he might choke

on his sorrow. The *hoca* stared fixedly beyond him, and but for his own distress, the young father of the dead infant could have read the panic etched in the old priest's face.

"Please—please—please," Erkmen sobbed. "If I must beg, I will!" With that, he backed away from the coffin and sank to his knees. Hands clasped, he raised them toward the *hoca*.

His heart like lead within him, İbrahim Hasan turned to the bereft father. "Rise, Ahmet Erkmen. Let us prepare the child for burial." He reached down and tore the hem of his gown, a cleaner swatch to wrap the infant. The resulting rent was not large.

There was not time for ritual ablutions. Carefully, Hasan lifted the tiny body. How insignificant the weight! Erkmen removed the newspaper and string and stuffed them inside his shirt. He placed the piece of cloth beneath Hasan's cradling hands and watched as the *hoca* began to wrap.

It was then he remembered the message. Erkmen reached inside his coat pocket and withdrew the folded piece of white paper. Cevdet Demirkol was in hiding and claimed to know where the Landing Place could be found. He'd always been a strange one, Cevdet. Working first for one side and then the other, whichever would pay his asking price. The friends had gone their separate ways once Cevdet began espousing revolution. Erkmen would deliver Cevdet's message and then be done with the man once and for all. Loyalty stopped at the gates of insurrection.

Erkmen supposed it meant a lot of money or

fame to the Americans. Legends, properly merchandised, were always lucrative. That was why he was being followed. Someone in Istanbul or some other capital stood to make or lose something valuable on Cevdet's "discovery" and needed to know his whereabouts. Erkmen cared little now whether he ever collected the fee promised him. He had no heir.

But a good Muslim keeps his word, he thought wryly. A good Muslim also prays faithfully and look what results! No belief was surely better than one that tortured and punished. He sighed heavily. Atheist or believer, Ahmet Erkmen was a man of his word. He folded the slip of paper twice more and placed it between the unyielding fingers of the infant. It would be far too dangerous and unhealthy to entrust the note to the defenseless old priest. But no one desecrated a Muslim grave.

The *hoca* raised an eyebrow at the note, then decided it must be a message of love and farewell. He concluded the bandaging, lifted the lid of the coffin, and placed the baby in the niche between the bound feet of the woman and the wall of the box.

"God is most great," he intoned over the boy. "Praise him and bless his prophet. Lord, this was to be your servant—" He faltered. "—and the son of your servant, the child of your community. His father has testified that there is no god but you, and that Mohammed is your servant and your messenger, and you know him best of all. Take this little one to your breast. If—if an offense has been committed to bring this about, then let the wrong pass without further punishment. O God! Deprive us not of his reward, and try us not after his death." He bent and kissed the tiny forehead. Tears of regret sprinkled the withered infant.

"I feel as if I've had the same child three times," said Erkmen sadly. "This one must bear the name we chose before there were any births. He is Mustapha . . . Mustapha Erkmen." He turned his eyes toward the ceiling and cried, "Mustapha Erkmen!" to whatever worlds would receive his son.

Quickly he rose and grabbed the arm of the startled *hoca*. "You must contact someone for me," he rasped, looking furtively over his shoulder. "Telephone Richard Bascomb, Enigma Society, Phoenix, Arizona, U.S.A. Tell him all is in readiness. The guide to the Landing Place awaits contact. His exact location can be found with the babe wrapped in swaddling clothes lying in a coffin. Zamira Erdemir's, Eyup Cemetery, Istanbul."

At the look of stunned disbelief on the priest's face, Ahmet Erkmen whispered desperately, "Don't fail *this* time, holy man. You must do this thing!"

Erkmen bolted from the room and out the way he'd come, running as swiftly as the rapidly swelling press of people would permit. The two men in black suits and dark glasses shoved and jostled their way in close pursuit. The wooden box seemed to float out the door behind them, suspended in air, eager hands fighting for a hold and the honor of bearing the coffin to the hearse for the trip to Beyazit Square.

Erkmen ducked behind a coterie of wailing women, their grief for hire by the wealthy, and plunged heedlessly down a blind passageway. Too late he saw the way blocked, and the sounds of his death merged unnoticed with the urgent roar of mourning beyond.

TWO kilometers away, a candle burned in the dilapidated shanty of Ahmet Erkmen, the coffee vendor. It would remain lighted for forty days, a beacon. Beside it sat his wife, a diminutive stoop-shouldered young woman with a wan complexion. She waited, as was her custom, for the newly released soul of her dead son. He would find it difficult to adjust to having lost his mother so soon, and his soul would return to the place of birth for comfort. She stared at the flame wondering at the loss . . . the meaning.

Mercifully, she did not yet know that the candle burned for two.

R

EG, MY BOY, you are one blessed bucka-
roo!" Richard Bascomb's booming bass vibrated the
telephone receiver. Though Danson held the voice of
the excited heavy equipment tycoon fully six inches
from his ear, the volume was little affected.

It was two days after his encounter with Arthur
Bryce before Reg finally got through to his employer
on a secure military line from Fireweed Air Force
Base outside Tucson. Bascomb broadcast a one-word
explanation for the delay.

"Arrangements, Reg, lad, arrangements! More
like *de*rangements! Like to have gone cuckoo trying
to crack the code of the Turkish Council of Minis-
ters. So many Ark-hunting flakes have fallen from
the sky in the last ten years, who's to blame the officials for being wary? The flakes give us all a bad
name, leave their garbage all over creation and back,
and walk off with priceless pieces of antiquity without so much as a 'May I?'

"Even with practically a presidential proclamation, it was like arm wrestling Paul Bunyan to get the clearance and requisition the supplies, but—hey!— do my machines move mountains or don't they?"

Reg attempted a feeble interjection, but Bombastic Bascomb was way ahead of him. "The world is drastically off course, Reginald—we both know that. And as we career toward oblivion, the great majority of humankind have become fatalists, fiddling while the place burns down around them. Who in the industrialized world really wants to clear the air when it means eliminating the automobile and our steel-belted independence? Who in the Third World gives diddly squat about ozone layers or thermodynamics or the coming Ice Age when their babies are screaming in hunger, their brain cells dying from malnutrition? What bejeweled sultan of the OPEC nations wishes to turn in his Rolls fleet as long as he's got the superpowers by the throat? And what potentate of any stripe would willingly surrender his foothold in Southeast Asia or the Middle East in some faint hope of bettering everyone's lot? Oh no, self-interest will motivate us to the bitter end, my friend. Noble sentiment is noble sediment in today's power game.

"But now let us play the game of 'What If?' What if an archaeological discovery were made of sufficient magnitude that it would command the attention of the entire world, cause it to pause in its mad dash to destruction, bring the mighty to their knees, and reshape the entire thinking of rational humanity? What then, Reg, my boy?"

Reg opened his mouth a split second too slowly.

"The odds are two million to one against dying of snakebite," Bascomb plunged on. "More people die from being struck by lightning or slipping in the bathtub, yet most people are deathly afraid of snakes. Why don't they face spiritual death with the same dread? The odds for it are fifty-fifty. Eternal life? A prayer away. Eternal death? Reject God, turn off the spiritual tap, say good-bye to heaven. What fools we are!

"But *now* they'll listen!" The triumph in Bascomb's voice added several decibels to the volume. "On Ararat, God's holy mountain, Noah's Ark stands revealed! It proves the Flood and that mankind came a flea's whisker from extinction because of the same wickedness and spiritual apathy we're playing with today. But in the Ark's wooden bowels, eight persons, four men and four women, along with members of every living land species of animal life, rode out the most cataclysmic upheaval the earth has ever endured. After 375 days entombed in this salvation ship, they set first tentative foot on a brave new world of their own creation. They and the creatures with them, prototypes of a new civilization, streamed down the mountainside toward an uncertain destiny but full of God's blessing and promise.

"Think of it, Danson! Now! Today! Revealed!"

Reg was faster this time. "How? How is it possible after all these centuries?" he managed quickly, still fighting a feeling of unreality.

"Heat, man!" Bascomb fairly exploded, barely able to contain his ebullience. "*Heat.* The same glorious, broiling, thermometer-popping stuff we Arizonians have always said was our best friend next to a cactus full of water. An unseasonably warm winter with less than half the normal snowfall, a dry spring, and an Omega Blockbuster and old lady Ararat sits exposed like a thief in church!"

"Omega Blockbuster?"

"That's weatherperson lingo for a monster high-pressure ridge that settles down like the lid on a pressure cooker, sealing off as much as half a continent from any hope of precipitation for up to three months or more. This one's been baking the life out of the Eastern Mediterranean north of the Red Sea and parts of Asia since mid-March. Particularly hard hit has been the area where northwestern Iran, Soviet Armenia, and Eastern Turkey join. Lake Van, Turkey's largest lake, is barely seventy-five miles from Mount Ararat and five feet below normal water level. And the mountain itself is the barest anyone's seen it in this century. The Kurdish nomads who roam the area are so afraid of the climatic change, they refuse to look at the summit, now clearly visible—in itself a rare, unsettling thing.

"Ararat manufactures its own violent weather. Evaporation from the semiarid flatlands condenses daily on the seventeen-thousand-foot icecap. Storms, insane in their fury, slash the mountain all summer long. It can be a hundred degrees on the plain while ten feet of snow are being dumped on the summit. But today it is calm, serene, *melting!*"

Danson wanted to shout aloud. Bascomb's optimism was catching.

"Time is of the essence, my boy," Bascomb marched on. "Omegas are as unpredictable as politicians. The Ark has been seen and *touched* by thoroughly reliable witnesses in my employ, and everything's been arranged. You must fly to Ankara via Istanbul posthaste. The necessary equipment and personnel are even now gathering for the assault on Ararat at the Turkish military base of Karakose, a hundred road miles from the mountain. Amazing what clout one has when one's machinery has been largely responsible for modernizing a nation.

"Members of your team are all fully knowledgeable in their fields, of course—archaeology, photogrammetry, paleohydrology, the usual assortment of geologists and chemists. You naturally have carte blanche for any staff changes you need. A Lieutenant Cayan is directing things at that end. Expert in all things Turkish, the good lieutenant will accompany you as chief liaison officer. And from what I understand he's a regular mountain goat.

"Since I'm familiar with your usual requisitions for materials, I took the liberty of sending a couple of dozen of everything to the base where you can finalize the outfitting of the expedition. The helicopters coming in from Jerusalem will be headquartered at Karakose, and the demolition team will join you at the Kent Hotel command post in Dogubayazit, your jumping-off place. The Ritz it isn't, but adequate for as long as—"

"Wait a minute, sir," Reg interrupted with sufficient force to slow the Bascomb barrage. "Is the Ark really stable enough to remove intact?" His hands trembled at the thought. If only Barbara, his wife, were alive!

"Some structural damage," Bascomb replied, a little annoyed at having his pace slowed. "Nothing you can't patch together. The timbers are said to be quite sound. Steel banding and the sophisticated harnesses on our Skycranes ought to keep her in one piece.

"There is—ah—one other thing you need to know. . . ."

At the worrisome pause on the other end of the line, the old "this-job's-too-good-to-be-true" feeling crept up Reg's spine again.

"Someone has already paid with his life for the Ark to be found. You've got to be careful, my boy."

"Climbing accident?" Reg asked quietly, well aware of the physical hazards posed by the fierce mountain.

"Murder," came the dulled reply.

Danson looked at the telephone receiver as if it were deadly in itself. *Am I really sitting here chatting on the phone about mountains and murder with a manufacturer of bulldozers?*

"Lieutenant Cayan will fill you in on the details. Suffice it to say there are those who do not wish the Ark to be found. Maintain a prayerful attitude while watching your backside. Turkish army soldiers will accompany your party, and you'll have a supply of Turkish barter sufficient to smooth your way past the Kurds.

"The wolves, bears, and poisonous vipers said to guard the mountain? You'll have to learn their language on your own."

"Why must I fly into Istanbul first?" Reg asked, afraid of the answer.

"An old Muslim priest named Ibrahim Hasan can take you to the hiding place of the man who will lead you to the Ark. We did not think it wise to discuss his information over the telephone—any telephone. Besides, meeting Hasan will give you opportunity to become accustomed to the land and some of its ways."

Was there an evasive note in Bascomb's answer?

CHAPTER

4

THE BOEING 727 Turkish airliner droned
through the heavens high above the ancient earth
and its vast natural storehouses. Most of those on
board were either tourists, oblivious to much but the
rising cost of film and airfare, or jaded businessmen
interested in little except Aegean villas and eighty-
proof Izmira vodka. How did the advertisements go?
"An idea, an attitude, a sensing of the pulse of a people bridging the civilizations of two continents."
Amazing what the copywriters could do for a bottle
of distilled beet juice.

A handful of passengers, however, were distinguished by occupation. Seat 1A first class held Ismail
Turkman, former religious affairs counselor to the
Turkish Embassy in Paris. He had a ragged furrow in
the flesh beneath his left armpit, compliments of an
Armenian Liberation assassin, who had ambushed
him just off the Place de la Bastille six months previous. Turkman had since been reassigned to the
cushy embassy post in Washington and was return-

45

ing home to Bursa for a two-week furlough. His slot at the French embassy had not been filled, and most of those reassigned to Paris in the wake of the shooting were less given to diplomacy than to muscle. The toll at the embassy over the last six years stood at four dead and three wounded, one critically.

Turkman would not have been comforted to learn that twelve rows behind in coach was one Sarkis Arak, prime exterminator with the Armenian Secret Army for the Liberation of Armenia. It had not been Arak who had clipped Turkman's wing that rainy day in Paris. The counselor was too small a fish for Arak to handle personally. That was why he would take the connecting flight from Istanbul's Yesilkoy Airport to Ankara International. The Turkish capital was liveliest this time of year, and if one wished to kill the president, one had to go where the president was.

In 9C economy class was Istanbul Chief of Police Kenan Terlimez. Foremost expert in the uses and abuses of *papaver somniferum*, the opium poppy, Terlimez was in an unusually cheerful mood for one so employed. He had just engineered a multimillion-dollar trade agreement with the Americans to supply them with 500 thousand pounds of opium. The U.S. Defense Department had been uncharacteristically cooperative and embarrassingly eager to meet the police chief's demands. They did not know how to barter, these Americans—everything was now or never. Their entire military structure was ultraconservative and highly alarmist. The director of the opium stockpile, already the world's largest, had been most frank about the sudden buildup. "Iraq, Libya, China, the Muslim republics of Eastern Europe—take your pick. Any one of them could exercise the trigger finger tomorrow. Bam! Nuclear exchange." The opium would be used to treat radiation burns.

The director was also shopping about for 1.5 million pounds of goose feathers for cold-weather ground combat in China. The Boy Scouts weren't the only ones prepared, he said. Down-filled sleeping bags, boots, parkas—small enough comfort in a protracted land war, but troop loyalty had been known to turn on less. Were there any Turkish geese for the plucking?

Stifling a laugh, Terlimez had assured the director that though feathers were not in his province, he would mention the need in Ankara. Then he had gone to a tiny back-street bistro to drink and laugh the night away.

But the night had not been without its demons, and it was perhaps that more than feathers that had caused him to get roaring drunk. The one concession he had made before the deal was finalized had been a considerable one. He would declare his own war on the illicit opium trade that flourished in the rotten guts of Istanbul, a highway of hallucination that stretched to the United States.

North Americans did not know how to enjoy their drugs without debilitating themselves, everyone knew, and Terlimez did not feel personally responsible. Asians for centuries controlled their enjoyment of the habit. The sale of opium to the Americans would provide the Turkish economy with a much-needed boost. He would ferret out the main supplier and apply some proven methods of persuasion and pray to Allah that it did not backfire. The suppliers could be deadly persuasive themselves.

The plane lurched badly and Reg Danson glanced up nervously from the newspaper. *Lord, keep an angel in the cockpit.* He always felt woozy on airplanes and tried to recall an article he'd once read on the worst airlines in the world. He could not remember how Turkish Airlines ranked but Middle Eastern companies in general did not rate well.

His mother said he still resembled the rugged actor type despite the galloping gray that surfaced guerillalike at each morning's combing. His wife, Barbara, had taken fiendish delight in what she'd called "the graying of America," helping him count each new silver streak and kissing away his little-boy hurt at finding it. She called it "surfer hair"—fine, sun-bleached, close-cropped, but please, dear Lord, not sparse, not yet!

His amber-brown eyes sparkled with an easy merriment, their gentle depressions free of the bagginess common to his overworked peers in research. A few feathery lines and a mild pothole or two in the general physique put the lie to the thirties—but not unkindly. And the chin and jaw were firm, no sag. At the first sign of jowls, he often joked, he'd skydive without a parachute. Besides, he was a prize church-choir tenor, a forceful talker, and no snorer, not so much as a single "Z" in his entire life.

He looked fondly at the young man dozing in the seat next to his. Anthony Danson was a lithe, handsome twenty-year-old, with a lean tanned face that exuded confidence even in slumber. The longish blond hair parted down the middle was clean and healthy. The slender hands and fingers extending from the sleeves of a well-worn army surplus flak jacket were strong but neat, the fingernails well kept and unbitten. *The life of protest agrees with him,* thought his father grudgingly.

The reasons for Tony's coming were complex and not altogether to Reg's liking. There in the seaside cottage, the astonishing news from Arthur Bryce the Ark hunter still ringing in his ears, he had seized upon the idea as a desperate attempt to bridge the awful gap that had separated father and son for too long. He had not even been sure Tony would accept. It had been nearly two years since they'd last talked at length, and Tony still blamed his father for his mother's death. "Some wild holy goose chase" was how he'd belittled the expedition on which Barbara had drowned.

Reg had surprised Barbara with a summer at Loch Ness for their anniversary. Out of the blue, he made her drop everything and go. Like some giddy gazelle, she danced on the sunporch and jumped into his arms. She insisted he carry her across every threshold in the house until they collapsed weak with laughter at the basement door. He splashed her with water from the dog's dish, and she grabbed a fly swatter and threatened to beat him within an inch of his life.

The flight, the drive along the shore of the loch to the ruins of Urquhart Castle, the intimate dinners in Foyers at the quaint Serpent's Neck Inn—all of it was tinged with a fairy dusting of mist and moonbeam.

For four glorious days they played before the

search team assembled on the shore of the Benedictine abbey at Fort Augustus. Divers of the British Loch Ness Investigation Bureau took up positions in the water in a gigantic oval at preset locations. Two large glass-bottom observation rowboats patrolled inside the ovals with high frequency, side-scan sonar units clamped to the gunnels.

Reg and Barbara, riding in the bow of the smaller rowboat, were armed with telephoto cameras and binoculars. They kept vigil for anything roused by the intense activity. Barbara made quarter-hour entries in the logbook.

The loch was unusually calm. Murky water and bits of vegetation slid lazily beneath the thick glass that formed the bottom of the boat. An occasional salmon kept pace below their feet, and Reg itched to wet a line. The streaming water and a constant flow of particles slipping into and out of view had an almost hypnotic effect.

At half-past two on the afternoon of the second day, the search team was one hundred yards northwest of the abbey's boat dock. "Ho! What have we here?" shouted the sonar engineer, almost stumbling overboard in his excitement. The Dansons held their breath. A massive object moved through the sonar beam thirty feet off the starboard bow.

"It must be fifty times bigger than the fish we've been picking up on screen," said Barbara in a hushed tone. Reg jerked the binoculars to his eyes and scanned the water for wave action. A dark, elongated shadow cruised the cloudy depths. "There!" he cried and pointed.

The sonar engineer radioed the starboard divers to look sharp. Before they could respond, the dark visitor passed beneath them in a shadowy glide.

"Another one!" sang the engineer, motioning to the stern.

Reg and Barbara spotted it in the same instant. An oily, mahogany brown back humped above water for three seconds before sinking from sight. "Talk about a moving target," gasped Reg, his shaking hands making the binoculars dance dizzily. The only view he managed to keep still for long was a floating mat of peat debris.

A diver bobbed to the surface by the boat and spat out his air intake. "Bloody peat particles!" he exclaimed disgustedly. "The thing was no more than twenty feet from me but might as well have been in the next county for all I could make of it. Reminded me of a great brown sea slug through that soup— can't know which end's the business end!"

Twice more that day the creatures registered on sonar but weren't visible to the naked eye. Each sonar blip scrambled the team to full alert but always seconds too late for a firm sighting. The sonar print-out showed heavy black splotches trailing thinner ragged ones as if someone had tipped over the ink bottle and then tried unsuccessfully to wipe up the ink.

That evening the Dansons returned to the little garret in the abbey, exceedingly thrilled over their first brush with "Nessie," the sea monster.

"Happy, love?" Reg looked at her appreciatively, thinking how tender and beautiful she was, yet perfectly willing to traipse into the oddest places in the name of discovery. She nodded contentedly and gave his neck a squeeze. "Music, maestro?" she asked.

He nodded.

"By Jeep through jungle in June . . ." She sang alto, he tenor. Let others swoon over Sinatra; the silly little ditty they'd composed together was their song.

"In rain, snow, or typhoon!" they yowled with mock intensity, shushing each other a moment later when they heard an answering liturgical chant from somewhere deep in the far recesses of the abbey. They snorted and cackled in their half-hearted attempts to muffle the duet.

"Give me a vine . . .," Barbara sang solo.

". . . and I'll swing through time," answered Reg in exaggerated basso profundo.

"And together we'll—do—just—fine!" they ended, cheek to cheek. They dissolved into laughter and wondered what the monks must think.

God was so good.

Early next morning they set out in a thick fog the British like to call "a green pea souper." The search team, still high on the thrills of the previous day, were suited up and fully loaded by the time the Dansons arrived at the boat launch. As was their custom, Reg and Barbara prayed on the reedy shore, arms around each other in what they called their "morning huddle."

In the larger boat dubbed "monster mother," the sonar engineer watched the praying couple. When they said their amens, he called out to the others, "Think I'd get some of that religion, too, if it meant starting me morning hugging a fine bird like the missus there!" Everyone roared, including the missus.

It was difficult going in the dense, swirling fog. The bright, fragrant air of the day before had been replaced by a wet, clinging oppressiveness that was almost like a cold steam. All was still and musty-smelling, a heavy mist turning them and their boats slick with moisture. The engineer bemoaned their lack of camera strobes for lighting the underwater darkness. That equipment had been somehow misdirected and was last seen on a train bound for the south of England.

The Dansons were split up, Barbara in "monster baby" and Reg in the "mother." They wanted to get to know the men better and to cover more territory than they could in the same boat. Perhaps it would double their chances of spotting the elusive creatures of the loch.

"Shouldn't you be wearing your life jackets?" the engineer inquired of Reg.

"No time," Reg said, climbing into the boat. "As it is, I'm slow enough getting the binoculars up when one of those things surfaces. A bunchy life jacket would make me totally useless. And Barbara says she can hardly see to write with one of those things on." He laughed. "Says it makes her feel like an expectant mother who loses sight of her toes for a good three months!"

Because visibility was so poor, the divers were pulled and the boats sent in opposite directions around a prearranged perimeter. They would keep in radio contact and return to the dock by noon unless a sighting was made.

They should not have gone out at all under the

conditions, but Danson was in charge and he felt a keen anticipation still surging from the previous day's sightings. *Just until noon,* he promised himself, *just until noon.*

Here the lake was no more than eighty feet deep, a far cry from the nearly thousand-foot depths farther out. There was the frustration. In so many deep caverns, shy creatures could escape electronic detection. The loch was twenty-three miles long, and Mount Rushmore could be tucked away in any of a hundred places.

"Plesiosaur's what we're after," said the engineer matter of factly. "Been spotted from Siberia to Scotland and anywhere else the waters run deep. Flippers, snaky neck, reptilian tail—all the signs are there."

Reg nodded in agreement. "Elasmosaur," he said, naming the particular type of plesiosaur thought to be native to the loch. Then he laughed dryly. "Kodak won't be using existing shots of Nessie in their commercials anytime soon."

The engineer chuckled. "No sir, not when the fuzz factor's high as it is." Both men had seen the provocative but impossibly grainy and blurred photos taken by a businessman, a mechanic, a medical student, a host of vacationing boaters, and a biologist or two. All were remarkably similar in shape, however, and in outline looked eerily related to the prehistoric monsters of childhood dreams.

The fog thickened. Radio reception was garbled and a clear connection so far impossible. Reg took a turn at rowing. Neither man heard the sound of approaching oars.

Barbara was lost in thought, sketching in the

margin of the logbook a sinewy creature, half submerged, half exposed, its long serpentine neck stretching over the marsh weeds at lake's edge. A tumble of vegetation was clamped in its jaws, a look of primitive satisfaction wreathing its blunt face.

Suddenly, the man rowing behind her gave a strangled yelp and began a frantic backpaddle. Barbara lunged for the binoculars as something parted the waters to their left. Nervous with excitement, she leapt to her feet at the moment they were struck amidships by the bow of the "monster mother."

The force of the blow nearly swamped the smaller craft. Barbara fell backward, struck her head a sickening blow on the starboard oarlock, and lurched over the side.

In the confusion and the covering fog, Reg heard first one plunging splash and then a second. He could not tell their significance. He dropped the oars and shouted, "Barbara, are you all right?" A tendril of fear wrapped itself around his neck and he could not breathe. "Barbara, answer me!"

The engineer ripped off the sonar headset. "We'd better go in!" he yelled. Both hit the water in a dead heat.

Progress was slow in their sodden clothes, but Reg quickly outdistanced the heavier man in the life jacket. He came alongside the oarsman from Barbara's boat, clinging to the gunnel, gasping and choking for breath. Reg grabbed the neck of the man's life jacket and screamed, "Where, man, where is she?"

The other man looked at him miserably. "Can't tell. Too dark. Hit her head. Might be unconscious."

Again and again Reg plunged deep into the loch,

oblivious to the other men joining the search. *My dear Barbara . . . gone . . . no, God . . . please, God . . . not this way.*

Then he surfaced, his lungs bursting, and all he saw was water and fog. No boats. No divers. No Barbara.

He didn't want to live any longer. He felt his muscles go slack, everything turning black. Water enveloped him like a womb. *Blessed is he who cometh in the name of the Lord. . . . Coming, Lord, coming.*

Strong hands reached for him. Air. Sweet, sucking lungsful. Life returning. Life without Barbara.

The local police dragged the lake for two days, but found nothing. Just as the monsters of the loch could hide with little effort, Barbara's slim, small body had found a permanent hiding place of its own.

Newspapers around the world carried the tragedy, and Tony, on a long backpacking weekend, read the story of his mother's disappearance at the tiny general store in Stoverville, Colorado. When he returned to his grandparents' home, his father had been there twenty-four hours.

The look on Tony's face said it all.

"Tony, I'm so sorry!" his father said. "We tried to locate you, but you hadn't checked in at the ranger station. Your mother—I—we love you!" He stopped, totally bewildered at how to say the loveliest, most valuable, most important woman in their lives was gone. He put a hand on his son's arm.

Tony knocked it away savagely. "How could you risk Mom's life on some holy wild goose chase? How could you just throw away my mother, your wife, all for the sake of some stupid sea serpent? Why didn't you take care of her? The newspaper said she wasn't even wearing a life jacket! Is that true?"

"Tony, I tried. It—it was a freak accident. You weren't there, you don't know how hard we—"

"*No!* Don't you give me your weak excuses! Did God tell you to go to Scotland? Did God tell you to take foolish risks? Is this just another of your mysterious acts of God?" Tony was crying, and his fists clenched and unclenched, as if to strike his father.

Reg, now weeping himself, forced his eyes to look into the searing anger of Tony's. "Look, buddy, this is not the time to blame God. We need Him; we need His comforting spirit. If you want to blame someone—"

"Oh, don't worry, Dad, I do blame you. *And* I blame God—and all the religious posturing and sloganeering done in His name. You've quit on the Smithsonian, you've quit on me, and now you've quit on Mom, and all in the name of following your destiny in Jesus Christ. And yet, for some equally unexplained reason, you're still around as unhurt as can be!"

Reg exploded. "Unhurt? Would you be any happier if we'd both drowned? Part of me died with Barbara, can't you believe that? You've got a lot to learn about love and personal sacrifice. I loved your mother more deeply than you could possibly understand. And it was God who brought us together, whatever you may think. And what do you know about taking risks and making commitments anyway? You and your ban-the-bomb friends? You broke your commitment to this family when you turned your back on me two years ago!"

Tony took a deep breath as if gathering courage. When he spoke at last, his voice was low and he did not look up. "We're no family anymore, Dad, thanks to you."

Reg felt the turning of a knife in his stomach. As if to steady himself, he reached for the corner of the battered upright piano in the comfortable old living room where Tony had sung "O Holy Night" at the age of five. Then he drew his hand back sharply, as if to lean were a sign of weakness. "I hope in time you will want to take those words back. For now, I want you to know that I love you with all of my heart. You are part of your mother and very dear to me. I can't fault you for wanting to blame someone for something neither of us can explain. But God's ways are mysterious. He did not promise us freedom from want or troubles or even destruction. But He did promise us His presence, that He would never leave us or forsake us. I am trying desperately to sense His presence in this. Sure, I'm very angry, and I feel cold to the death inside. You hate me and Barbara's gone. That doesn't leave a guy a whole lot to live on."

Tony turned to leave, hesitated, then mumbled, "I'm sorry, Dad. I just don't have anything to give you right now." He shuffled out, shoulders slumped in an awful attitude of ruin. Reg wanted to hold his son and cry with him until the terrible dread lifted. Instead, he could not move and held himself against the scream that threatened to rip his heart in two.

After the memorial service for Barbara, Tony had

plunged headlong into nuclear protest while barely maintaining a *C* average in his archaeology studies.

When classes officially ended for the spring quarter at Portland State, Tony stayed on to lead SUBB—Students United to Ban the Bomb. When Reg phoned the dormitory from the Oregon coast he had to shout to make his wishes known. The loud babble of voices in the background was occasionally punctuated by someone attempting to restore order. Amid the din and demands for quiet were cries of "Peace!" and "No nukes! No nukes!"

Tony's resonant voice finally came over the line. How it had deepened! For a moment Reg was too overcome with emotion to speak. The "hellos" became indignant, and he struggled to answer. The exasperated voice on the other end must have turned on the crowd, for Reg had no difficulty distinguishing every word of the shouted, "*Will you shut up for once!?* Yes, who's calling, please?"

"Tony? It's me, Dad. How are you, son?" He could hear a mighty expulsion of breath.

"Geez, I'm sorry, Dad. Didn't mean to shout like that. Uh, how ya been?"

"Fine, son. Sounds like your little party's getting a little out of hand."

"Oh, that. Yeah, well, when you feel strongly about something, I guess you've got to take a stand, however loudly you might come across. You oughta know about that."

Reg winced at the pointed reference to the Smithsonian affair.

"Listen, son, have you got a minute to talk? I've got a proposal I think you might be interested in."

There was a moment's hesitation. Reg had approached Tony before in the hope of drawing him into a father-son exploration partnership.

"Gee, Dad, you called at kind of a bad time. A group of us are taking off to the G.E. plant in Pennsylvania to smash a few missiles they've got stored there—"

"Tony! What in the name of reason are you into? You can't go around breaking into atomic installations. They'll have you in prison so fast! Then where will your good intentions be?"

"Save it, Dad. We've got divine sanction on this one. Father Dan and Phil Berrigan are leading the charge. Besides, a little time in the slammer didn't seem to hurt St. Paul's career any."

"Don't get cute with me, Tony. God has no truck with vandals or pseudopriests who hide behind a cloak of respectability while subverting our democratic system!"

"Thank you, John Birch. Listen, Dad, if you're through preaching, I'd like to get on with my subversive activities."

Reg Danson took a deep breath to regain control. "Sorry, Tony. Let's start again. It hurts me that our few conversations always end this way: you going off to ban another bomb and me feeling like I've just had stomach surgery with a dull knife. Can't we just this once let some healing take place?"

The breathing on the other end was erratic. Reg couldn't be certain above the steadily rising noise in the dorm, but he thought he'd heard a sob. "Listen, Dad . . ." The voice was strangely tight, yet containing a familiar little-boy tremolo out of the past, which stabbed Reg with icepicks of memory. Tony did not go on.

"Please, son, let's try to make it work this time. I—I need you, Tony. I've got a difficult assignment in Turkey that requires your mountain climbing expertise. Better than any summer school. You'll get to rub shoulders with the cream of archaeologists. Just the thing for show 'n' tell when you resume classes in the fall!" He chuckled lamely at the thin joke, while praying urgently for a miracle.

"Okay." The suddenness of it, the weary, defeated tone, caught Reg totally unprepared. Had he misread his son's silence these past years? Had his own foolish pride contributed to it?

When the shouts of "No nukes! No nukes!" began again, Tony decided to go to a quiet coffee shop nearby and phone his father back. Reg filled him in on the incredible conversation with Richard Bascomb, and Tony agreed to join the expedition.

"Priests Arrested in Attempted Missile Sabotage." The *London Times* headline snapped Reg out of his daydream. He straightened the newspaper and read, "Norristown, PA (AP)—Police have identified two of the eight persons apprehended in a hammer-wielding attack on missile parts at the General Electric Reentry Division assembly plant in nearby King of Prussia. They are the brothers Berrigan, Philip and Fr. Daniel, who, along with six others including a lawyer and a mother of seven, broke into the plant in an attempt to damage plans and nuclear nose cones. Officials at the plant say the intruders splashed their own blood, previously collected in baby bottles, over valuable documents. . . ."

"Quite the nice writeup, don't you think?" Tony was sitting up, reading over his father's arm.

"I was thinking how close you came to being issued a prison number."

"Yeah, you're right. They almost always get the stiffest sentences for break-and-enter of a munitions installation! It's a crime akin to murder! Mothers and priests are a potential threat to our national security, you know. Why, I'd give 'em five to ten years in jail at least."

"They are a threat when they take it upon themselves to undermine our system. Look at them. Burglars. Conspirators. Those missiles are necessary to preserve that precious peace you're always marching about."

"You sound just like another famous burglar, Dad. Richard Nixon was his name. How come he could crash the gates in the national interest and we can't? He's pardoned and we're imprisoned."

"All right, Tony, that's enough. I'm not about to feel sorry for people who willingly taunt authority or deliberately break the law; I don't care how honorable their intentions. I don't excuse Nixon any more than I do your priestly pals. And I'll tell you another thing. To God a clerical collar and a gold crucifix are certainly no substitutes for responsible citizenship."

"Geez, Dad, don't be so stuffy! If we who have the greatest amount of freedom and peace in our land are not the prime movers in the shedding of that peace all over the face of the earth, what hope has humankind? General Electric is more than toasters and waffle irons. It's one of the top five weapons manufacturers, into genetic engineering—Dad? Dad, are you listening?"

Reg nodded absently, his gaze fixed six clouds off the right wing. "I was just thinking how we haven't talked like this is years—you know, about really important things."

Tony heaved a sigh and nodded. Then he looked at his father and grinned impishly. "Remember how I used to climb in bed with you and Mom on Saturday mornings, and you'd pretend you were going to fillet me with your fish knife? You'd say, 'Hold him down, honey! We've got to get this one in the pan before he gets away. He's a mighty tasty specimen!'"

"Do I ever! I'd accuse you of being in violation of the Geneva Convention for using morning breath as germ warfare."

"That wasn't half as bad as the time we went camping and ol' Ruff 'n' Ready Danson slung his hammock between two trees. That night a big old black bear shuffled into camp and decided to nibble at the big bulge hanging down from the middle of the hammock. You went into orbit and almost got beaned with the cast iron skillet Mom fired from the tent in self defense!"

They both dissolved in gales of laughter, punching and poking one another. People around them turned. A matronly passenger in outlandish sunglasses across the aisle sniffed disapprovingly and gave the flight attendant an "Aren't you going to do something?" look that sent father and son into fresh hysterics.

Religious Affairs Counselor Ismail Turkman set

down his drink. The laughter made him think of his own family and the son who had been killed putting down a Kurdish uprising. Police Chief Kenan Terlimez shook his head in wonder at how seemingly carefree Americans were—unless, of course, they were government bureaucrats in search of goose feathers.

Terrorist Sarkis Arak shifted in his sleep. He dreamed of guns and who the next president of the Republic of Turkey would be.

A THOUSAND miles away in the inky night an emaciated peasant girl heard drunken laughter beyond the door of the squalid hut. It was not her Ahmet. This, the third day of her vigil, the candle had long since become a sooty puddle of hardened wax. She had not eaten. There was no food. The grief for her dead child had been swallowed by dread for her lost husband. He loved her little or not at all, but he fed her, he kept her.

And the ice high on Mount Ararat continued to melt.

CHAPTER
5

T HE UNPAINTED, drooping tea shop was far off the traveled path. Its equally threadbare clientele referred to it as *bitkin*, exhausted. Adnan, the owner, spent much of the day passing out crude handbills to overweight Texans and British women in floppy hats, inviting them to "sip tea in peace away from the crushing crowds, yet not far from the Grand Bazaar." They asked him in casual drawls and clipped precision if he sold film or hamburgers. He always smiled in pained apology and they never came. "*Only* tea?" Only tea.

Meanwhile, Adnan's dozen usuals sat at the table with the broken leg or the one stained dark with the blood of Ziya, the coat hanger merchant, in an argument over politics. They helped themselves to glasses of tea, swatted flies, and waited for the day to end when Adnan would return and bring them news of foolish tourists endlessly snapping fuzzy photos of one another. The tea rooms in the Bazaar sold over a thousand glasses a day. Adnan was lucky if he sold a hundred and spilled but ten.

Occasionally, there was a pause in the loud sipping of tea and the arguing—for the men never conversed, only argued. Then the stale atmosphere of the stuffy little shop squashed beneath the Hotel Babadan, a fourth-class hostelry billed in the Turkish Travel Guide as "plain but clean," turned decidedly judgmental. The men glanced knowingly at a tattered curtain at the rear of the shop. The fabric hung limply over the doorway to the dusty storeroom, where Ibrahim Hasan, the Muslim priest, sought refuge. Adnan, the shopkeeper, felt a holy obligation toward the priest. A little kindness in the right places might cancel out at least a few of a tea man's indiscretions. Surely the righteous would drink tea in Paradise, would they not?

Ibrahim Hasan dreaded those moments of incriminatory sipping. Outright accusation would have been more tolerable to the defeated holy man. But this rudeness with the lips somehow underlined the magnitude of his crime. At such moments he envied the Christians their forgiving God, their compassionate Savior. He wished for a gentle shepherd with wounded hands to touch his shoulder and say, "Come, Ibrahim, let us drink tea together. I have already paid for your heinous transgression. The sin is forgotten."

But Christianity was an opiate. He was Sunni Islam. For him there was no savior, only one's own ability to fulfill the requirements of a demanding God. To fail was to face the crushing and all-consuming fire. And he, Ibrahim, had failed. He had prayed, and death had taken an innocent child within its mother's womb. He would burn.

Hasan shifted uncomfortably now as if upon the spit of Allah's cooking fires. From his narrow cot in a flea-bitten corner of the storeroom, he could watch the men in the tea room deposit an occasional coin on a lean little pile at a counter near his curtain. They would pause, the tips of their own shoes sometimes edging under the curtain into his meager sanctum. They peered accusingly through the tired cloth before returning to their accustomed seats. At those moments, the unwillingness to forgive tortured the broken inmate more than any thought of future hell. But even they were fleeting bits of time compared to the endless hours he spent loathing the *hoca* who willed the death of little children. Ibrahim Hasan could not forgive himself.

The evening of rug weaver Zamira Erdemir's burial—he could no longer recall the words of comfort he had mumbled over her grave—he had stumbled into the night and wandered alone along the Golden Horn. The sounds of ships' horns, the twinkling lights, the mocking cries of the gulls left him raw and bleeding inside. Laughing school children ran past onto the Galata Bridge, their merriment adding to his pain.

When it became dark, he stood near Tokapi Palace, listening to the sucking sounds of the Sea of Marmara at his feet. He felt he should jump and end a miserable life, but he could not. Fear shook him until he almost fell in. He prostrated himself and ground his face into the earth and stones, moaning and grunting and crying out, wishing for death, hoping for clemency, vomiting up an empty life.

Afterward, he crawled and ran and mewed his way to Adnan's shop where he had spent the last three days nearly immobile, rising only to relieve himself into a tin can kept on a nearby shelf. The shopkeeper asked no questions. Allah would reward handsomely the providing of refuge to one of God's dependents.

"Seek amidst that which God has given you, the Last Abode, and forget not your portion in this World, and do good, as God has been good to you. And seek not to work corruption in the earth; surely God loves not the worker of corruption." The words of the Koran stung. He would wear his two pieces of unsewn cloth for penance. He would not eat, clip his nails, cut his hair, hunt, argue, or dwell on sexual matters as was prescribed for one on a holy pilgrimage. Not that it would do him any good. Allah would simply allow him to starve to death on his cot. Workers of corruption could expect no surcease.

The sound of an auto in the rough alleyway outside was rare enough for both customers and prisoner to take note. A battered and oft-patched *dolmus*, or Turkish taxi, ground and whined its dusty way around dogs and garbage and an abandoned Buick, nearly plowing into a scarecrow of an old man shuffling diagonally across the roadway. The *dolmus* lurched to a stop inches from the ancient pedestrian's knees, throwing passengers and luggage and an emaciated chicken cursing and squawking against the back of the front seat.

The driver nearly leaped through the open window in agitation, screaming unintelligible Turkish at the old man who leaped onto the hood of the cab with remarkable agility and jumped up and down. The driver climbed out the window and reached for the old one prancing on the hood with exaggerated grace.

From there the spritely elder leaped nimbly atop the roof of the *dolmus* and taunted his purple-faced pursuer in a chiding singsong. When the driver jumped to the roof, the old man skipped to the trunk and did his dance there. The driver, making a suicidal dive for his tormentor, grabbed an armful of nothing and ended in a bone-jarring skid down the alley on his chin. The prey cackled riotously from the corner of a building before disappearing in a flurry of flapping coattails.

Reg Danson disengaged himself from the tangle of chattering passengers and irate fowl and stood gratefully before the open doorway to Adnan's tea shop, brushing the dust and chicken droppings from his rumpled suit. Bascomb had warned not to get in the way of a Turk when he was either romancing or driving a taxi, and Danson could now understand the wisdom of at least half the admonition. There had been no cash meter or speedometer in the cab and only one speed—faster. Above the windshield inside had been carefully painted a single word: *Insallah*, "If God wills it." The Turks were the original kamikazes.

Once his heart rate was nearer normal and the *dolmus* had departed, tires spinning, Danson entered the dimly lit shop. Conversation abruptly ceased. All eyes were upon the rumpled American, save those of the one who had bet money the old man would escape the burly driver. He counted his winnings.

"Ibrahim Hasan?" Reg's voice sounded strangely flat, out of place. Eight pair of coal-black eyes stared unblinkingly. *What exotic plot might these ruffians be hatching?* wondered Danson uncomfortably. One of them at the blood-stained table asked in a thick accent, "Texas?"

Reg shook his head.

The questioner's countenance darkened, but he jerked his head toward the curtained opening.

Reg pointed at the curtain and gave his benefactor a questioning smile.

He was rewarded with an indifferent nod.

Crossing to the curtain, Reg felt like the little boy in the Christmas play trio who suddenly cannot remember which of the three kings he is supposed to be. He breathed a silent prayer for wisdom before he parted the curtain.

The air was rancid. At first he could see little more than some broken crates and a leaning shelf of dusty tea glasses in the faint light. As his eyes adjusted to the gloom, he saw the sparse figure of a bearded man dressed in dirty muslin and lying on a bed of boards and sacking. About his head was twisted a once-white turban. Crammed into a corner of the dark room, as if he too had been stored, the wretched man was barefoot. His face was mournfully devoid of hope.

"Ibrahim Hasan?" The man did not move or show expression for a moment; then great tears spilled onto his beard.

"Teşekkür!" the holy man rasped. "Thanks!"

Reg went to the man's side and grasped the out-stretched hands. The man wept bitterly, hugging Reg's hands to his breast. *"Teşekkür! Teşekkür!"*

"Mr. Hasan, do you know why I am here?"

The old Muslim nodded. "I am so glad that you have come all the way from America. It shames me that I must receive you in so squalid a manner. I have suffered a great defeat. . . ." He broke down again, sobs of grief wracking his body.

Reg longed to bridge the spiritual gap that sepa-rated them. A man was emotionally disintegrating before him. He prayed for words of healing, and a poem came to him, one he'd been taught by a con-verted Muslim girl who had emigrated to the States from Iran. Her American friends brought her to church, and Barbara helped her commit her life to Christ. The poem, written to the Prophet Mohammed, became for her praise to God's only Son.

Reg held the holy man's hands firmly and looked into his eyes. Then he began the poem, speaking softly at first in a rhythm that was slow and sacred. "All things created joyfully acclaimed him, sorrow was done, new life the world was flooding."

The sobbing slowed, and Hasan turned to his visitor in wonder. "The very atoms joined in mighty chorus," Reg's voice swelled with emotion and enthu-siasm, "crying with sweetest voices: 'Welcome, wel-come!'"

The *hoca's* voice cracked forth, taking over the lines. "Welcome, matchless sultan, thou art wel-come! Welcome, source of knowledge, thou art welcome! . . ." Hasan's eyes grew large and bright as the devotion worked its way into his soul. "Wel- welcome . . ." he faltered.

Reg joined him, and together they cried lustily, "Welcome, thou, Nightingale of Beauty's garden! Welcome to him, who knows the Lord of Pardon. . . ."

Then from beyond the curtain came a gruff cho- rus of two or three voices: "Welcome, thou, moon and sun of God's salvation, Welcome, who knowst from Truth no deviation. . . ."

Hasan could no longer speak. He looked from the curtain to Reg and back, tears again flooding his eyes. The fullness of the ragtag chorus permeated the other room with a holiness long absent.

Reg looked deeply into his new friend's eyes and spoke the last lines low and with fierce intensity: "Welcome, the rebel's only place of hiding, Welcome, the poor man's only sure confiding. . . ." He squeezed the timeworn hands and whispered, "It's Jesus, Ibrahim—it's Jesus!"

The old man looked back at Reg, his eyes for a moment full of a burning power of their own. Then it was gone, and he turned to the wall with a groan.

REG Danson and the subdued old priest walked in silence for a long while, the *hoca* readjusting to the use of his legs and thinking back on the sacred moment in Adnan's tea shop. Might Allah have sent an American to take him beyond the Prophet to the Messiah? Preposterous!

Istanbul was at its intoxicating best in the late afternoon. Children of every shape and size formed a running subpopulace to the business flow, herding their hoops with sticks and gambling away their marbles at every corner. One whippishly quick sprite guided his hoop between the spindly legs of a camel grazing in a back-street yard. The creature stared with baleful eyes, but trampled too late.

Men bent double under huge loads of firewood hummed cheerfully to themselves while the ferry boats tooted and zigzagged across the Bosporus Strait to the mystical shores of Asiatic Turkey. Here in European Turkey, two legless beggars raced down the sidewalk on roller skates fastened to their stumps, nimbly capturing coins held out by the appreciative crowd. They roared past, laughing outrageously.

At the Blue Mosque of Sultan Ahmet, Ibrahim pointed to shaggy-haired dropouts of European society lounging about, ever reaching for hashish despite the vigilant Istanbul police.

Suddenly, from above, came the clarion call of the *muezzins*, singing the invitation to prayer from the balconies of minarets all across the city. Many of these were now electronic with tape-recorded prayers fervently announced over public address systems. The one above them, however, was live. This was the third prescribed prayer in the Muslim day, just before sunset. After sunset and again at the close of day, the faithful would pray the fourth and fifth prayers facing Mecca and giving thanks to Allah. After a few minutes, Ibrahim arose from the sidewalk where he had knelt, and he and Reg continued their roaming.

The Grand Bazaar was ablaze with sound and color and cascading fountains. More than four thousand shops were spread over eighty-three streets and sold everything from hookah pipes to suede suits to gold rings and Turkish slippers to icons, onyx vases, furniture, and copper trinkets. A tiny girl in a brilliant red dress ran up to Danson, clutching a jewel-encrusted dagger in her grubby fist. He patted her head and shook his own no. Next she ran to a man with five cameras festooning his neck, and he fished in his pockets for cash. Strange musical instruments twanged and wailed. Carpet merchants haggled in English, Swedish, French, German, Italian, Russian, Spanish, and Japanese. They watched a Londoner pay five hundred pounds sterling for the toil, skill, and patience of one woman's entire winter sewing.

Danson and Hasan escaped down the Passage of the Flowers to a little cafe delightfully dubbed the Pandorosa. Inside they found a table for two in a small private alcove where they could at last hear above the din.

The cafe, or *taverna*, was pleasantly alive with the soft murmur of diners of several nationalities. Reg guessed that the couple nearest were Swiss, while the family of six beyond sounded of German extraction. The two black-suited men occupying a table behind the family were certainly of Eastern European stock, their square builds and stolid expressions reminiscent of Eastern bloc weight lifters he'd watched compete in the Olympics.

He liked the exotic, crossroads-of-the-world feel of the place. And he especially liked the bright fuchsia rugs and flickering candlelight from red sconces deepset into the walls to give the room a rich, ruby glow.

Even the *hoca's* downcast features were converted to a ruddy affability in the shimmer of light. He reminded Reg of an Islamic St. Nick in a loose-fitting muslin robe and a profusion of beard in gray and black. His "stocking cap" was a tight-fitting turban, but no matter. The nose was browner and leaner than Nick's, but the face was broad and kind as a baker's and must once have been jolly. Missing now, though, was the merry twinkle in the eyes. The eyes that met his were tired and tormented.

"A mighty meeting place for deeds of every shade," said Ibrahim, jabbing a thumb in the direction they'd just come. "The Bazaar was probably once the livery and carriage stables for the Byzantine Empire. What may appear to you an elaborate tourist trap is actually the heart of Stamboul, a giant marketplace where the pride of Turkey goes on display. Cabbages two feet in diameter, eighteen-inch carrots, five-pound peaches! Apples, quince, apricots— Allah's bounty from the fertile Anatolia region. And tulips, Mr. Danson, tulips of indescribable beauty! Did you know that tulips originated in my country? Yes! The Dutch borrowed them from us. They were once a symbol of Turkey as they are now of Holland. We even refer to the reign of Ahmed III as the 'tulip period.' Oh, it was a marvelous time of good taste and courtly manners, literature and the arts flourishing. The court amused themselves in the royal tulip beds, which were illuminated at night by the glow of candles fixed to the shells of roving turtles. Turkey has given the world many things, my friend— watermelons, yoghurt. . . ." He paused in his vehement rambling and flushed. "I am sorry, Mr. Danson. These are inconsequential matters. I should be exalting our social and cultural advances. We did, after all, give the world its first female supreme court justice. But we are so much people of the soil.

"Agh! At any rate, I should not babble so. I apologize. Perhaps it is the lack of food. . . ."

"Say no more, Mr. Hasan." Reg motioned to a waiter. "Please, Mr. Hasan, I am at your mercy. Order for us. I have but one request. Order plenty, I'm starved and I'm paying!"

The old man beamed with obvious enjoyment at being able to play host. He spoke rapidly in Turkish to the waiter, and soon they were enjoying lamb kebab, slices of various meats, juices succulently intermingled, and *Hünkar Beğendi*, a dish with eggplant base that translates, "His majesty liked it."

"You may order a glass of water with your meal as I understand is the American custom," said Hasan, "but I warn you . . . no ice and heavily chlorinated."

Reg declined, and they ordered *ayran* instead, a sharp, milky beverage made from yoghurt, water, and salt. For dessert, *helva*, a pastry made with sweetest Royal Honey and pistachio nuts.

When at last they were satisfied, Hasan sighed. "I did not mean to be rude toward your Jesus, Mr. Danson. It was very kind of you to inspire me with my own faith's holy poetry. But I fear our worlds are too far apart for instant reconciliation. You see, at the moment of my nativity in nineteen hundred and twenty-nine, my father proclaimed me to be among the chief of Allah's dependents. Imagine. Holding a squalling, bloody little bundle toward heaven, umbilical cord trailing, and announcing me to be servant of the One True God. Aiyee! Such faith. Blind, misdirected, ill-conceived—" Hasan's voice caught and his mouth trembled.

From the far side of the room the shrill notes of a primitive kind of violin began to sound. Six men stood, stepped onto a small raised platform, and linked arms. Dressed in black with silver trim, they quivered in time to the string vibrations.

"The *Horan*," said Hasan, seemingly glad for the diversion. "A Black Sea dance performed by men only. Later tonight will be the belly dancers." He laughed as if enjoying some private joke. "Come back in the spring, my friend, and I will take you camel fighting. Much more humane than bullfighting or American boxing. Male camels spar until one establishes its supremacy. The loser is immediately dragged away so that neither beast suffers permanent damage."

Reg made a face and both men laughed. "Too many wonders at once," Danson noted dryly.

Hasan agreed. "As I was saying, we followers of Mohammed are a strong-headed lot. We've had to be. The Prophet had to speak in a rudimentary style to bring understanding to an idolatrous people, the Arabians. Your Christ went among the Jews, an enlightened people, and therefore spoke eloquently. They were students of the Torah who accepted the prophet Moses.

"Unlike them, the Arabs were murderers, thieves, and prostitutes of the worst ilk. The harem system allowed men to feed their perversions. A man could even take his father's wives upon the father's death. All the son was required to do was to place his cloak on the shoulders of the one or ones he desired and they were his. Sons lying with their mothers, Mr. Danson. Mohammed said enough, if you are just you may have four wives and no more. But 'none is righteous, no not one.' That is your St. Paul speaking, is it not?"

Reg nodded.

"Eventually, true followers rarely took more than one wife unto themselves," the old man added. "Still, in some ways we have not come so far at that. Because a good reputation and virginity are the prerequisites for a good Turkish marriage, doctors can yet be found who for a fat fee will surgically restore a girl's physical virginity. What fools we can be!"

He took a sip of his *ayran* and continued. "Mohammed wrote of rivers of limpid waters in heaven because the Arabs had no clean water. He spoke of rivers of honey in heaven because there was no grass in Arabia and thus there were no bees. Honey was an exquisite luxury. He spoke to their conditions. Admittedly, he brought no real new revelation. Essentially, he only seconded what Christ had already said. He brought order out of chaos in a land that desperately needed a legalistic morality to bring back its sanity. Christianity, with its lofty, self-righteous exclusivity would have gotten nowhere with the hot-blooded, degenerate Arabs, Persians, Turks—just as it does not today. You blame Islam, I blame conditions."

The waiter brought tea and Reg swirled a steaming glassful before he answered, "Christ claimed to be equal with God, Mr. Hasan. No one is too rough to receive redemption. If that were so, His death would have been very much in vain. We Christians say we are children of God; Muslims say they are the slaves of God. What do you say, Ibrahim Hasan?"

He was sorry he'd said it the moment it was out. The abject misery that again flooded the old man's eyes made the silence between them palpable. "I'm sorry," Reg hurried on. "I didn't mean to be rude. I'm just tired from the long journey. Forgive me, Mr. Hasan, please. What information do you have that should bring me ten thousand miles?"

The old man looked dejected as if the clock had struck midnight and the ball was over. "When first I laid eyes on you, Mr. Danson, I felt an odd mixture of hope and regret. Hope, that you might restore my vision. It was a supernatural moment there in the tea shop, east meeting west, Christian changing the tasteless water of a defeated Muslim into the triumphant wine that Mohammed promised his people. In the Grand Scheme, I think we are not that far apart, you and I.

"But then came the regret—that a young man of your compassion and insight should expend his energies in search of a myth, at best a spiritual allegory."

Reg began to protest, but the *hoca's* upraised arm stopped him. "Don't misunderstand me, Mr. Danson. Moses, your prophet and ours, told of a very real flood and the building of an Ark in great detail. Our Koranic account fleshes out the pathos even more by relating a conversation between Noah, the distraught father, and a wayward son who perishes. Noah calls to his son from the Ark already afloat: 'Embark with us, O my child, and be not with the unbelievers.' His son haughtily replies that he shall climb a mountain and there be safe from the waters.

Noah reminds him that no unbeliever will be spared. And then comes one of the most terrible lines in the articles of our faith. Even as they were talking, 'a wave passed between them, and he was among the drowned.'

"So upon the event we are in total agreement. But to say that it was a flood that engulfed the entire earth or that so many animals of each kind were taken aboard or that the Ark itself is frozen now at such and such an exact location is religious nonsense. You Christians love your hocus pocus but surely you cannot swallow a picture of Moses as some itinerant magician whose snakes happened to be bigger and more voracious than those of the Egyptian wizards? His spiritual victory over the pharaoh was couched in human terms to make it understandable to the easily misled Israelites.

"Surely the real miracle of Christ was not in literally feeding five thousand—of course they were fed, *spiritually* fed—but in his ability to turn twelve crude fishermen and tax collectors into lions, in his defiance of the Roman machine—worse, of the Jewish machine—and in his eloquent revelation of a higher plane even though he, himself, was roughly clothed, of no class or formal education.

"Forgive me, Mr. Danson, but I cannot believe in the gimmickry of God. Miracle or myth, the Ark of Noah is more significant to me as an ark of salvation than as an actual ship with a prescribed number of animals that is now wedged neatly between the peaks of Ararat. The covenant God made with Noah is far more important. Serve God and he will spare you annihilation—that's the essence of the story.

"I realize those are strong words for one so recently bereft of spiritual direction. Forgive me if I speak too boldly, but I think your time might be better spent in salvaging disillusioned priests than in stalking literary illusions." The friendly brown face broke into a smile, and Danson chuckled.

"Glad to see your Islamic stubbornness is intact, but you are blind to a couple of essential facts, Mr. Hasan. Christ promised to return to this earth when conditions of spiritual darkness are identical to those in Noah's day. What's to say He wouldn't take the Ark out of the deep freeze at that time to remind man that He keeps His promises?

"Show people a wooden boat the size of a modern aircraft carrier suspended in a glacier fourteen thousand feet up the side of a mountain, 150 miles from the nearest living trees of a similar kind, and they will reevaluate the whole idea of God and what He expects of us."

The *Horan* ended to enthusiastic applause, except from the table where the two men in suits sat stirring cups of coffee absentmindedly. They seemed oddly out of place in the cafe, neither ordering food nor conversing with one another. They might have been strangers waiting for a bus.

The waiter returned and freshened Hasan's and Danson's drinks. "Tell the cook the meal was delicious. Tell him *elinize sağlik!*" Hasan said to the man. "Health to your hand!" The waiter bowed slightly and left. Reg smiled at the quaint Turkish praise.

The two studied each other a moment before Danson leaned forward and grasped Hasan's arm.

"It's there, my friend. It has to be. More than two hundred individuals since the great earthquake of 1883 swore to have seen or touched it. Three of them, all men of outstanding character, have found hand-hewn timbers, wood of an incredibly durable type not found growing anywhere in the world today. Dating shows them to be of ancient vintage.

"Believe me, Ibrahim Hasan, as surely as God is in His heaven, *something* is on that mountain. For centuries people of that region have sworn that their ancestors made pilgrimages to the holy boat."

"Ah, yes," said Hasan unimpressed, "but they are Armenians, an emotionally erratic people—"

"—and Christian," interrupted Danson. "Admit it. Historians have proven that Turkish prejudice against the Armenians is no more rational than Nazi Germany's against the Jews."

"Not Islamic historians, my friend," said Hasan heatedly. "We're not speaking here of religious differences or even cultural misunderstanding. We're talking here of plotting, of political insurrection, of treason with the Soviets. The Armenians never were quite comfortable with the 'infidel' Turk in their midst, nay, their government." The *hoca* trembled with anger, pulling his arm roughly from Danson's grip. "They are not a people to be trusted."

Danson persisted. "The Ark is not Armenian any more than it is Chinese or Scandinavian. It is for all mankind. Because we have taken sides, it has remained hidden to the world at large, can't you see that? Are we to be denied its potential to mend a broken world by our personal biases? Give me what I have come for, Mr. Hasan, and I'll leave for Ankara.

Then you have only to wait for the news." Danson sat back wearily. His emotions had been run through a spiritual blender the last few days, and he had little heart for politics now.

Hasan eyed him curiously. "I'm afraid it's not that simple. Did your Mr. Bascomb inform you as to the whereabouts of the information you seek?"

An uneasy feeling settled over Reg like a dark cloud. "He told me I had only to seek you out, that you possessed a paper that tells where I will find the man who can take me to the Ark."

Hasan laughed grimly. "Not that easily, Mr. Danson. The paper you seek is not with me. It is with Zamira Erdemir."

"Then we must go to her and get it," Reg said testily.

"Aiyee. That is easy to say but difficult to do. We must first exhume the body."

"Exhume the body!" Shock slammed the base of Reg's spine. He spoke slowly. "You mean the paper is inside someone's coffin?"

Hasan nodded and quickly told of Ahmet Erkmen, the coffee vendor, his murder, his dead son, and the danger to anyone possessing the note. Danson felt ill. He was expected to rob a foreign grave and remove the evidence from the hand of an infant corpse.

Reg Danson also felt a moment's disdain for Richard Bascomb, who was making him do this. For do it he must. To turn back now would be to deny the Lord, risk losing his son and the fragile relationship they had begun to rebuild, and miss the opportunity of a lifetime to reveal to the world the greatest testimony to God's power and grace in two thousand years.

"It's all right, Mr. Danson," Hasan went on. "No one ever desecrates a Muslim grave; therefore the police never patrol the cemeteries after dark. We can work undisturbed. Besides, we'll each have a captive audience of one. We can try to convert the infidel in one another. Rewards aplenty in heaven for such a prize. Think of it!" He smiled slyly, and Reg could not repress a grin.

"You are so right, my dear pagan friend. Lead on!" Danson paid the check, and they headed for the exit.

Behind them, the two men in black suits also made to leave. While the one settled their bill, his companion put on sunglasses and stood outside picking his teeth, watching the old man and the American walk away in the direction of Eyup Cemetery.

CHAPTER

6

REG DANSON and Ibrahim Hasan went to a tool shop, purchased a shovel and a pair of sturdy work gloves, and after nightfall slipped into Eyup Cemetery.

Reg hurriedly followed the holy man to the foot of Zamira Erdemir's burial plot. All about them headstones tipped and tilted at crooked angles because Turkish burial custom decreed that death must be as filled with ups and downs as life.

The ghoulish fingers of stone, stuck crazily into the bumpy, uneven ground of the grave sites, gave Danson the awful sensation that the deceased spent their evenings squirming about underground, disturbing the earth above in their restlessness.

Danson did not care for this business at all. It was grave robbing, open and shut. Generally, he accepted the necessity of graveyards as long as it was broad daylight, you knew the deceased, and someone else did the digging.

Tonight was pitch black, the deceased was a

Turkish celebrity he'd never met, and the shovel in Danson's hands was not for spading the radishes.

"We should have gone straight to the local authorities," he said in a hushed tone.

"Aiyee, they would take a very dim view of this," Hasan replied. "It is highly unlikely they have any official knowledge of your expedition and highly likely I would spend my remaining days in a dank, rat-infested cell for allowing a second unauthorized body to invade Zamira Erdemir's private vault."

Both men were trembling despite the hot night. Surely no one could sleep on such a night, and they would soon be discovered.

"Help us, oh God, and give us strength," prayed Reg fervently, gripping the shovel for dear life. "Forgive us for disturbing the dead, but help us quickly find that which we seek."

"Allah, blessed be your name, grant us your favor this night," Ibrahim prayed just as passionately. "We are sorry men on a sorry quest, and without you we are truly undone."

Reg became sorrier by the minute.

Hasan stood sentry over the horrible scene, the white of his turban a ghostly halo in the darkness.

I wish Tony were here, Reg thought. The young Danson was back at the hotel poring over maps and Turkish tour guides, oblivious to his father's midnight deeds. All he knew was that Reg was off gathering intelligence vital to the expedition. Reg stabbed the shovel into the loose soil and winced. *Some intelligence!*

"Be glad you are not digging in Aksoy Cemetery for the Criminal Offenders," said Hasan, in an attempt to be cheerful. "Last week we buried three men there for rape. Such a crime is a felony in my country."

"Rapists get the death penalty?" Reg asked, trying to take his mind off the grisly undertaking. Not exactly the conversational turn he would have chosen, but appropriate, perhaps, under the circumstances.

"Yes, but that is not how these three died. They were shot to death by the father of the young sisters who were violated. Such revenge for a felony is not itself necessarily a crime in a Turkish court of law. It is the same for arson and armed robbery if an innocent one dies. The girls' father will not be brought to trial."

On Danson dug, listening to the holy man's steady chatter about Turkish justice. It was somehow comforting and steadied the nerves. A dog barked an alley or two away. Distant music and laughter drifted down from an open window. The laughter turned to accusation and an answered cry of indignation. The shouting intensified until the male and female antagonists stopped abruptly, then erupted in gales of tipsy good humor. The hoot of a ship's horn reminded Danson he was not far from the sea. The thunk of his shovel striking wood reminded him he was not far from two dead bodies.

The hair at the back of his neck stood at attention. Pure dread seized him and his heart rammed against his chest. He forced himself to clear the soil from the lid, then tossed the shovel from the gaping hole.

Lifting the lid was one of the hardest things he

had ever done. The fumes of death made him sick. Retching, he averted his eyes and felt about the cloth shroud at the foot of the coffin. He touched the parchment scaliness of the child's hand and pulled back. He hardly dared breathe and had to will himself to reach again and pull the scrap of paper from between the stick fingers. As if refusing to relinquish the message, the rigid little body rose an inch or two before falling back with the hollow rustle of an abandoned wasp's nest.

"Oh, God!" Danson cried. "God, why this?" Uncontrollable shudders rattled his body, and the precious paper fluttered to the ground. Hasan scrambled down by his side, picked up the paper, and flung his arms around his terrified friend. They clung together in the mutual grave of Zamira Erdemir, the great and beloved weaver of carpets, and little Mustapha Erkmen, the unfinished son of a poor coffee vendor.

Reg Danson and Ibrahim Hasan hastily replaced the coffin lid and the twice-turned earth, then fled the land of the dead. At three in the morning they sought the closest refuge from the terrors of the night. They beat on the door of Adnan's tea shop until the protesting proprietor saw who it was and let them enter, no questions asked. Their ashen faces said all there was to say.

Hasan crawled back into the wretched sanctuary of the storeroom. Danson, still in his suit, filthy and stained, stretched out on the table upon which Ziya had bled. Neither man slept, only remembered.

7

JUST AFTER DAWN, Danson rose exhaustedly from the table. Hasan was gone, having slipped silently away to be first at prayers in the mosque. Two immediate needs warred within Danson. He hungered for the sacred, restoring silence of a church, yet craved a bath—the one to cleanse his soul of the feeling a sacrilege had been committed and the other to cleanse his body of the decay and unholy fragrance of Sheol. The rotting odor made the other more pressing, so Danson headed for the hotel.

A quick scrub would do for now. Back in their room, Reg did not awaken Tony. His son's mouth gaped wide, and the windy snores of one who'd studied late escaped noisily. Danson changed into brown slacks and a tan polo shirt, after first soaking his head in a basin of cold water. He scoured his hands and nails with a brush four times over and still they felt defiled. Only time could wash away the grit of the grave.

The spiritual cleansing was next. Danson left

the hotel and headed toward some minarets to the north. It was Monday. Of the few Christian churches in Istanbul, none was open on Monday. A mosque would have to do.

Istanbul was home to four million inhabitants and more than six hundred mosques. Early as it was, the steps leading to the magnificent marble vastness of the Mosque of Sultan Ahmet the Conqueror were empty of gawking tourists. Later, they would form great gaggling lines at the entrance and would scoop up cases of miniature Korans and multicolored post-cards. Bare female shoulders would be covered with the cloaks of modesty now hanging in wait on racks just inside the cool atrium. Overalls were provided for men and women in shorts.

Danson walked up the stairs to the entrance. He saw a pencil-thin young man wash his feet in a foun-tain provided for that purpose before entering his house of worship. Foreigners were not required to bathe, but Reg would have to remove his shoes.

The mosque (from which the official pilgrim-ages to Mecca in the days of the sultans used to be-gin) was an elaborate shrine to one of history's supreme egotists, the Sultan Ahmet, who believed himself invincible because of an unusual success at war. The tile, the ivory, the mother-of-pearl, the acres of carpet—all the opulent handiwork was not so much for the honor of God as for dazzling the jaded sultan, God's "Shadow upon Earth." Beside the pulpit was the royal box where the sultans could enter on horseback.

Even the number of minarets on this mosque ex-pressed the emperor's conceit. Sedefkar Mehmet

Aga, the architect, was ordered to make the minarets *altin* or golden. He mistakenly thought he had been told *alti*, which is Turkish for the number six. The old Islamic law strictly forbade any mosque to have more than four minarets so as not to exceed the five of the greatest mosque of all—the tomb of Mohammed in Mecca. But the sultan loved the plans for six, and six were built. To defy the sultan was tantamount to defying Allah. The wise men of Mecca quietly added two minarets to Mohammed's mosque, and the score remains seven minarets to six in favor of Mohammed.

Danson felt immediately dwarfed upon entering the great hall of worship built on the ruins of the Church of the Apostles. Four colossal pillars supported the immense domed ceiling while shafts of light from 260 windows played capriciously over the rich layers of marquetry and marble. He went to his knees beneath the vast expression of the divine. There were no icons here, no saints, no crosses. No pews or organs or choirs or sacramental observances. No talk of the mark of the beast, the Second Coming or the Lamb's Book of Life. Only a quietness and a calm that was sufficient. The great hall was starkly empty to the eye, yet overflowing for the spirit. Reg's prayer was one of thanksgiving that God honored his having come here. Silent sacred echoes reverberated in the hallowed air. The child from whose hand he had taken the paper was no longer a rotting corpse but the infant messenger of blessed truth.

The paper. That morning he had put it in the pocket of his slacks where it remained unread. He was able to read it now. It would be safe to do so here on this great open plain where the faithful had been prostrating themselves for centuries. He removed the crumpled note and read:

> See Keeper of the Castle, Valley of the
> Fairy Chimneys. *Ille illa!* Without fail!

The hasty scrawl made no sense. *Guessing games,* he thought in exasperation. He could only hope that Hasan, when he found him, would be able to shed some light on the strange words.

A sudden, overwhelming sense of his filthiness made his skin crawl even though he had scrubbed so vigorously in the hotel room. He would go to a barber and then seek out the *hamam* or public bath house. Every pore begged for steam cleaning.

Reg left the mosque beneath a cloud of pigeons and followed the enormous Aqueduct of Valens towering as much as nine stories above. Built by the Emperor Valens in A.D. 375, the aqueduct supplied the Byzantine and later the Ottoman imperial palaces with water. Four very long blocks later he stopped a man with a brass flagon of fruit juice on his back and drank his refreshment from a glass cup on a metal saucer. He asked directions to the nearest *berber.* The man grinned and pointed across the street to a green door.

The way to the green door led past hanging strings of spicy sausages, slabs of cured beef covered in red pepper and smelling of garlic, and hairy goat hides filled with cheeses. Reg was still off his appetite, but the enticing aromas pricked his senses and made him feel better.

The barber was a wizened gentleman who, as it turned out, had performed circumcision on Ibrahim Hasan and followed his career as a *hoca* with great interest. Only a holy man near perfection would have been allowed to officiate at the funeral of Zamira Erdemir; thus the barber considered that he had left a permanent mark on no less than a minor prophet of God. Danson held his peace and nervously watched the single-edged razor fly about his head like a buzz saw. The man seemed totally unaware of what the blade was doing, had been doing for more than half a century, and for the first time in his life Danson prayed earnestly for the safety of his own ears.

"*Saatler olsun!* May it last for hours!" gushed the barber, seeing Reg to the door with the standard good wishes for someone just emerging from a shower, a shave, or a haircut. With vigorous gesticulations of the razor, the wiry little barber pointed the way to the lovely long low building with domes near the mosque from which Danson had recently come. The Hurrem Sultan Hamam was the beautifully restored bath built in 1556 by Suleyman the Magnificent for his wife, Roxana. In an age when bathrooms were unknown in Europe, the elaborate baths defined the Islamic ritual of bodily cleanliness.

Reg enjoyed the return trip, the heated air distinctly kinder to his razor-cropped scalp. He supposed he ought to keep an eye out for anyone who might be tailing him. Should he take a more devious route? He smiled. Too much television.

He passed an open air studio where calligraphers turned the written languages into masterpieces and artisans crafted the most intricate illuminated miniatures. Next door at the Kristal Kahve, men sat sipping coffee and smoking their hubble bubble pipes, the tobacco smoke drawn through the water in what had all the appearances of an optical illusion.

By the time he reached the baths, Reg was on the verge of feeling carefree for the first time in a long while. He passed through the ornate marble archways and was greeted inside by a grinningly pleasant little man no more than four feet tall, his turban set at a rakish angle.

The little man snapped to attention and gave Reg a disarming salute. "America?" he asked, arching his eyebrows in a comical parody of Groucho Marx. Reg nodded. "Texas?" The question was asked as ingenuously as the first. Reg smiled and shook his head no. *What is this national fixation with Texas?*

"Bath?"

"Yes, my friend."

The little man, who was the cashier, saluted again with his left hand, leaving the right free to receive payment. Then he issued Danson a large white towel wrap and led him by way of a pink marble hallway to a private dressing cubicle. In large cities like Istanbul, separate bath houses are provided for men and women. But Reg had heard that in small towns with only one bath house, different days are assigned the sexes. *Women are even-numbered days, men odd.* He smiled at the thought. It was like water rationing in California. Odd-numbered addresses water on the first, even-numbered the second, and so on.

Everything about the cavernous bath house was ornate, and it was not difficult to imagine the sultan's court indulging in this most ancient of customs. Tile and marble, gold and brass trimming, floor and ceiling, everything was finely crafted and meticulously maintained. Even the dressing benches were of a finely worked wood, deeply stained and brilliantly lacquered to a shine.

Reg undressed and wrapped his waist in the *pastemal* or towel. It was early yet, and while he heard some distant voices echoing faintly from another quarter of the bath house, he heard or saw no one close at hand. Padding back to the hall, a passageway as tall and broad as a railway concourse, he imagined a rich, continental accent announcing the arrival of the Orient Express.

The sign on the wall read "This Way" in Turkish, English, French, Japanese, and Arabic. An arrow pointed the way to a half dozen pink marbled alcoves beneath skylights of stained glass. The only furnishing in each was a huge *göbek taşi* or belly stone. Upon these heated stone slabs, the customers perspired away their impurities while undergoing a vigorous rubbing down by *tellaks* or bath house attendants.

Danson's attendant was a giant of a man, well over six feet tall and fully three hundred pounds if he was an ounce. Himself barefoot and naked to the waist, the *tellak* glistened in the steamy heat, his muscles bunched and hard, his considerable stomach overflowing the confines of loose-fitting muslin trousers. With a curt nod and no speech, the attendant swept a thick arm over the stone, indicating that Reg should lie down.

Reg did so, face down, wincing not unpleasantly at the touch of hot rock against his skin. "All areas of the body rubbed except the face, the waist area and the bottoms of the feet," a sign at eye level read in the same five languages.

Reg was soon perspiring madly. The attendant was thorough and uncompromising at his work. The canvas washcloth was an extension of the massive paws and left no uncharted territory save for those already mercifully declared off limits.

Under the relentless scrubbing, large gray beads of dirt and dead skin rolled off Reg's back and legs. He clenched his teeth, the washcloth grinding into his shoulder blades, the attendant grunting at his labors.

Ah, Tony, I beg forgiveness for all those times I so roughly wiped your nose and the dried food from your little face. I'm paying now!

Steam swirled dreamily about the grunting Turk and his paying victim, enveloping the stone in primordial clouds of hundred-degree mist. The big man snorted and complained under his breath. "*Çok pis*, very dirty!"

The echo of distant voices grew more distant still. The canvas cloth ground into the nape of Reg's neck, meaty, probing fingers expertly searching muscle and sinew for a familiar nerve. A prickly numbness spread outward from his savaged spine producing a delicious tingle and a welcome change from the brutal scraping.

Are we nearing the end of the torture, herr commandant? Did the swine confess? Reg smiled dreamily, looking into a vat of unconsciousness he very much wished to fall into.

Eyes squeezed shut, beefy face sweaty and grim, the big man above strained, bearing down on the nerve with the blunt thumb of his right hand, holding it steady with his left.

. . . plane leaves for Ankara one P.M. . . . mustn't be late . . . got to find Hasan . . . shhh, so sleepy . . . Reg vaguely sensed the sudden release of pressure. When the sausagelike fingers slid along his neck and wrapped around his throat, he was riding an overweight gull out to sea.

Danson's head and neck exploded in pain, the finger vise closing off his trachea. He fought to lift his head, his arms, anything, but his muscles would not respond to his commands. Fear and anger welled up in him at the ignominy of dying helpless, face down, half naked. His eyes bulged; his face was a florid purple; still the meaty fingers bored deep into the soft tissues of his neck. Praying madly, he fought to tense his muscles and force the loathsome fingers out. Blackness assailed him in waves, but he willed himself to remain conscious.

The towel slipped to the floor, Danson jumping and slapping against the smooth stone, fighting strangulation. His body paled as the blood flooded the upper torso, rushing to the scene of mortal struggle.

Dimly, as from a great distance, Danson felt his left leg striking against the big man's thighs. A powerful resolve and an abhorrence of this evil, so concentrated he could taste its bitterness, surged through his weakening body. *God of my needs, give me strength*, he prayed. With a mighty gathering of will and energy, Danson swung his left leg back and drove it forward with a roundhouse kick that smashed into the giant's groin. The attendant roared and lurched sideways, clutching his pain, crashing head-first to the stone floor. The enormous head bounced once with the soft crack of a dropped watermelon.

A terrible roaring filled Danson's mind. One nagging thought fought to be heard through the sweeping nausea, the gasping, raking chokes, the colossal relief in being alive. *The note . . . where is the note?*

He rolled off the stone, landing on the unconscious attendant's quivering belly. He lurched unsteadily to his feet and doubled over instantly from the crashing pain at his temples. Half running, half stumbling, he staggered past the anterooms and dressing cubicles along the main hall. The cool marble reminded him of gravestones.

The note! . . . God, please, the note . . .

It was excruciating to swallow. His throat felt mangled. *Why aren't there other people here?* He tried to yell, but all that came out was a weak gargle. *Almost there.* His head started spinning, the ceiling and floor exchanging places.

Movement to the right. His cubicle. A man with his pants, running. *Stop!* He thought he'd yelled it, but there was no answering echo. Only the hollow footfalls of the escaping thief. *The note . . .*

He fell headlong into utter darkness. The fall continued for thousands of feet down a mountain that would not reveal its treasure.

8

BRIGADIER GENERAL OZDEMIR SEKER was in the foulest of moods. As chief of army propaganda for the Koraltan government, he deserved better than what this day was serving him raw. From the moment his alarm clock failed to awaken him, the general felt an ominous foreboding about what the day held in store.

Seker watched and precisely at eight that morning, the Rolls Silver Cloud glided noiselessly to the curb in front of the elegant two-story Victorian house next door. General Turan Tokay, flawlessly attired in medal-laden uniform, stepped smartly from his front door to the waiting limousine as he did every morning, nodding ever so slightly to the military chauffeur, who stood rigidly at attention until the general was inside. Then he closed the door with a soft, expensive *schlunk!*

The acrid taste of hatred for Tokay canceled out the flavor of General Seker's toothpaste that morning. His starch-necked neighbor positively clanked with honor and bravery when he walked. But General Seker knew how much of that metallic nobility had been purchased through bribes, kickbacks, and extortion. General Tokay was ten years younger, yet he had risen to the rank of chief of general staff in the Ministry of Defense in half the time it had taken Seker to attain his tiny niche in the small, ill-funded, and distinctly unglamorous department across the hall.

General Seker dressed as smartly as he could; the coat that had always hidden his frayed cuffs was itself beginning to fray. At precisely eight-thirty, his Rolls Silver Cloud would arrive for the fifteen-minute drive downtown to the seat of government and the stuffy office across the hall from the door through which his neighbor passed half an hour earlier. On closer inspection, had they cared, the inhabitants of all the other Victorian houses on the street would have noticed a striking similarity between the first chauffeur and the second. They would have discovered that not only the chauffeurs but the limousines they drove were one and the same. Sharing the ride would have meant intolerable loss of face. It was the last symbol of status left to General Seker. When the day arrived that he was forced to ride with General Tokay, and it would surely come, he would kill himself.

When the mantel clock chimed the half hour, General Seker opened his front door and stopped short. There was no car. The street was empty. For another half hour he stood in the doorway and stared at the spot where the Rolls Silver Cloud should be. The telephone rang six times before he moved to an-

swer it. It was his secretary explaining the delay—
flat tire.

Rolls Royces do not get flat tires, he mused sarcastically. Who had ever seen a man in a silk suit by
the side of the road changing the flat on his Rolls
Royce? They were invincible, above the petty break-
downs and cheap delays of lesser autos. This was Tokay's doing—Seker was certain of it. Deliberate
humiliation was in Tokay's arsenal of tricks. In fact,
General Tokay was not above slashing the tires himself.

At last a sheepish chauffeur rang the front door
chimes at nine-forty-five, laying his tardiness to the
tire and the need to clean up after the incident. A
streak of grime adorned his nose, but Seker said
nothing. He was too busy second-guessing Tokay.

Upon Seker's arrival at his meager office, his secretary informed him that the chief of general staff
wished to see him immediately. *The murderous
deed to be done at last,* thought Seker gloomily. The
first time he had spoken face to face with Tokay had
been two years before when the military wrested
power from then President Kemal Gurun, a dodder-
ing old recluse, whose chief concern in life seemed to
be the air pollution in Ankara. Dev-Sol, the orga-
nized union of Marxist rabble, had been pounding
down the doors to the chambers of the Grand National Assembly. General Tokay, then commander of
the army, had ordered the doors swung wide. The
mob's seething fury swarmed into the chambers,
changing rapidly to wide-eyed terror. A battery of artillery was trained on them from atop the banks of
legislators' desks. The shrieking crowd had turned

back on itself. Fourteen peasants had been trampled to death, and half a dozen more were critically injured without a single shot fired. Since then Tokay's elite "Sons of Justice," ruthless guerilla fighters culled from the ranks, had rounded up fifty thousand suspected terrorists. Of those, five hundred had been publicly executed, another two thousand quietly "removed."

Tokay had been widely hailed—by his countrymen and by the United States government—as a savior. He had broken the back of Marxist insurrection. He was granted free reign to adjust the military infrastructure to include those he trusted most. He saw in then-Colonel Seker a loyal party man, who only made waves in the water polo tournament at the officers' club pool. Perfect for the propaganda department, Tokay decided. Flatter him with a promotion and he would "yes" you until the day he died.

Seker had indeed been flattered and at first endeavored gladly to paint the picture of government and military solidarity as crisp and clean as the daily memos from Tokay instructed him to do. But with increasing dismay, he watched Tokay build a tiny fiefdom across the hall. Requisitions for equipment and supplies were grossly inflated, the superfluous goods sold internationally at black market prices and the profits used to maintain Tokay's Grecian villa on the Isle of Rhodes. Dissenters were whisked away for a weekend of wine and women on the sun-washed shores, returning refreshed, their former complaints magically forgotten.

President Koraltan did not question Tokay's extracurricular activities; neither did the defense minister. They had never been to the villa but had heard the adoring references to "Tokay the Great" in the office buildings and bazaar stalls of the land. He was good for public relations. With inflation running at 100 percent and unemployment at 25 percent, public relations was tops on the Koraltan government's list of priorities.

Seker had never been to the villa either, but for vastly different reasons. The president and the defense minister did not require invitations. It would be an unnecessary expense. In some ways it would be equally impractical to invite the chief of army propaganda. Seker knew that Tokay could crush him as easily as a bug beneath his heel if he chose to do so. Attempting to discredit Turkey's national hero would be professional suicide.

But Tokay had felt pity for the meek little man across the hall and had extended the invitation to Villa Monolithos—the "Great Rock"—on five separate occasions. Five times it had been refused. Rather than anger, Tokay felt a kind of bemused admiration for the other's silent protest. At least Seker did not totally lack intestinal fortitude.

Wondering why Tokay wished to see him, Seker felt physically ill. He frantically searched his memory for any transgression against the chief of the Ministry of Defense. None came to mind, but then Tokay was not known for needing evidence to eliminate someone.

Seker stepped shakily through the doorway into Tokay's office, a futuristic jumble of chrome and suede. The chief of the general staff of the Ministry of Defense stood with his back to the door, staring stolidly out the floor-to-ceiling window opposite his desk. Hands clasped behind his back, he twiddled restlessly with a miniature Rubik's Cube. The door closed behind Seker, and Tokay turned.

"Drink?" he asked, face gravely set. Tokay looked as if he were fighting food poisoning. He was a tall man and fussily conscious of preserving a military erectness. But today, he was strangely stooped and haggard-looking. Seker declined the drink and wondered at the man's pallor.

"This detestable heat," mumbled Tokay obliquely, glancing at the digital clock on the desk. "Just ten and already hotter than an itchy Kurdistani!"

Seker could not believe this was the same man who had so arrogantly sauntered from his home that very morning. The man before him, ostensibly the commander of the fifth largest standing army in the world, was reacting schizophrenically to something. Might the axe finally have fallen?

"We placed first in the polls again," Tokay said huskily. "According to the American Freedom Foundation, the sharpest loss of civil liberties for the year occurred in 'militarily repressive Turkey.'" Tokay's voice tightened, taking on an air of mock pride. "We are far in front of El Salvador, Bolivia, and Haiti in all categories, with a particularly fine showing in suppression of the press and manipulation of the judiciary."

Tokay whirled around from the window and slammed a fist into the desk top. Seker jumped. "Pompous idiots!" Tokay seethed. "Crying over the rise in international terrorism while branding us, who are doing something about it, as tyrants. Did you know that according to their grand four-color charts, only a third of the world's population lives in freedom, and you and I are not included, Seker? That's right, the Turks, who of all the Muslims were first to abolish fanatical theocratic rule, opting for democracy instead—and who were first to abolish the veil and give women back their humanity and their dignity just four years after they were given the vote in America. Do they ever speak of the Turks who fought their guts out in Korea, whose courage resulted in the highest casualty rate of any United Nations member engaged in the war? Where is their thanks for that?

"Ah, but forgive me, General. We are not here to discuss popularity polls." Tokay straightened a little. "Issues of far greater importance concern us this morning. The Kurdish separatists are in an unholy alliance with Armenia, Muslim and Christian in the same bed. A quarter-million of them are poised in the east for an assault on our border. Baghdad, in spite of hating the Kurd dogs as much as we, is backing the coalition in case they succeed in securing the Anatolian Plain. Moscow, well under the table, is supplying limited weaponry and some intelligence in the same eventuality. They've never given up a scheme to secure access to the Persian Gulf and its oil by way of an ice-free port in Abadan, and while they'd have to get past Tehran to do it, this might be one chess move closer to realizing it. It could serve to appease the countries of Georgia, Armenia, and Azerbaijan by bringing them into the stew. A destabilized Eastern Europe is like a loose cannon in a crystal factory, and Moscow's willingness to parlay with Islam makes me doubly suspicious they're after a way to tie the cannon down."

Tokay paced, fingers flying over the Rubik squares in nervous agitation. The rapid clicking of the cube filled the silence. "Think of it, General. Moscow, the Kurds, the Iraqis, and the Armenians hold a fat poker hand among them. Our own National Salvation Party looks at what's going on and says, 'This is our chance to restore Islamic law and governance to Turkey and to destroy the democratic and secular overseers we have hated for far too long.' So they convince our Sunni Muslim majority to join the coalition and the eventual march to the Gulf. Before long, General, you and I could be pushing pencils in Istanbul."

Seker wished he'd had breakfast that morning. Bad news on an empty stomach was asking for ulcers.

"U.S. President Pierce has issued a warning to all parties that his nation's interests in the Middle East will not be compromised. But who can second-guess a putrid Kurdish alliance such as this? We may well be on the brink of war, General!"

Tokay gripped the back of the desk chair. His knuckles showed white. Seker's voice came out in a barely audible whisper. "What would you have me do?"

"Koraltan has called an emergency session of the National Assembly for one o'clock. At that time, we must be prepared to deliver in writing the status of Turkish Armed Forces today. Exactly what is that status, General?"

Seker swallowed dryly. While Tokay strutted and played the role of commander-in-chief, Seker had been devoting the bulk of his time to what he smirkingly called his "import-export business." Fortunately, in the dreadful scenario unfolding around them, Turkish militarism was its strong suit and thrived despite the excesses of some of its key personnel. Turks gladly sacrificed to defend the homeland. National smokers had paid for the Air Force when parliament declared a half-century ago that all packets containing twenty cigarettes would henceforth contain but nineteen. The government used the twentieth to raise money to buy fighter planes. Regardless of Tokay's ignorance, Turkey's defense preparedness was excellent. Seker cleared his throat.

"One quarter of the national budget has gone into defense maintenance, including replacement of obsolete equipment and staff training. Currently, there are 566 thousand personnel on active duty including 470 thousand army, 51 thousand air force, and 45 thousand navy. Nearly 1 million are in active reserve with an additional million inactive but trained. Add to that another 50 thousand national police and 125 thousand paramilitary gendarmerie, and we could mobilize a force well in excess of two and a half million within a minimum seventy-two hours."

Seker warmed to his subject, recognizing for the first time his advantage over his younger commander. It might take a war, but Seker was going to shine at last. "Army has sixteen infantry divisions (two mechanized), one armored division, nine separate infantry brigades (four mechanized), five separate armored brigades, one commando brigade, and four SSM (surface-to-surface missile) battalions; plus two infantry divisions on Cyprus.

"Air Force has eleven forward ground attack squadrons, three fighter-interceptor squadrons, two reconnaissance squadrons, five transport squadrons, and eight SAM (surface-to-air missile) squadrons; equipment inventory includes 309 combat aircraft.

"Navy has northern and southern sea area commands and a fleet command—a war fleet, submarine fleet, mine fleet, landing units, and two ASW (anti-submarine warfare) aviation squadrons. In addition, there are twenty-four civil airfields and ten major and thirty-five minor seaports available for military use."

General Tokay, who had paced all through his subordinate's unfaltering monologue, stopped and looked at General Seker. "Congratulations, General. You are well informed. Have it typed immediately and six hundred copies printed for this afternoon's session. I will place the entire military on red alert."

General Seker was about to close the door behind him when he remembered another matter that might prove important in light of the new developments. "Excuse me, General Tokay," he said, poking his head back into the room. "There is one other thing. A representative of an American expedition to Ararat is due in my office this afternoon to seek a government permit to climb. I assume you wish me to send him packing. It wouldn't do to have this mongrel coalition mistake the intentions of a pack of glassy-eyed relic hunters—"

"No!" shouted Tokay, anxiety making the cords of his neck stretch taut. He straightened to full height. "You will do nothing of the sort. Accord the representative every courtesy and issue the permit without a moment's delay."

"Yes, General, of course—as you wish." Seker closed the door hastily. His astonishment was total. Allow a team of Americans to swarm over the face of a mountain within thirty-five miles of a massing enemy force? Either Tokay was insane or he had exposed but a tip of the iceberg to his chief of army propaganda. Seker sensed he had been told less than Tokay knew.

CHAPTER 9

CEVDET DEMIRKOL felt the razor sharpness of his father's scimitar for perhaps the thousandth time since he had descended beneath the earth, and again he was comforted. The wooden cross clutched to his chest made him feel less hunted. They had come for what he knew, stalking him among the passageways and endless caverns of the Fairy Chimneys. Three of their bodies would likely never be found, hidden as were other secrets in one of the thousand subterranean Christian churches honeycombing the area.

It helped him to recite: "A poor man watched a thousand years before the gate of Paradise. Then, while he snatched a little sleep, it opened and shut." The old Persian proverb kept him alert.

He licked the water from the walls eight stories beneath the sunbaked land of fantastic shapes carved by man and nature from volcanic tuff less than two hundred miles from Ankara. Local wine, cheaper than hauled water from the valley, supplemented

ground moisture. Fruit and vegetables awaiting ex-
port to Europe in vast neighboring storage caves gave
sustenance. Only Lord Onouphirius, the eccentric
Armenian monk with allegiance to no government,
knew his precise location. The farmers who rented
the most accessible caves were themselves fearful of
the bizarre landscape, preferring their lower orchards
and alfalfa fields to the dreamland above. The fifteen-
hundred-square-mile moonscape of Cappadocia was
said to make mystics of men and widows of their
women.

But Cevdet found nourishment for his soul
among the monasteries and Byzantine frescoes of
these holy holes. If ever he had need of such sanctuary, it was now. Above and beside him in vivid colors
that almost shone in the half-light from four ventila-
tion shafts were lively renderings of the raising of
Lazarus, the miracle of the loaves and fishes, the
healing of the blind, the Crucifixion and Resurrection. Painted by centuries of Cappadocian Christians, the caves lent solace and asylum, as had the
Roman catacombs, and for similar reasons. Roman
persecution, Byzantine oppression, Turkish-
Ottoman excesses—all had served to drive as many
as thirty thousand Christians below ground. Christian murals in the mountains of Allah. It was to Cevdet a delicious irony.

The meticulously honed blade of the scimitar
reminded him of his immediate peril, and he relished its precision. His was a warrior family. His
great-grandfather, son of Christian parents, had been
taken into slavery as a small boy by the Turkish Janissaries or "new troops." Sent to live with a Muslim

family, he had been converted to Islam against his will, then taken to Constantinople to train for the Janissary Corps. These elite troops swore a vow of celibacy, prayed furiously, and practiced "mortal combat" on one another. They not only became the most feared body of troops on the face of the earth but dangerously independent. To display their displeasure with a government decision and forewarn of an impending coup, the troops dumped their giant soup kettles in the barracks square. Having become virtually unmanageable by 1826, hundreds of them were cannonaded to death by the sultan. Ever willing to place such massacres in the best light, Turkish historians referred to the execution as "The Auspicious Incident." Cevdet's great-grandfather survived the massacre but fled the corps. He changed his name, married, and fathered sixteen children.

Cevdet's grandfather voluntarily became one of the last of the Janissaries, renouncing his vows only after the corps was officially disbanded. Cevdet's father was a much-decorated major general in the modern republic's land forces. Cevdet himself, after majoring in history at university and serving the obligatory twenty months with the army, was confused and hurt over his nation's bloody military past. His great-grandfather nearly murdered, his Armenian ancestors annihilated by the hundreds of thousands in the 1890s and again in 1915, his indoctrination into the much-touted *jihad* or Muslim holy war that transcended nationalistic lines—all served to create in him a core of mistrust and a fierce independence, what he cynically called the "living Janissary spirit" of his forefathers.

That commando spirit had sent him parachuting into Dezful, Iran, on the side of the Iraqis in their prolonged war. To him, the ayatollah was deranged and as bad for public relations as the bloody sultans ever were. As a member of the elite unit called "The Daggers," he was to help cut the pipeline that carried 70 percent of Iran's basic stock of kerosene heating fuel and thereby cripple its theocratic government. Soviet MiG-23s, surface-to-surface Scud missiles, and T-55 tanks had kicked in the front door to the city, but the infantry failed to show. While The Daggers awaited troop support, the Iranians completed a twenty-four-inch pipeline from Isfahan to Tehran, making the taking of Dezful purely academic.

However stillborn his paratroop exploits, Cevdet's reputation as a fearless and principled fighter reached the ears of Richard Bascomb, whose earth movers and engineers were transforming the ancient land with dams and factories and technology. More importantly, the incredible thing that Cevdet believed more strongly than his own existence had brought Bascomb fully alert.

"Never mind where I am for now," Cevdet had curtly told Bascomb on the phone from Ankara four days ago. "Others have known; others have died. What you need know is that the Ark of Noah exists. For how long, however, I cannot say. There is much unrest in my country, and there are many whose fevered imaginations crawl with reasons to destroy anything at all."

A band of usually dauntless Kurdish nomads had ridden their mounts to the point of death to reach Cevdet with the news. Their wild eyes and nearly incoherent telling of what they had seen bore testimony to their discovery more eloquently than reasoned words. They had ridden unnoticed past Turkish soldiers guarding the base of the mountain from unauthorized intrusion. The Kurds were a law unto themselves, and rather than risk random and brutal attack, the Turks often looked the other way.

To the Kurds, Mount Ararat or Ağri Dağh was a place of dread, the mountain of evil. Many would not even look upon its slopes for fear of being struck dead. The only way to reach it was to be pure as a young child, free of all personal evil. Despite the Kurds' reputation for wiliness, even they were honest enough to admit none of them qualified.

But something unsettling was happening to Ararat. Its hood, normally buried in blackened mists, stabbed by periodic flashes of lightning, had been clearly visible for more than three weeks. Though they'd heard the centuries-old tales of terror, one balmy night of drinking drew the Kurdish band up Ararat's lower slopes, then ever higher into the rocky realm usually hidden from view. Laughingly they chased and prodded one another higher still, a massive moon lighting their faltering, drunken way.

They had stumbled headlong into the shape. Its squarish contours and wooden feel defied any natural formation. It loomed above them in the darkness, the roof starkly defined in moon glow, in a niche of glacial rock fourteen thousand dizzying feet above the valley floor at the foot of Abich II Glacier. They fled in terror to the more familiar dangers lower down the mountain. For forty-eight hours they neither slept nor ate before their hellish dash to Cevdet's camp. At every hoofbeat they imagined the mammoth ship overtaking them and burying them beneath its judgmental slide into the present.

A sharp scraping sound jerked Cevdet upright. The cross of gopher wood, sliced into being from the Ark itself, banged against his chest—his heart hammered back.

Great-grandfather, great-grandfather, grant me the courage of Ham, Shem, and Japheth to conquer the approaching evil as surely as they fanned out across a new washed world to claim it for the Lord God of Righteousness!

Cevdet crouched, body taut, sword poised to slash intruding knees, felling the marauders and allowing him time to reach their throats.

Then came a dull rapping as of wood against stone, Cevdet counted five blows, then strained for the voice to follow.

"It was said that Mohammed used three weapons—a tongue, a whip, and a sword—" intoned an ancient shrill voice, scraped thin by years of valley dust and chanting.

"—but that he only used the second or third when the first failed," finished Cevdet, slumping emotionally drained and relieved against the cool cave wall.

The little procession that entered Cevdet's sanctuary was led by an impossibly shriveled little man, the self-proclaimed Lord Onouphirius, enveloped in thick priestly robes, a gnarled wooden staff in his clawed hand. He seemed to glide across the rough cave floor as if on wheels. He cocked his head to one side, eyes tightly shut, and from his tiny puckered mouth came a string of words half sung, half chanted:

> We will make the path to happiness easy and safe to all such as fear Allah, and give alms, and believe the truth proclaimed by Allah's messenger. But we will make easy the path to distress and misery for all such as are niggardly, are bent on making riches, and deny the truth when it is proclaimed to them. When these last fall headlong into hell, their wealth will avail them nothing. In the burning furnace they shall burn and broil!

Ibrahim Hasan and Reg Danson waited quietly at the entrance to the room, struck dumb in the other world created by sword, priest, and subterranean frescoes of another time.

The wizened priest rushed to Cevdet and knelt by his side with alarming swiftness. He wrapped the skeleton of his scrawny hands around Cevdet's wrist and planted thin lips on the back of the strong fingers.

"Let me kiss the hand of valor," he murmured in a high-pitched whine, "and heaven shall be my reward!"

As old as he was, Lord Onouphirius sprang to his feet and peered fiercely at Danson from the depths of the brown goat's-hair cowl wreathing his face.

"He knows of the ship in the sky," whined the priest. "He says it must no longer remain our shrine alone but must be given to the world to heal the insanity. I spit on man beyond the valley, but Allah's warrior must be believed. Go at once and may the mother of mountains suckle you in your quest!"

Danson met Cevdet's drilling gaze and saw in it a blaze of commitment stronger than fear, mightier than death. The Bible was full of it, but he'd never met it face to face until now. Momentary panic pricked his spine. Suddenly Cevdet's link with the divine omnipotence that empowered Noah and his sons to defy global catastrophe dwarfed Danson. His own faith was pitifully meager when confronted with this valley and this mountain that Noah walked. These people, whom Noah begat, were soldiers of the soil, keepers of the eternal secrets entrusted to Noah's issue. They groaned when the earth groaned, rejoiced when it blossomed forth in rejoicing; for millennia the Mystery had been safe with them. Now Danson came with his corporate financing, his sophisticated gadgetry—Arthur Bryce had contemptuously called it "expeditionary tonnage"—and his technocratic philosophies and artificiality to pluck the Mystery eons old, yet mystically fresh, from its sacred moorings. Reg no longer knew if he could.

Cevdet saw the uncertainty in Danson's eyes and spoke. "You are no longer in your element, Mr. Danson, and that unsettles the spirit. The Evil One would have it that way. Consider, however, how the nineteenth-century Chinese warlords fought their bloodless battles. Rivals met in a tent and went through an elaborate tea ceremony, each leader dropping hints as to the number of his men, the size and fire power of his weapons. The one outclassed would admit his enemy stronger and deserving of victory and pay reparations. The two enemies then parted, no loss of life, all-important face having been saved. Let us go to Mount Ararat as to tea. We will meet the enemy, remind him that Lord God the All-Powerful is with us and that the ship is His. The Evil One *is* severely outclassed, Mr. Danson, is he not?"

Before Reg could answer, Lord Onouphirius spoke in his familiar singsong. "If you are ignorant of the state of the ant under your foot, know it resembles your own condition under the foot of the elephant. The Evil One is an ant; God is an elephant. Let us be done with this discussion!"

With that the priest glided out of the room and up the passageway, pushing Hasan ahead of him. His muttering echoed back to the two men left behind. "You're too quiet for a holy man. You haven't done anything Allah won't forgive, unless of course you've become a merchant. You haven't, have you?"

Hasan's answer was lost around another turn in the passageway. Cevdet smiled, and Danson helped him to his feet.

Reg, his eyes grown more accustomed to the light in the grotto, marveled at the yellows and browns in the fresco of the Last Supper Cevdet had been leaning against. What faithful follower had been driven underground to paint such a tribute to his Lord? There were thirteen present with Jesus on the cave wall—The Twelve joined by Lucifer, glowering satanically in the background, his features closely resembling those of the haughty sultans in paintings Reg had seen in the Grand Bazaar.

Reg's hand moved to the large, roughly hewn

cross around Cevdet's neck. He could not resist reaching out to feel its form.

"Grasp it firmly, Mr. Danson," Cevdet urged, "for you yourself have now touched the Ark, and there is no turning back!"

CHAPTER 10

THE SWELTERING TARMAC at Karaköse
teemed with life. Two dozen laborers and scientists
with clipboards and water flasks wrestled expedition
supplies into place. Tony Danson, shirtless, a red ker-
chief tied about his forehead, inspected the scientific
equipment, survival gear, and climbing apparatus assembled for loading aboard military transport vehicles for the three-hour journey to Dogubayazit and
the beginning of the ascent. Stoves, lamps, butane
canisters, lightweight tents, sleeping bags, back-
packs, mountain boots, crampons, and ice axes lit-
tered the area in the frying heat of late afternoon.

When his father had suggested Tony go ahead to
the staging site and monitor preparations, Tony felt a
surge of pride and fear. To be so trusted was remarkable, considering the badly burned bridges in their
relationship. To move among scientific and military
experts as a twenty-year-old mountaineering authority was pretty heady stuff. In a group of thirty anti-
nuke protestors he knew his bearings; here his

stomach knotted with the fear of not measuring up.

"Mr. Danson! Come please."

Tony ducked beneath the awning and entered a makeshift field hospital. On ten beds lay the sweating bodies of the main Ark removal team. The five Israelis, three Iraqis, and two Americans were connected via nasal tubes to tanks of air-oxygen mixture. For most of a week they had been undergoing a program of lung-heart regeneration developed in Germany. Heavy vitamin doses and several hours of air-oxygen intake were followed with mild drugs to increase blood flow throughout the body. The effect would be to return the oxygen supply to the organs with levels normally found only in the young. Result: prolonged strenuous exertion at high altitudes without adverse physical deterioration.

The Dansons, Cevdet, and Ibrahim Hasan, as late arrivals, would be "bled" on the climb to keep their blood from thickening. High altitudes stimulate overproduction of red corpuscles, turning the blood to sludge and depriving tissues of needed oxygen. Removing some of the thick blood "sludge" and replacing it with plasma would increase muscle performance and exercise tolerance. The process reminded Tony of Antarctic ice fish, which possess no red cells at all. They are active in water only two degrees above that at which no life could be sustained.

One of the Iraqis was demolition expert Ahmed Karim Kassem. He motioned Tony over to his cot and handed him a lightweight transmitter.

"Are you familiar with the Pieps 2?" he asked in a voice made flat and tight by the plastic tubing in his nose.

Tony nodded. "I've read about them. First opportunity to use them though." The radio transmitters were Austrian-made and designed to operate on two alkali-manganese batteries for at least five hundred working hours. Upon entering the hazardous snow zone, each member of the party would switch to the transmit mode and become individual broadcast beacons. The intense heat would have by now weakened the snow pack on the upper slopes, making avalanches a treacherous possibility. Should an avalanche bury someone, the others would immediately switch to the receive channel and search in the direction of the increasingly loud beeping signal. Victims as deep as one hundred feet had been located in less than five minutes with the system.

"I'll feel a lot safer with these babies along," said Tony, flashing a friendly smile at Ahmed. He was met with a curious gloomy stare that made him shiver despite the heat.

"There are no trees on this mountain," said Ahmed in his tight monotone. "No shelter, no wood for fire. Water is almost as scarce; the porous volcanic rock absorbs it as fast as it melts. Yawning crevices are everywhere camouflaged by a thin layer of snow crust. Snow and rock avalanches are triggered by the mere sound of two men conversing. It is Satan's mountain!"

Tony glanced at the man in surprise and alarm. Ahmed Kassem was a pragmatist, a veteran of wars and paratroop drops under heavy enemy fire. Yet he was trembling now at the simple mention of a mountain.

"Must be a cold coming on," Ahmed rasped, attempting to shrink away from Tony and the terrors beyond. "Hotter than the flames of hell and I catch cold!"

Tony offered to find him a blanket, but Ahmed only murmured for him to check the probe poles. The seven-foot, sectional aluminum ski poles were tied in three bundles. They could be threaded together to create a search prod for buried equipment—and bodies. Tony shuddered. Ahmed's dark mood was catching.

Tony reached for a tube of PABA gel and spread it liberally over his bare skin. Without the sunscreen, his fair North American hide would have been blistered, peeled, and bloody from the relentless sun. As he rubbed he chided himself for catching Ahmed's superstitious fears. Everyone in this land had a touch of the wall-eyed crazies as far as Tony was concerned. Passions, curses, and Koranic pronouncements seemed to be standard equipment in the Fertile Crescent. So strong was the spell that Tony kept looking at everyone he met to see if his throat had ever been cut.

Feeling sheepish, he grinned and thought of the genuine danger he had experienced. Hurtling at a hundred miles an hour down the sheer granite face of Yosemite's El Capitan made the romp up Ararat a Sunday outing. Take fifteen hundred feet of gut-tearing free-fall in ten seconds and the snap of the chute a slender twelve hundred feet from the ground—now that was pure, undiluted terror. A day's strenuous hike up, a two-minute ride down. He'd been jailed twice and fined two hundred dollars, in his mind a small price to pay for the exhilaration of a death dive and resurrection. Cliff diving was a criminal act only to those too cowardly to themselves sail off the ends of the earth.

A jeep careened into the compound and lurched to a halt. Reg Danson, Ibrahim Hasan, and Cevdet Demirkol stepped down and brushed clouds of dust from their clothing. Reg stretched mightily, wincing from the pain of travel and the bath house massage. *Who tried to kill me?* he asked himself again and again. *Did Cevdet get them all? Dear Lord, assassins!* He was worried for Tony and the others, but it was too late to turn back now. Besides, they would be safe once they began the ascent.

A soldier in spit-shine military attire, a rifle slung familiarly over one shoulder, spoke to the new arrivals, then led them off in the direction of the camp command post.

"Wait'll my dad gets a load of Lieutenant Cayan," said Tony aloud, smiling impishly. "It could change his entire outlook on the military establishment!"

"Or confirm his worst fears," said Kassem with a soft snort.

DETERMINED to have answers, Reg followed the soldier to the large headquarters tent. Too many pieces of the puzzle still did not fit. It was entirely too easy. Why was the Turkish government being so very accommodating to this expedition when it had sent so many past American-backed Ark teams packing? Astronaut James Baldwin had made half a dozen attempts and been bureaucratically blocked at nearly every turn. Arthur Bryce had been coming to the mountain for forty years and leaving empty-handed. Now suddenly the way was cleared for a brand-new exploration team, and not only would they be allowed to remove Turkey's most precious archaeological treasure, but they were being supplied security troops and outfitters compliments of the government. The unanswerables were beginning to mount.

While Hasan and Demirkol waited outside, Reg entered the tent. Inside, a strikingly beautiful woman in a white aviator's jumpsuit sat writing at a battered metal desk amid stacks of wooden crates, cartons, and boxes. Jet-black hair fell to her shoulders and reflected the soft lamp glow in blazes of shimmering light. Green eyes as clear and captivating as cut emeralds, yet bearing a warning, glanced up as he entered. The cheekbones rose high and proud. The sculpted chin, the flawlessly smooth throat—Reg felt his pulse quicken. Lieutenant Cayan must be highly regarded to rate an aide as lovely as she.

The woman rose to eye-level with Reg and extended her hand. "Lieutenant Nilay Cayan," she said briskly. The voice was caramel studded with thorns. "You undoubtedly are Reginald Danson."

Reg shook the proffered hand and wondered at its firmness. The nails were immaculate in clear polish, the fingers slender and warm. He barely recovered his surprise in time to say yes before the lieutenant continued.

"All supplies have arrived as requisitioned; all personnel are present and briefed. Our drivers have slept and are prepared to move out in convoy immediately. Best to move quickly while the weather is with us and the brigand Kurds are holed up counting the day's take. As you Americans are fond of saying, delay would be counterproductive."

Lieutenant Cayan made a sweeping gesture at the cartons stacked about the desk. "At my suggestion we have added several hundred portions of high-energy trail food—a blend of cocoa, chocolate, peanut butter, chopped walnuts, raisins, coconut, and brown sugar. Three rations a day will keep us alert and fortified. I can spare two weeks, Mr. Danson, and then I have other pressing military matters."

Reg felt his ire rising. "I take it, Lieutenant, you do not place much credence in our mission?"

"What I think matters little. I believe it was your own director of the University of Pennsylvania museum, Froelich Rainey, who, when asked what he considered the prospects of finding the Ark, answered, 'Absolutely anything is possible in this world, but if there's anything that's impossible in archaeology, this is it.'" Her eyes were like emerald drill bits aimed at his skull. "Forgive me, Mr. Danson, but I understand you chase a fair number of legends."

Reg prayed for the strength to quell his anger at this infuriating beauty. "I investigate the unknown if that's what you mean, much like Columbus, Marco Polo, Pasteur, Madame Curie, and others. I regret I am unable to list a single Turk among them, however. Repression does not breed discovery." He might have felt shame at his tone, but he guessed this woman respected vinegar.

Her faint smile betrayed nothing. She dismissed the stolid soldier at the tent door and motioned Danson to a chair. After pouring tea, she leaned against the desk and stared at the canvas ceiling. *Not many women could look as stunning in coveralls and black army boots laced to mid-shin,* thought Reg appreciatively.

"I need not defend my land to you, a foreigner," she began, her words carefully measured. "Turkey is an exquisite country, keeper of ancient treasures beyond human belief. Discovering the world is round or a reliable source of silk for the garment trade is but mildly interesting when compared to the incredible contributions of Islam. We produced the leading physicians of Asia, Africa, and Europe. Ophthalmology was our 'discovery,' the gift of sight to the needy without number. We have penned lyric poetry to lift the hearts of humankind. At least twenty-five written languages were used in the Ottoman Empire. Suleyman I was named the Brilliant for his splendid military strategy by land and sea. Your society is blind to the contributions of our culture, for all you see is the blood. Odd that a Christian culture such as yours would be squeamish on that point. Without shed blood, where would either of us be?"

"We who are Christians are covered by the shed blood of God's sinless and only Son," Reg replied, sipping carefully at the scalding contents of his tea glass. "Your salvation seems to depend on being covered in the blood of as many people opposed to Islamic goals as possible. Suicide bombings are rather common among your people, are they not?"

"A people of principle and passion believe there is a higher law than mere passive civil disobedience," Lieutenant Cayan responded, her eyes never leaving Reg's for a moment. "Westerners place an abominably high price on the value of human flesh; no wonder you are such easy prey for terrorists and kidnappers of every persuasion. To die for a righteous cause, now *that*, Mr. Danson, makes sense of our existence. But you Americans have lost touch with that ideal."

Curiously, something did not ring true in the lieutenant's recitation of Islamic glory. It lacked conviction; it sounded too practiced, too Chamber of Commerce. For the first time since they'd met, Lieutenant Cayan's gaze dropped, and she turned hurriedly to arrange the papers on her desk.

"Tell me, Lieutenant, why the welcome mat?" Reg sipped tea and waited.

"I am not certain what you mean."

Reg felt she was stalling. "Why accord us a military escort into one of the world's most militarily sensitive regions? Why pour tea in a tent when I am, by your own admission, about to waste two weeks of your valuable time? Why, in short, give me the time of day?"

Lieutenant Cayan's eyes sparked. Any trace of uncertainty was gone. "Expediency, necessity, compromise—take your pick, Mr. Danson. Turkey is coming into its own, and we desire to take a more strategic and deserved position among the world's powers. To that end we must begin to fashion a global communications system of satellites capable of handling not only scientific, meteorological, and experimental functions but increased domestic, international, and military communications duties.

"The fly in the ointment is that we are relatively late bloomers as these things go. Already upward of a

hundred operating satellites occupy the choicest orbit, a narrow belt some 22,300 miles above the Equa-
tor. The prime radio frequency band they use is
nearly saturated; a very few 'parking' slots remain.
We remove all bureaucratic obstacles to the Ark,
NASA pulls the necessary strings to grant us parking
privileges. A small concession given the rewards,
wouldn't you agree?"

"Unless we find the Ark," Danson replied evenly.

Lieutenant Cayan ignored the remark.

Reg persisted. "What of any number of trigger-
happy splinter groups this region seems so blessed
with? I believe Cevdet Demirkol and I have already
made the acquaintance of some." He rubbed his tender neck. "Isn't there a danger they might misinter-
pret our presence? For that matter, how will Muslim
fundamentalists take to our removal of the greatest
of holy antiquities?"

"We have one of the largest standing armies in
the world," she said, refilling his glass, "second only
to that of the United States within the NATO alliance. The Third Army is headquartered at Erzurum
120 miles to our west and is on emergency mobiliza-
tion as of yesterday afternoon. Its command covers
the former Soviet trans-Caucasian border and the
historic invasion routes from the east. Tens of thousands of troops are being deployed throughout the
harsh mountains and deep valleys of eastern Anatolia against threatened Kurdish insurrection and militant Muslim intrigue. The Third Army knows the
rugged terrain and inaccessible areas of the eastern
border. Massive use of armored vehicles is prohibi-
tive in this stern and unforgiving land. But we have

trained huge numbers of mounted cavalry who can negotiate the treacherous ravines and towering escarpments as nimbly as fairy sprites. Enemies of any stripe face virtual annihilation should they foolishly attack the Anatolia!"

Reg smiled from behind his glass despite the sobering news of unrest. He had little difficulty imagining this woman, saber clenched between her teeth, astride a wild mountain steed charging full tilt into enemy territory. Woe to the Kurds!

Nilay Cayan wrestled with just how much to tell the handsome American. The Kurdish-Armenian alliance could strike at any time. The Third Army was actually swarming to the Turkish border with Iran, a scant twenty miles from Dogu-bayazit at the foot of Ararat. There they would remain, she fervently prayed, until her American guest had enough of the terrible mountain, the satellite agreement had been forged, and she had been promoted to major, perhaps even lieutenant colonel. She would be halfway to general then, a living mockery of the bloody sultans. She, a woman.

Cayan decided against telling Danson of precise world events. There was a media blackout throughout Turkey for the time being. No newspapers. No telephones in Dogubayazit. No way for him to learn the full extent of the truth. The powerful Moonstar satellite radio transmitter-receiver accompanying the expedition would enable Danson to speak directly with the U.S. president if need be, but she was certain Thurston Pierce would do nothing to jeopardize Danson's quest for the holy grail.

"Are you prepared to go to war over a wooden

boat you do not believe is there?" asked Reg, absent-mindedly twisting his wedding ring.

The fascinating woman's countenance darkened. "I never said I did not believe in the Ark. What I do not believe is that it is lying there to be picked up like a child's toy on the stairs. But of course it exists. I've walked on it."

THE SWEAT TRICKLED from Danson's armpits. His palms felt moist and unfamiliar in the thick atmosphere of the tent. The ring on his finger slid off and on easily. He tried to control his exasperation at this woman who was as maddening as she was beautiful. Her supply of bushes to beat around seemed inexhaustible.

"Walked on it?" he asked dumbly.

"I do not bruise like a woman." The lieutenant's sarcasm jabbed at Danson's resolve to stay calm. "I grew up on Ararat. My family are Armenian Christians, my parents even now citizens of Nakhichevan, Armenia. The name of the town literally means first camp of Noah. We had a farm near Igdir on the north of Ararat until the memories sent my parents away. One day when my father was plowing a formerly unused portion of his field, the blade turned up human bones. Hundreds of them. It was a shallow mass grave of Christian Armenian women and children murdered by the Turks in the pogrom of 1915 and 1916.

"They left me with an aunt who taught me that the only way to undo the slaughter of a million and a half of our people was not to run off as my parents had done but to beat the Turks at their own game. I went away to school, I joined the military, I seized every opportunity to fling their Muslim hatred back in their faces. I not only removed the veil, I made them eat it! One day I shall command the Third Army. For now, I must snatch away the Ark and send it far away from destroying hands. They literally skinned some of my people alive, Mr. Danson. They would not think twice of using the Ark to heat their tea water."

She visibly trembled and Danson ached to ease her torment. *Slow down, Reg. Oh, Barbara, sweet Barbara, if only you were here.* He fiddled with his ring and said softly, "When did you walk on the Ark?"

"I was but a girl of six or seven when my uncle hoisted me onto his shoulders and walked the familiar Armenian Trail of Fruitfulness, down which it is said Noah and his sons and the animals marched to begin anew. It is not a difficult climb for someone who is reasonably fit. The climb was off limits to foreigners, even in those days. But no one would question a peasant farmer, a little girl, and a donkey.

"After three days' hike, we came to it, looming there in a cradle of the mountain, surrounded by the stone altars of the faithful who had been coming there for tens of centuries. It was like stone itself, petrified and hard to the touch. Someone had piled a ladder of rocks against the side of the boat, and I scrambled up. I was perhaps sixty meters in the air and scared to death.

"It was so huge to my childish eyes, so dark green and holy. All I could think to do was to kiss it. I did. I knelt there on the roof in the freezing cold and kissed the Ark."

Reg leaned forward, eyes aglow. "What did you see up there?"

"A great flat expanse, little tufts of grass, patches of snow, and covered holes that had been shaped, fifty or more, spaced at regular intervals down the center. A large, gaping hole had seemingly been chopped in the roof, but I was too afraid to peer inside. At my mother's knee I had learned of a great shaggy beast that inhabits the interior and gobbles those who would tamper with the mysteries of heaven. My uncle stood a hundred meters from the Ark, afraid of a consuming fire should he linger too close too long. I began to cry, and he called me down. We knelt at an ancient tumble-down altar and wept. We were there no more than an hour when Uncle herded me down the mountain away from that holy place."

Danson stared at the beguiling woman who was overcome by the profound recollection. For a moment he saw the slighter, more delicate vision of Barbara standing there, the ready-for-action twinkle in her eye, the cuffs of her pants stuffed into the old hiking boots scuffed and worn by adventure. *My Lord, how I ache for her!* He twirled the wedding band and thought of whale bones and sultry jungle nights.

A flash of orange . . . on the shore . . . "Shouldn't

*you be wearing one?"... "No time... makes her feel
pregnant..."*

Reg shook his head to clear it. Those thoughts
had arisen frequently since Tony's return. He had to
concentrate.

"Does that ring perhaps squeeze you too
tightly?" Cayan's lovely face, suffused in lamplight,
betrayed nothing.

"I was just thinking of my wife and how she
would have loved to be here, to hear you speak of the
Ark, and to anticipate the climb up Ararat."

"Yes, I heard of your wife's death and I am sorry,
but I do hope your being here is in no way due to
romantic readings of Genesis and fond recollections
of expeditions past." The hard edge to the lieutenant's voice reminded Danson she was there because
she'd clawed her way past men and mentalities too
weak to stop her. Friendship was out of the question.
Professional tolerance, maybe.

"Ararat is unforgiving," Nilay Cayan continued,
pacing the small space behind the desk. "She is pre-
dictable only in her cruelty. Some two hundred outside explorers over the last century have reported
seeing the Ark, yet none—not nobleman, peasant
farmer, or military reconnaissance team—has been
able to verify or authenticate the sightings for an international audience. Photos, maps, official reports,
interviews, and countless other documentations, including the eyewitness testimony of a U.S. Air Force
crew flying a B-17 over the mountain in 1943, have
all been mysteriously lost or destroyed. The recollections of an old man and a little girl are dismissed as
religious superstition. Whether of heaven or of hell,

there is a supernatural conspiracy to keep the Ark locked away. Why should this expedition succeed?"

"Before you tell me of the ferocious beasts that stalk the mountain and the storm winds of Hades that devastate its heights, tell me what actual hope we have of finding the Ark, in your estimation." The impatient anger in Danson's voice brought the unfathomable smile back to Cayan's lips.

"Twenty percent," she replied. "I am not given to padded estimates. Perhaps the Ark is only accessible to the simple and unencumbered. Sophisticated equipment and scientific credentials do not impress this mountain. It can change its shape at will, say the Kurds, and is by no means the same mountain today that it was when I was a girl. Still, never have the political and climatic conditions been this favorably combined. Let us depart before the demon legions have time to regroup."

"Then you tend to think the hedge around the Ark has been placed there by evil forces?" Danson persisted.

"God is greater than Satan times two," she answered, arranging an army cap on her head. "He has often allowed the devil to restrain people and actions in some divine working of the cosmic plan. I say we go there, then draw our conclusions."

Danson followed Cayan into the white heat of daylight. After being introduced to Ibrahim Hasan and giving a cursory nod to Cevdet Demirkol whom she already knew, Cayan drew Danson aside.

"Demirkol will be of limited value with the Kurds, but surely you're not proposing we take this holy man up the mountain? We can ill afford dead weight and another mouth to feed."

Reg had heard enough. "Lieutenant, I appreciate all your efforts in marshaling supplies and personnel, but let's not lose sight of the fact that I am the leader of this mission. The financing is from my organization, and I say who goes and who stays. Ibrahim Hasan, at great risk to his personal safety, relayed the message that brought us here and was instrumental in leading me to Cevdet, who was in hiding. Hasan has earned the right to make the journey."

Lieutenant Cayan appeared not to be listening; she was peering instead through the shimmering haze to the east toward Ararat. "Ever ridden a donkey, Mr. Danson?" she said.

"Once, in Jordan on a dig. What's tha—"

"You're about to again," Cayan interrupted, a dreamy quality to her voice. "Stubbornest animals alive, so they say. Some claim that the true Miracle of the Triumphal Entry on donkey back was that Christ made it into Jerusalem at all."

Reg said nothing, wondering at two weeks in the wilds of eastern Turkey with this annoying woman.

"Seriously, Reginald Danson, don't you think it significant that God would choose to place the Messiah on the back of the stubbornest creature in His kingdom?"

"I couldn't disagree more," Reg said coolly.

Cayan, unaccustomed to having even the least of her observations contradicted, looked sharply at him. "Why is that?" she demanded.

"Well, Lieutenant, it's this way. Surely if God

had intended to use His most obstinate creature to bear the Messiah, He would have placed Christ on the back of a woman." He smiled ingratiatingly.

Lieutenant Cayan frowned a moment, then laughed in delight. She grasped his hand and clapped him on the back. "Welcome to Turkey!" she exclaimed with radiant warmth, "Welcome to Turkey!"

Her touch was electric.

CHAPTER
12

VOLCANOLOGIST GEORGE LACEY whistled slowly through his teeth. The report from the Instituto Internazionale de Vulcanologia in Catania, Italy, left little room for doubt. Something earthshaking was developing in the Alpine-Himalayan belt.

He grinned weakly at the pun. It would be no laughing matter if what appeared to be brewing in fact blew its cork. Of the thousands of volcanoes on earth, 502 had been active in recorded history. Of those, 98 were located in a belt that extended from southeastern Europe through the Mediterranean and southern Asia into the old East Indies Archipelago.

Something was definitely shaking along this strand of lava pearls. The seismic readout provided Lacey at the Scientific Event Alert Network in Washington, D.C., looked as if it had a severe case of measles in the southwest quadrant of the Eurasian Plate. Earthquakes by the hundreds, each marked with a tiny dot, over a seven-day period. Their increasing frequency and intensity indicated rapid movement of magma only twenty-five to thirty-five miles beneath the surface—and rising. What on earth—or under it—was going on?

Lacey was handed a collaborating dispatch from the boys in the Departamento de Petroligia y Geochemica in Madrid. Even at that distance from the ruckus, seismometers were dancing the watusi. The dispatch included reports from the global satellite surveillance monitors that confirmed the worst. That part of the world was set to rock and roll.

"God have mercy!" Lacey exclaimed aloud with a fervency he hadn't felt since Sister Sylvia Parker, his Sunday school teacher, had awarded him a transistor radio for reciting all the Beatitudes without a single skip.

He knew that the Alpine-Himalayan belt included one in six of the most violent and deadly eruptors in all of history. In 396 B.C., Mount Etna in Sicily spewed forth a stream of lava twenty-four miles long and two miles wide that was said to have stopped the Carthaginian army in its tracks. Nearly six centuries later, Italy's Mount Vesuvius annihilated the ancient cities of Pompeii, with a snowstorm of superheated ash, and Herculaneum, with a wall of mud.

Java's Mount Tamboro exploded in 1815, losing more than four thousand feet in height. Its "neighbor," Krakatoa, detonated in 1883 with the force of five thousand megatons of TNT, and the noise was heard nearly three thousand miles away. Hundreds of thousands perished. A one-hundred-foot tidal wave swept entire villages into the sea. The immense ash

cloud turned the sun blue and the moon a vivid
green.

And all of them had been thought to be dormant
or extinct before the devastation. The most dreaded
disease among volcanologists was complacency. The
more geologically stable the region appears to be, the
greater the need for vigilance. Who can find work as a
volcanologist in Great Britain? Yet that nation's rock
contains massive evidence of countless volcanic
eruptions.

Lacey whistled again. Accompanying data from
three rural reporting stations in eastern Turkey,
where the seismic disturbances were clustered, cited
examples of one of the more controversial indicators
of impending earthquakes and eruptions: animal pre-
monition.

In Takuriengiz pigs were biting each other like
dogs. At Omerabal, rats were milling in the town
square, and serpents from the surrounding hills slithered through the streets. Several dogs in Baskale had
to be shot, so crazed was their howling.

"Gone mad," muttered Lacey distractedly. He
didn't share his colleagues' disdain for animal behavior as a reliable signal of impending doom. Much of
nature turned strange before seismic upheaval. Wells
would cloud up; groundwater would sharply rise or
fall; lightning would strike from a clear sky or bolt
from the ground. Earthquake scientists in China believed the signs in 1975. They observed geese flying
into trees, chickens refusing to roost, and snakes
crawling from their burrows only to freeze to death
on the snowy ground. Officials evacuated tens of

thousands from the Haicheng area just before a massive temblor 7.3 on the Richter scale destroyed half the buildings where 500 thousand people lived— with few victims because the animals were believed.

How long do we have now? Lacey wondered. The warnings could come a month in advance. Most came just a few days or hours before disaster. For some, there had been no warning at all.

Sirens were going off this time. That portion of Turkey was a regular seismic breeding ground. Within the last fifty years, more than half a million lives had been lost in the devil's triangle formed by the borders of Iran, Turkey, and Soviet Armenia. The earth had opened again and again with a great roaring and rending, swallowing people and livestock whole.

This series of tremors was different in one important detail. The old man beneath the Alpine-Himalayan volcanic belt was hitching up his pants with a vengeance. One titanic yank and Mount Ararat, one of the most massive mountains on earth, was going to blow her lid. From the looks of the rapid seismic build-up around her skirts, she'd take fifty cubic miles of real estate with her.

The volcanic notches in the Alpine-Himalayan belt are unevenly spaced and, in the main sections of those two mountain ranges, far apart. Repeated folding and overthrusting from the movement of crustal plates had left a greatly thickened crust beneath these regions through which molten rock had been unable to penetrate.

But a seeping crack in the earth's shell had occurred from a head-on ramming of the Australia

Plate and the Eurasia Plate. The rupture reopened the ancient scar tissue that had blocked fault access to the surface vent of Mount Ararat.

Molten rock, superheated to a temperature of two thousand degrees Fahrenheit was speeding toward the surface on a cushion of pent-up gases. It could burst forth in a hellish rain of boiling mud, suffocating ash, and incinerating lava, cremating any living thing. Billions of gallons of melted snow would roar down onto the Anatolian plain and lay waste to farms and towns and populations without prejudice. Tens of thousands would die.

Mount Ararat, where the ancients said that life began again, was contemplating murder.

"Shades of Noah's Ark!" Lacey muttered, searching the geologic history charts for Ararat. There she was, lying along a complex earthquake fault system, twisting and turning east to west. Known as the Ararat-Alagoz Fault, she was massive. The more publicized San Andreas Fault in California paled in comparison.

Very few people outside science realized, but Lacey knew, that there is ample volcanic evidence that Ararat was once submerged. Pillow lava—interconnected, saclike bodies of lava formed only under water—are exposed as high as the fifteen-thousand-foot level. Sedimentary rock, which can only be deposited by flood waters, has been found at the fourteen-thousand-foot snowline, rich with the fossilized remains of sea creatures.

Volcanic eruptions had rocked Ararat numerous times after the Flood, but decreasing in frequency and intensity until at last subsiding for centuries between. That it should come alive again uncovered a terrifying image that haunted Lacey still.

Ten years before while gathering data for the U.S. Office of Geochemistry and Geophysics, he had stood at the edge of Ahora Gorge, an ugly gash miles long and thousands of feet deep torn from the north side of Ararat by the last eruption in 1840. Probably four or five cubic miles of rock and volcanic debris had burst from the mountain, leaving that awful wound in its side. To peer into its black depths was unsettling then and unnerved him still. There was something evil about it. Scientist or no, some things beyond the laboratory defied explanation.

And now something was welling up inside that awful mountain that would maim and ruin everything in its path.

"Get me the Turkish Embassy now!" Lacey barked into the phone. His pulse raced. Not that alerting the Turkish authorities would change much. You don't defuse a volcano; you run for your life. Maybe, just maybe, there would be some life left in eastern Turkey if the warning could be sounded in time.

HAYRI Erbakan felt the hot earth through the thick soles of his bare feet and skipped to a little hummock of withered grass. He had lived high on the flanks of Ararat his whole life, as had his father and *his* father before him. They had relied on the goats for their livelihood, and the goats counted on the spare vegetation for theirs. Much of the year it was a hot and searing place, this year more than usual. But never, never, had Hayri shivered in the cool before sunrise and found it nearly impossible to stand still in one place.

There was fire in the soil.

"Anlamiyorum," he whispered fearfully. "I don't understand. The goats were behaving badly. They bleated piteously and stepped gingerly over the terrain. Suddenly one would leap straight into the air as if struck by a snake and the others would frantically knock into one another. Half a dozen of the dams had stopped nursing, and two prize milk goats had dried up overnight.

Hayri winced and shifted feet on the hummock. He felt the ground shudder. Was the devil that everyone said lived in the mountain coming to the surface? He pulled his tattered cloak more tightly about him and prayed for the dawn.

CHAPTER
13

PRESIDENT THURSTON PIERCE listened dispassionately as Secretary of State Frederick Delaney outlined the situation in Turkey. The president liked the news from the Turkish Ministry of Defense. The Kurdish Alliance had halted its advance and was keeping a wary eye on Ararat. Even the unwashed hordes respected a volcano in its insanity. They felt the quakes; they knew the dangers; and they bore the terrible personal loss. The vast majority of people killed in Ararat's bloody history were their ancestors, their loved ones. For now, they would wait and watch.

The president, however, did not like the news from the volcanology experts. They believed that Turkey and her allies were jumping from the frying pan of war into the fire of natural catastrophe. The Alert Network people were adamant that Ararat was on the verge of eruption and that the entire Anatolian plain must be evacuated without delay.

The Turkish attache in Washington was on the line awaiting further clarification before contacting Ankara. What of the archaeological expedition wending its way up Ararat? Surely it would need immediate notification, and of course Turkish military helicopters would be dispatched within the hour to evacuate.

Delaney finished his report and looked to the president for reply. If he expected a rapid response, he was disappointed.

Pierce made a tent of his fingers, tapping them together, his head bowed. When at last he looked up, there was a trace of weary resignation in his countenance. Delaney relaxed. For a moment there, he thought the president was going to refuse the request.

"You ever wanted anything so badly you'd compromise your principles to get it?" The president's words were spoken in a hushed monotone. Delaney started to reply but was cut off by a wave of Pierce's hand.

"I don't mean ordinary, everyday things like money or presidential appointments," he went on, "but extraordinary things like eternal youth, worldwide fame, immortality . . ."

"Mr. President, the Turkish attache is wait—"

Pierce jumped to his feet and slammed the desk with the flat of his hand. His eyes were fiery; his voice was threatening. "Hang the Turkish attache! We're not talking about a few backwater peasants whose lives on that Godforsaken plain don't mean spit in the international scheme of things. What we *are* talking about is the bloody Ark of Noah! That's what's at stake on that mountain, and that's what I aim to have in my possession.

"Don't you see? We've been given a reprieve from God. He's stalled the Kurds without a shot being fired. And there's no guarantee of an eruption. It's an inexact science at best. A few barking dogs, an earthquake or two—no need for panic in that!"

Delaney kept his emotions in check. "Mr. President, you cannot bargain away the life of even one person in the event of such a disaster. The international code of honor gives precedence to mercy and compassion over all other considerations in time of emergency. Women and children are sitting ducks—"

"Your nobility is admirable, Mr. Secretary, but ill-placed. And don't lecture me about compassion." Delaney had never seen the president so remote, so hard. Pierce walked over to the window and spread the blinds. The sunlight lanced the dim room, cutting the antique oak desk in two and illuminating the pen and pencil set with the bronze presidential seal. All was quiet save for the ticking of the mantel clock and the distant hum of a vacuum cleaner.

Pierce sighed resignedly and fixed Delaney with a pained smile. "Actually, your concern is perhaps more ill-timed than ill-placed, Mr. Secretary. To be sure, we must do everything we can to reduce potential loss of life and property among the Turkish citizenry. Tell the Turkish attache that all U.S. military bases have been alerted to an impending eruption of Mount Ararat and are placed at President Koraltan's disposal. Should the opportunity arise, you might voice again America's opposition to continued martial law in the fifteen provinces in which the Kurds reside, but I will leave that to your discretion.

"And Fred, one other thing." The old strength had returned to the commander's voice. He stood more erect and his eyes flashed enthusiastically. "Be certain Koraltan understands that it wouldn't take much cooperation to up America's aid to an even ten billion. Might come in handy in a disaster." He let the blinds snap back into place, and the room dimmed.

"Alert the International Red Cross that evacuation centers may be set up at the air bases of Elmadag, Incirlik, and Diyarbakir. U.S. military transports including naval vessels are standing by to airlift supplies and evacuees. Contact the American Red Cross for current status of blanket and first-aid inventories. But whatever you do—" and here the president's voice iced over "—do nothing to alert the scientific expedition now scaling Ararat."

Delaney started to protest, but the sudden flood of red in Pierce's neck and face stopped him. "Under no circumstances is that expedition to be told." Pierce's voice was low and menacing.

"Those people are professionals, you stupid fool," Pierce went on. "They knew up front there would be grave risks. Take the leader, Reg Danson, a hunter of cryptoantiquities. How many of those do you know? He's tramped through some pretty dank places in quest of hidden things. His wife died while they were out searching for some long-necked throwback out of a kid's picture book. Oh, he knows the risks all right—and is plenty willing to take them.

"Believe me, Mr. Secretary, those kinds of people

don't appreciate bureaucratic meddling. The less they hear from politicians, the better they like it. They see us as regulators, intruders, i.e., *the enemy*.

"No, we need to leave them to their research, their explorations. It's the stuff of life to them. Stop them, and they cause some international stink over government interference in their search for the global good. If they find what they're looking for, they are hailed as giants of discovery. If they die on the hunt, they go down in the books as heroes of mankind. For them, it's a win-win situation."

Delaney snorted, thrust his hands in his pockets, and stared at a painting of Lincoln delivering the Gettysburg Address. "It's a win-lose situation for us, Thirsty. If they find the Ark, you sew up the election. If they die in a volcanic holocaust that you and I kept from them, we both go to a common grave that you dug. You want to gamble with your life, be my guest, but I must draw the line when it's my neck in the noose."

His face suddenly drawn and haggard, he looked at Pierce with an expression the president hadn't seen since they were classmates at Annapolis. A hazing of "Thirsty" Pierce's devising went sour, and the plebe was crippled for life. Pierce's father smoothed it over with both the academy and the parents, and the papers were none the wiser. It had been the devil, though, keeping it concealed from the opposition party during Pierce's rise through the House, the Senate, and finally, the White House, but a handler of Delaney's caliber kept tight accounts. Secretary of state had been payoff number one for Delaney. Number two was to be named Pierce's running mate this time out.

"Freddy." Pierce's tone was the old manipulator's mixture of honey and oil.

"Forget it, Thurston." The dejection in Delaney's voice matched the dread in his heart. "I don't even know those people. I have no desire to see them killed. Have you any idea what you've become?"

Pierce fought the rage welling in his chest and placed a hand on his friend's shoulder. "Where has sentimentality ever gotten us, pal? I don't want anyone to die either, but do you have any inkling what Noah's Ark in the Smithsonian would do for America's prestige? And where will you and I be if the mountain blows and the Ark is destroyed and word gets out that we were within mere days of preserving it for all time? We'll be cleaning toilets at the highway rest stop."

"With a clear conscience," Delaney said dispiritedly.

Pierce squeezed his friend's shoulder. "Hey, Freddy, snap out of it. We may be worrying over nothing. Volcanoes have threatened to blow before, only to let off a little steam and then go back to sleep for another thousand years. Even if the worst happened and we lost the expedition, a solid case could be made that it was necessary to sacrifice the good of a few for the potential good of many. How much historical precedence is there for that? Plenty!"

To the president's disgust, the secretary of state started to weep. "I can't keep covering up for you, Thirsty. You're doing this for your own prestige. I will have my resignation on your desk by three o'clock this afternoon. You can say the long hours were taking their toll on my family and that I've decided to return to my law practice in Boston. Whatever happens in Turkey, I won't say a thing."

The president removed his hand from Delaney's shoulder. When he spoke, his voice was quiet, but the menace had returned. "I can't let you do that, Mr. Secretary. Too many unfortunate accidents happen in Boston. Besides, my ducks are now in a row for the election. You are one of my ducks, Freddy, and if you decide to fly, I'll have to shoot you down. You understand."

When he at last looked up, Delaney's eyes were red-rimmed and moist. "Oh, I understand all right," he said softly. "I understand perfectly."

14

I
N THE DAY of overwhelming calamity, some men shall be made to eat thorns and to drink from a boiling spring."

Lieutenant General Nikolai Shkidchenko sat chest deep in the river and mumbled the Koranic paraphrase as a curse. His churning bowels felt as if they'd dined on nothing but thorns and boiling water for four days. The high-powered binocular view of Ararat's brooding heights did nothing to settle a rebellious constitution.

The word from Detente College in Moscow was to stop the American discreetly, but as swiftly and surely as a howitzer would a canary in a cage. The college, despite its friendly name, was a cover for a powerful clique of former Red Army insiders who were deadly determined to ride out the republican fervor in Eastern Europe. They were former high-ranking officers of the Supreme Command of the Socialist Republics, popularly known in back rooms as the Soviet Mafia. They had fed and been fed by the great bloated maggot of the Soviet military machine for nearly three generations, and they would be there at its resurrection.

Truth was, in the millions of offices of state bureaucracy throughout the fifteen so-called "independent states" once corralled by Soviet conquest, communism still controlled the flow of paper clips and human lives. Survivors, nationalists, the holdouts would not sell out to the West. Human perfectibility by human means was no dead ideology.

A few years of a bankrupt free-market economy and rudderless social reform, and a half-starved, once-Soviet citizenry would be beating down the doors of the Kremlin to put communism—and its inherent socialist security—back on the throne.

So went the theory. But back on the throne meant back in the hot seat of trying to exact loyalty from an impossible 160 diverse ethnic groups scattered across the vast land tracts from Siberia to Moldavia. Shkidchenko punched the water with both fists as if to blacken the eyes of all who refused the hammer and sickle.

Yet perhaps the biggest and most troubling unknown threatening to compromise the entire plan of communist renewal were the sixty million Muslims who inhabited the vast eastern territories of the former Soviet Union. Their allegiance had always been shaky at best, but give them the holy Ark of Noah to rally around and the zealots among them would have their mandate.

Tough, fearless mountain and plains dwellers with direct lineage to the ancients abounded in Eastern Europe's and Central Asia's ridiculous expanses. Their loyalty was to nothing but their past and their land. For their communist "conquerors" they had only contempt. Five million Azerbaijanis had warily guarded the Soviet Union's oldest oil fields along the western shores of the Caspian Sea. The nomadic Kazakhs, six million strong, roamed the vast plains from the Volga in the west to the Altai Mountains in the east. Two million Turkmen, lords of Kar-Kum, one of the largest deserts in central Asia, prowled the southernmost republic. Another two million Kirghiz controlled the Tien Shan and Pamir mountain ranges on the border with China. They were masterful weavers of carpets and breeders of cattle, yet they numbered not a few assassins among them. Ninety-three percent of Tajikistan was mountains. Every attempt at an accurate census among the millions there had met with hostility and failure. Uzbekistan, the most economically important of the Central Asian republics, had also been among the Soviet Union's most recalcitrant conquests. Though most of its fifteen million inhabitants had helped produce 67 percent of their overlord's cotton, 50 percent of its rice, and 33 percent of its silk, they were a murderous and anarchistic lot. Show them Noah's Ark and every turbaned, bearded, son-of-a-goatherd one of them would stampede to slaughter the liars who had enslaved them.

And the thought that some of the maverick republics might actually possess the beginnings of nu clear capability was far too horrible to consider.

Shkidchenko shifted irritably in the water, and a

cloud of thick silt welled up between his legs. The coarse uniform rubbed his body raw. Blast the intolerable heat!

Officially, there was no Ark. Only of necessity had Christianity been given unprecedented entree inside Russia since the collapse of the union. It was a salve to the moderates, which ought to be removed once democratization ran its course. But the discovery of Noah's Ark would jeopardize recommunization. The Nations for Christ Congress in Riga, Latvia, had shown that. Thousands of gypsy evangelists, pentecostal rabble rousers, and irascible Russian Orthodox priests had gathered to train willing workers in a subversive scheme to plant churches throughout the land. The Ark would become their battleship, and they would ride it into bloody skirmish after bloody skirmish.

Oh yes, if Shkidchenko let this one get away, he would taste the full wrath of the Soviet Mafia.

Before him, south across the Aras River from Artashat Military Outpost, Republic of Armenia, loomed the incredible bulk of 16,950-foot Mount Ararat, in volume perhaps the largest single mountain on earth. And because it rose abruptly from a flat plane, rather than from foothills like Mount Everest, it was technically the tallest mountain on earth. Though stinging sweat burned his eyes, Shkidchenko strained to peer into the very hold of the dark object barely discernible, but geometrically defined, not three-quarters of a kilometer from the summit. *Precisely where Father said it was!*

He belched, and the taste of bile inflamed his acute discomfort. It made him think of the fat-faced police/politicians who believed they could erase human faith by erasing the Ark. How he wished they were here to bake and sizzle in the monstrous heat with him and the 2,433 men of the Seventh Regiment consigned to this inferno. But such assignments were the only way, they said, to justify continuing to employ hundreds of thousands of military personnel and prevent their flooding a jobless civilian market. Imbeciles!

Forty men had already succumbed to heat stroke, and a dozen more were showing signs. All seventy men of the engineer company, stripped to their underwear, had to be sprayed constantly with water pumped from the river as they wrestled two self-propelled bridge sections into place.

A ZSU 23mm automatic cannon aimed at the head of Boris Nekrasov, the effete editor of the army newspaper *Krasnaya Zvezda*, was the only antacid sufficient in power to quell Shkidchenko's roiling innards. Nekrasov had called for the immediate destruction of "anything on Ararat that in the slightest resembles a wooden vessel so that these persistent rumors inciting incursions by CIA operatives in scientific guise might once and for all be laid to rest."

The old guard Kremlinites had eaten it up. Trying to forget the debacle in Afghanistan and retrieve as many of the fleeing republics—and as much of their badly bruised pride—as they could, they were quietly backing the Kurdish Alliance in its latest move to strong-arm its way into eastern Turkey. The Seventh Regiment would continue on under separate command to bivouac near the Kurdish forces. But that slimiest of Turks, President Koraltan, had chosen to allow this latest relic search at the very moment the Kremlin-supplied insurrectionists were amassing along the border east and south of Ararat. Intelligence indicated that the American-led expedition had a strong chance to succeed and thereby polarize the critical Armenian Christian and Muslim fundamentalist allies. The whole plan would fall apart.

Fortunately, thought Shkidchenko, *I am an entrepreneur.* The word was a good American import and an antidote to the general's increasing distemper. If he was going to risk the mountains of Ararat, he was going to have more to show for it than a few dead archaeologists. He would have his moment of glory.

His father's glory had been snatched from him long before. Shkidchenko remembered the once-proud man excitedly retelling the find of the century, aging military medals glinting in the firelight of their humble farm cottage in the Georgian republic. Sitting there in the shallows, the curling green waters oddly tepid for a mountain stream, the general could not stem the rapid flow of memories.

He was again sitting in the old porcelain bathtub, his ears assaulted by the rough washcloth wielded expertly by his mother. Peter Shkidchenko, who had looked so very much like Russian royalty in the faded military photographs, paced the floor, prematurely stooped, obsessed with what he'd seen many years before, silenced by the uncompromising Bolsheviks.

His father, kneeling beside the tub, eyes pleading, asked in a quavering voice, "You believe me, Nikolai, don't you? I saw it, I touched it. I entered and saw the cages, felt the cypress wood, collected the pitch with which it was varnished."

. . . Wearily Nikolai Shkidchenko lay back in the soothing waters of the Aras River, feeling its gentle swirl and suckle, seeing another bath in another time . . .

"We of the Fourteenth Railroad Battalion of the White Russian Army were headquartered at Bayazit in 1917, just southwest of Greater Ararat," intoned Peter Shkidchenko, his eyes taking on that faraway look that had always frightened Nikolai as a boy. "Czar Nicholas sent a dispatch recounting an aerial sighting of the Ark by First Lieutenant Zabolotsky of the 3-D Caucasian Aviation Detachment.

"Our orders direct from the blessed czar himself were to mount an immediate ground expedition to substantiate the claim. Some 150 army engineers and specialists were chosen for the ascent.

"We began the climb in two columns, one of fifty men and mine of one hundred. The fifty were prevented from reaching the site by a vast swamp swarming with bloodthirsty mosquitoes and literally undulating with the squirming bodies of deadly puff adders by the thousands.

"But we of the one hundred at last rounded an immense rock outcropping and came face-to-face with the Ark of Noah! We had braved snowstorms and falling ice and had literally cut a stair-step trail the last half kilometer. Yet our half-frozen, rock-torn bodies were forgotten in that incredible moment.

"Think of it, dear Nikolai! Without a word of command, we as one removed our hats in reverence. A few went to their knees. Many more crossed themselves, and whispered prayers were the only sound to break the awesome holiness of that place.

"The ship was huge, fully 160 meters long. One end was in ice, but we were able to enter through a broken hatchway near the front. Stretching before us was a wide corridor with rooms of various sizes located the length of the vessel. One huge room with a high ceiling was separated from the others by a fence of giant tree trunks as if elephants or even greater beasts had been stabled there. All about the walls were wooden cages. A great pile of broken partitions was stacked at one end of the corridor.

"The whole thing was marvelously preserved with a dark brown waxy substance. Nearby we found a stone altar with what proved to be a Sumerian inscription telling of the Deluge. I could have died then and been a very happy man!"

The bath water went chill before the telling was done. The light soon went out of the old man's face. As he toweled dry his naked and shivering son, his face darkened with a powerful anger and a sadness thick and ruinous. He recounted the jubilant trek down the mountain, the joy turned to ashes when they found Moscow aflame with revolution. The drying became steadily rougher with the remembering until the recounting of the official courier's death by firing squad at the hands of Trotsky's henchmen caused pain that made little Nikolai Shkidchenko cry out. Instead of hugging his trembling son to his breast as Nikolai had so wanted him to do, his father withdrew, bewildered, displaced, forgotten. To have seen the Ark, then be denied the opportunity to tell eager audiences every holy detail, was payment in hell.

As young as he'd been, Nikolai never doubted for a moment the truth of his father's experience. The Ark *was* there. But what of it? You could not survive Red Russia banking on religious symbolism. There had been no money, no gain, barely subsistence to be found in anything remotely religious.

Curse Koraltan the Turk and his issue for seven generations plus one! Shkidchenko shifted uncomfortably and smiled sourly. He liked that curse. Since the fanatics considered seven a holy number, he added the eighth generation to thumb his nose at the zealots. Stupid games.

He needed to pull himself and his men together. Myth or miracle, their assignment was to wipe the Ark and its seekers from the shoulders of Agri Dagh and rise another rank in the army of a restored communist union. An increase in pay, reassignment to a comfortable desk in an air-conditioned office where it was neither hot nor cold, eventual burial with honors alongside numberless others who had toed the party line. Glorious future.

What were the chances of that? The pathetic remnants of Hitler's S.S. still held out for a restored fatherland, and for what?

Nikolai Shkidchenko shook a dripping fist at the mocking mountain. The Ark's presence there meant what? Could he cross the border, ascend the mountain, throw himself at the feet of the American, defect? God might forgive, but the Soviet Mafia never would. Perhaps he should repent now in the shallows of the Aras River, then fling himself into the current and drown. At least then he would be food for the vultures downstream.

The words of his mother's prayers returned to him. "God preserve Nikolai. Spare him from Satan's talons. Find him worthy to enter your kingdom." Lieutenant General Nikolai Shkidchenko, for the first time since military training camp, desperately wanted to cry.

A sound behind him, like someone clearing his throat, made Shkidchenko jump. He quickly splashed water in his face. "Yes, what is it?" he roughly demanded. The medical orderly moved to the edge of the water.

"Please excuse the interruption, General, but five more men have fainted, and I regret to inform you that Colonel Rujansky has died of heart failure. We can do little in this heat."

Shkidchenko felt a flash of sorrow for the young man before him. Rujansky had really died of self-hatred years ago when he had turned in his Baptist wife for holding secret worship services in their tiny apartment. Today, she could hold Bible studies in Gorky Park.

The handsome young soldier was clean and virile and deserved more than to die here in this blast furnace at the whim of some geriatric committee of hypocrites without a cause for whom the wilderness was the suburbs of Moscow.

"Tell Colonel Solkov to have the men put on their clothing and immerse themselves in the river until nightfall. We will mobilize at dusk."

The orderly saluted smartly despite his own

acute discomfort and returned to his charges at twice the speed with which he'd left them. Shkidchenko rose stiffly from the river, feeling a crippling weight far greater than wet clothing. He hoped his operative had infiltrated the Ark expedition by now.

Of course he must storm the mountain and put an end to the Ark. It was not a question of fighting God. The events surrounding the Ark were ancient history; to conclude that they yet held relevance was religious nonsense. Millions of angry peasant assassins on horseback, now *that* was something to avoid. Besides, why would the holiest of high places be on that Godforsaken mountain? Few things made less sense than that.

CHAPTER

15

REG DANSON had no right to feel this ebullient. The expedition's line of march stretched impossibly long, the challenge ahead was impossibly great, and Lieutenant Nilay Cayan of Turkey's Third Army was impossibly beautiful.

Worse, after a half day's struggle in the searing heat, the faces of many of the men in his command were as dark and foreboding as the dread land they traversed.

They had begun their ascent of Noah's mountain from a sterile plain. There was a dim and gloomy cast to the countryside despite the sun's glare. The effect was of shadows where nothing was sufficiently high to cast shadows, save for the men. Oddly, their silhouettes were pencil-thin and pitiful under the tyrant sun. And for all the light, Ararat refused to reveal her hoary head and shoulders, encased as they were in inky cloud and swirling vapor.

Nearly oblivious to the austere terrain and his glowering marchers, Danson was drunk with excitement. He was within twelve thousand feet of Jehovah God's prize!

Not Babylon, not the pyramid tombs of the pharaohs, not the Great Wall—what, then, could begin to approximate what was about to be unearthed—un*iced*, on Ararat? Easter Island, Pompeii, Stonehenge? Some interesting riddles there, perhaps, but nothing earth shattering. The rubble of Jericho, the long-submerged streets of Sodom and Gomorrah, the eerie emptiness of Masada? Minor league archaeology. The scrolls of Qumran? The blessed Scriptures gave no blessing to those who would not believe them. Daily they were explained away by the heathen for whom they were but the wishful words of man.

No, it would take the Ark of Noah to bring the world to its knees. Undeniable, visible, believe-it-in-Missouri proof that God is alive and well and involved in the affairs of humankind.

He felt a magnetic pull, an unspeakable attraction to the thing in the ice. Was he not in a real sense a son of Noah returning to the scene of the liberation of his forebears?

The saddle sores pierced his euphoria, and he shifted the lean flesh of his backside once more. The small female donkey glanced soulfully back at him.

"Step lively, old gal," Danson crowed. "We'll soon see the stalls where your grand ancestors may have munched the grass of Eden!"

Lieutenant Nilay Cayan, astride a red donkey with the disposition of a cornered cobra, gave a sharp jab to the recalcitrant animal's protruding ribs and marveled again at Danson's unreserved gaiety.

Couldn't he sense the heaviness? A band of ill was drawing more tightly about the expedition as the day wore on.

She'd first noticed it when they had entered the sunken land ring around the base of the mountain. Instead of forming its own watershed radiating out from the base of the mountain as is usual with peaks its size, Ararat drains beneath the plain at its feet and the runoff joins the flow from the surrounding range to the Aras and Tigris and Euphrates rivers. In all likelihood, the original drainage system was established in the days of Creation, and Ararat itself rose in a volcanic eruption during the later Flood.

In the catastrophic deluge, Ararat formed and cooled, and the molten magma drained back into the lower crust, leaving a gigantic ring of hollow crust around the base of the mountain. The crust collapsed from the weight of the rock strata raised in the upheaval. This collapse left a sunken ring for the hem of Ararat's skirt that, poorly drained, had become swampland, infested by savage insects and poisonous vipers. Nilay could remember her uncle lifting her to his shoulders and running through the sour swamp country to fend off bites.

Today, the swamp was strangely dry. No whine of insects broke the oppressive stillness. Not a single snake crossed their path. The vermin seemed all the more lethal by their conspicuous absence. The air was heavy, and the unseen band grew tighter.

"Why the smile, Reginald Danson? Are you always this pleasant at the jaws to hell?" Cayan kicked her mount to stay even with him.

Danson hesitated a moment, then answered. "I'd

be disappointed if Satan didn't pull out all the stops
to discourage us, Lieutenant. But understand this.
Nothing—not storm, guns, or a ninety-foot, fire-
breathing Lucifer—will deter me from laying hold of
the Ark. That's God's lifeboat up there, and when He
brings it alongside, I'm jumping in!"

*. . . orange . . . life jackets . . . slick brown backs
humping through the loch . . . gray, sightless
fog . . . empty boat . . . can't breathe . . . Barbara! . . .
my wife . . . grab on, dear life . . .*

Lieutenant Cayan stared at the strange look on
Danson's face, then spurred her mount on ahead.
Tony pulled abreast of his father.

"Hey, Dad, you look like the trail food doesn't
agree with you. You okay?"

Reg nodded and managed a weak smile. "Sure,
buddy. You got hardening of the rump yet?"

Tony grinned. "Not exactly ships of the desert,
are they? I think mine's got marbles for vertebrae.
Every time I come down, that's what it feels like I'm
landing on!"

They laughed and rode on for a while in silence.

"Dad?"

"Yeah."

"Do you miss Mom?"

Reg looked sharply at his son and saw the sadness in the handsome features, so much the image of
his parents. The magnetic hazel eyes were Barbara's.
"I'd like a dollar for every time I've wished she were
along," he answered. It wasn't quite what he'd meant
to say or the way he'd meant to say it.

Tony looked abject and forlorn. He said nothing
for a time, then fished in his shirt pocket and drew

out a folded sheet of pink stationery. He passed it to his father.

"It's from Mom. It's the last thing she wrote me before . . . the accident."

. . . others wear orange . . . too bulky for the Dansons . . . jungle jeep . . . sinking deep . . . we're not a family anymore . . .

Reg reined in his mount and sat trembling, the familiar scent of Barbara light upon the well-worn note. Fumbling, he unfolded it. In her beautiful flowing script, she had written:

> My Dearest Tony, you are much in my thoughts this evening. Your father and I are leaving for Scotland tomorrow. He is so full of fun these days, and I have to say that gallivanting about in search of solutions to the world's puzzles beats cleaning the cat box.
>
> You should see Dad getting ready for this. He's like, well, like a certain young man I once knew who absolutely loved having his birthday gifts hidden. Remember how your father would spend half the morning writing up funny clues that would send you off on your own private adventure? One clue led to another and finally you'd find the new skates in the wash machine or the basketball in the china hutch, and you'd come back beaming as if you'd found a candy mine.
>
> I wish he wouldn't rush so. I just know he's going to forget something important someday. But you know, Dad. Old 'We can always buy a toothbrush en route' Danson.
>
> Be proud of him, Tony. He wants that just about

more than anything. Nothing's so important that you and he should stay angry at one another this long. You don't have to agree with a person to love him. He needs to know that he matters to you.

Well, honey, be sure to change your socks and let us know your summer plans. Maybe we could rent a beach cabin and go crabbing, just the three of us?

I'll see if I can't find a Nessie doll for your collection (ha!). Meanwhile, I know you've learned the alphabet, so how about stringing some letters together and sending 'em my way? Love, kisses, and general mush. God bless you, honey. Mom.

P.S. I learned the other day—don't ask me where—that a gallivorous creature is one that feeds on gall tissue. File that away under "weird," will you?

Reg's eyes blurred with tears. He refolded the note and passed it back to Tony.

"Did you ever change those socks?" Reg asked, attempting to lighten the weight they both carried.

Tony didn't answer immediately, as if undecided what to say. When he did speak, the words burst from his lips like ricocheting bullets. "*Did* you forget something important that day at Loch Ness?"

Reg was instantly livid. "Don't talk to me like some third-party investigator! I don't need to keep telling you again and again that it was a freak accident, totally unexpected."

"The unexpected always did kind of creep up on you, didn't it?" Tony shouted back. "This time you remembered your toothbrush, but you forgot the life jackets!"

Reg resisted the urge to just ride away and never look back. "So that's it? All of our life boils down to that one thing, does it? Or is it maybe that you have a hard time admitting that your attitude, your absence from home these last few years, is without excuse? That what Mom was trying to tell you in the note is that your staying away was hurting her, never mind me? And now you can't bring her back and give her the loving son she should have had at home all this time. You wouldn't let her be your mother when she needed you, and now when you want to, there's nothing you can do about it!"

Tony set his jaw, the muscles clenching spasmodically. "You'll be sorry you said that, Dad. Very sorry." The malice in his words lingered long after he disappeared into a knot of riders ahead.

Lieutenant Cayan dropped back and said, "Ah, impetuous youth. Without them, we would still be in the Dark Ages."

Reg smiled ruefully and ran a hand through his dusty hair. "Animal parents never seem to have this trouble. They grab the kid by the scruff of the neck, give a shake, drop him on his head, cuff him in the rear, and throw in a hefty roar for good measure. End of story."

"Well, the two of you have the roaring down perfectly," she said, with a smooth, beguiling laugh that softened the military edge and made her seem like a carefree teenager out for an afternoon's ride.

Neither of them saw the flash of the dagger nor

the black form hurtle without a sound onto the back of the little female donkey. With one fluid motion the form slammed against Danson's back, one hand snatching the reins, another placing the razor edge of a dagger against the hollow of his throat.

"Move and he dies!" the rider shouted, wheeling the donkey about to face those near soldiers who, having overcome their surprise, were frantically leveling their rifles and machine guns at the attacker.

Cayan quickly rode between Danson and her troops. "Hold!" she commanded. "Drop your weapons!"

As they reluctantly complied, the intruder pulled the knife away, gripped Danson's hair, and lunged to the left, pulling his captive to the ground. With lightning speed he returned the knife to his victim's throat. For one split second Danson entertained a nauseating vision of his severed head lying in the dust staring blankly back at him like a discarded chicken's.

"Please do me the kindness of remaining still," hissed the voice in his ear. With a knee placed firmly in the small of Danson's back, a secure grip on Danson's scalp, and the knife at Danson's throat, the man in black bowed toward the east. *I'm a human prayer rug*, Danson thought humorlessly. His nose and mouth were caked with dirt, and breathing was difficult. While he coughed and sputtered, his attacker prayed on.

Instead of instantly rushing to Reg's aid, Cayan's troops remained as motionless as stone. Heart pounding, Danson brushed at a noisome fly.

"I would refrain from movement of any kind," said the voice in the dirt. "Death from swatting a fly bears no honor!"

His prayers completed, the man bolted from the ground. "Back on the beast!" he commanded. Danson shakily mounted and spat dirt. His captor took three quick running steps and resumed his place at Danson's back, the dagger once again cool and securely in place.

The man gave a ferocious kick to the donkey's belly, and the little animal bolted cross country.

It was Danson's turn to pray. He felt that at any moment the donkey would stumble and the dagger would slice his jugular in two. *God, help me. Give me Your calm assurance.*

They raced swiftly upward, the sweat-soaked kidnapper holding his prisoner tightly pressed to his body so that they rode as one. The man of the mountain smelled of ten thousand nights away from home, soap and water an infrequent luxury.

A familiar tune flitted in and out of Danson's distracted consciousness. The ground blurred beneath them, but he was comforted. The dagger nicked his flesh and drew blood when they plunged into a narrow gully, and still he was unperturbed. It was maddening. What was that song?

. . . drive a big old Cadillac with wide wheels . . . rhinestones on the spokes . . . Now he remembered! *I've got credit down at the grocery store, and my barber tells me jokes . . .* He'd expected "Faith of Our Fathers" or "Victory in Jesus," and instead God had brought to mind an old Roger Miller tune Tony'd sung around the house as a sprout.

The charging donkey began to wheeze, its sides heaving with exertion as the terrain steepened. *I'm the number one attraction at every supermarket parking lot.* . . . A chuckle began to well up in Danson at the vision of Tony, in the blue pajamas with the bunny feet, belting out "Kansas City Star" while his mother threatened to call out the "high sheriff" and his father sang falsetto accompaniment.

. . . *I'm the king of Kansas City, no thanks Omaha, thanks a lot!* The song was not confined to his mind any longer. He was back in Philadelphia again, curator of a dinky, dingy country museum, crazy in love with Barbara and Tony and God and trying to get the priorities straight. There was that old Philco cabinet radio with the short-wave band and the roll-up wooden knob cover his grandpa had bequeathed him. Roger Miller was coming out of it, and little Tony was struttin' his stuff.

Danson began to sing aloud, oblivious to the breakneck scramble up the mountain, only slightly aware now of the dagger of death riding at his throat.

"Kansas City Star, that's what I are! Yo-de-le-de-le-de, you oughtta see my car, I drive a big old Cadillac with wide—"

"Silence!" The roared command bounced off the walls of Danson's cerebellum and sent his dream of Tony scurrying off to bed.

The steaming mount faltered at an almost perpendicular three-foot rise before it stumbled and scrambled over with a last desperate lunge. The blade nicked Danson again, but the sight before him numbed the pain.

It was a village of crooked houses, clinging

somehow to Ararat's unyielding rock. The wooden poles holding up the crude roofs were twisted and knotted, having been hauled from the valley floor at great effort. Uneven ladders, with missing rungs, leaned precariously against the walls. Windows, not quite square, were ill-fitted with glass panes deliberately caked with mud for privacy. A jumble of loosely fitted stones, sparse sod, and packed earth completed the architecture. Here and there several houses abutted one another and shared a common roof.

Five-gallon military canisters of water, hauled from the river far below, were all the exterior decoration of the meager dwellings. A few scrawny sheep and goats grazed on the wretched ground cover.

In the center of the compound, in sharp contrast to the drab, sloppy residential district surrounding it, was a stark-white tent, taut and commanding. In front of the tent were half a dozen tables at which men in soiled turbans, brownish jackets, and baggy trousers sat smoking and playing at dice. They leapt to their feet at the sound of the two riders and, as if one man, drew identical curved daggers from their cummerbunds.

Danson could now clearly recall the words to "Faith of Our Fathers" and began to hum the tune in earnest. He fully expected another snarl in his ear. Instead, the dagger left his throat and his captor dismounted.

Clearly the chief among cutthroats, the man strode to his fellows, who parted for him and bowed their heads ever so slightly in homage. He turned and gave Danson a superior look. He was an imposing figure, fully six-and-a-half feet tall, back broad, legs long and heavily muscled, eyes blazing with the light of a hundred thousand campfires. A broad nose and a lean face were held hostage to a ferocious countenance. Skin burnished the color of teak was overcast by a wicked scowl that, added to high, sharp cheekbones, thickly furred eyebrows, and contemptuously curled lips, gave the distinct impression that here was a man who seldom gave back the prisoners he took.

The man swept past his minions into the tent. Without a word, they followed.

Danson waited for what seemed an eternity. A hot wind whipped his hair on end. The donkey's labored breathing began to slow. No one entered or exited the tent. A murmur of male voices ebbed and flowed.

Was Reg free to go? Should he just leave, or would they have him eviscerated before he got fifty yards? For that matter, why hadn't the rest of Reg's party come after him?

It felt as if something brushed across his shoulders. A sudden chill gripped his belly, and he turned to look behind him. Nothing. The stark plain had disappeared, and in its place was a sea of gray. The world below had ceased to exist.

He turned back. A great creeping slug of gray was swallowing the tent whole. It rolled over him and the donkey, and it smelled of frozen caverns and subzero meat lockers where nothing lives.

Danson felt a cold more paralyzing than the brittle bone-cracking chill of Antarctica, more stupefyingly frigid than the great Chamber of Frost in the Blanca Caverns of Cozumel, Mexico, where the conquistadors laid their dead priests to preserve them for the Second Coming.

"Daddy! Daddy!"

Danson whipped around in his saddle. "Tony? Is that you, son?" The only sound was the hissing of the mist, strangling the stones, filling the volcanic fissures with false moisture. He searched the soupy gray for blue sleepers.

. . . orange life jackets . . . can't find fault in the fog . . . a real green pea souper . . . shouldn't have gone out at all . . . don't drown, I love you . . .

Tendrils of blackened fog entwined donkey and rider. No longer were his surroundings relevant. Tent and valley and the very mountain itself were illusions in the malevolent mist. The little donkey began to snort and skitter sideways, its hide quivering. The nervous dance became a desperate dervish as the frightened animal sought direction in the blank world it had entered. It abruptly reared and Danson lurched into nothingness.

16

STRONG ARMS ARRESTED Danson's fall and threw a heavy shawl of animal skin over his shoulders while others captured the donkey's reins and led the crazed beast to a rude corral of stone and wire.

Danson faced the fierce genie of a man who had snatched the leader of the Noah's Ark expedition as easily as a baby from a crib. The river of fog streamed between and past them on all sides. It was as if they had agreed to meet on a cloud. The only assurance the material world had not vanished was the sensation of standing on something solid. But to stand was a supreme act of faith, for the only visible reality was in two faces and the fog.

"A thousand pardons, Reg Danson," spoke his mountain host in a deep, resonant voice. "Welcome to the northernmost outpost of Kurdistan. You and your expedition have disturbed our *sarbasti*, our freedom. You have allowed Turkish slime to corrupt our mountain. I did not survive the mustard gas of the butcher Saddam Hussein in Iraq or leave ten of my children in a stinking tent city of ninety thousand Kurdish refugees along the southern border with Turkey only to be overrun here by an American and an Armenian woman who imagines herself a man.

"I do, however, apologize that you cut yourself shaving!"

A wide grin flashed across the darkly cunning face of the Kurd. Danson involuntarily felt the dried blood on his throat. The fog was beginning to dissipate, the cold evaporating with it. The rocks, the leaning houses, the tent reappeared, and the mist slithered over the edge of the ridge and was gone. Heat, made still more criminal by the contrasting cold, squeezed the oxygen from the air, which was already thin enough at eight thousand feet.

His lungs aching, Danson forced civility. "Not at all. It serves me right for attempting to make myself presentable while racing my donkey. Next time, I shall take pains to separate the two activities.

"Now if you will excuse me . . ."

The Kurd's hand gripped the hilt of the dagger sticking from his waistband. With great effort, he calmed himself.

"It would be of no advantage for you to leave without tea—or the reason you are here in the armed camp of Muhammed Barzani, son of General Dara Mustafa Barzani, supreme commander of all Kurdish freedom fighters!" He swept the dagger from his cummerbund and inscribed an elaborate arc in the air, finally pointing the knife at the tent and bowing low.

Danson hated the delay. He liked the blinding flash of sun on the dagger even less.

Inside the tent, Danson was surprised to see a young woman preparing a tray arrangement of peaches, sliced honeydew melon, and grapes. Her long hair was caught in two dozen intricate braids that formed a rich, brown latticework over the exceedingly unadorned but roughly serviceable frock she wore. Her face was lovely but somber. She placed a stack of thin pancake bread beside the tray and poured several glasses of tea. Then she backed to a foam rubber mat where she sat rocking yoghurt in a goat-skin bag to make butter. She neither spoke nor was spoken to.

A dozen men filed into the tent behind Danson and his host. They all took positions on plain, foam-rubber mats while Barzani motioned for Danson to sit on a startling blue Persian carpet in the center of the bare stone floor. The others might have been there as Barzani's protection or his counsel, each with a bandolier of ammunition criss-crossing his chest. Rifles and light machine guns were piled near the tent entrance.

The woman served them all tea, fruit, and bread, again wordlessly. When she came to him, Danson smiled appreciatively. She cast down her eyes and hurried on to the next.

"There is a saying that goes, 'The Kurds have no friends,'" Barzani spoke, sinking cross-legged to the rug. "I have found it so. Your Christian Crusaders cried, 'Death to Islam!' yet my people under the mighty Saladin repelled them. Not until eight centuries later did we finally extract a promise from a conquering people to give us a permanent homeland."

"I don't see what that has to do with the continuation of our archaeological project," Danson responded, more irritably than he'd intended. The pain in his chest had been building, and he gulped his tea to relieve it.

Barzani's wicked face loomed inches from Danson's. "It was your kind that broke the promise," he hissed. "The guarantee Treaty of Sevres in 1920 was signed by the Allies and the Turks. But you see the extent of our grand nation!" He motioned about the tent, the bitterness poisoning his voice. A loud murmur of angry assent rose from the others, even the once-silent woman.

"A Muslim would never break his word," Barzani continued. His countenance changed from fury to sadness. "Now my people sleep in bat-infested caves; Turkish militia use our children for target practice. My wife has been 'pregnant' 150 times with ammunition smuggled to the brave ones fighting in the Zagros Mountains. The Iraqi dogs want our oil without paying royalties. As long as we are a nonpeople with no country or government of our own, they may steal what is ours without compensation. For this, they have paid with their lives like the rabid dogs they are!"

Danson gulped his tea glass dry, and it was instantly filled by the woman, who this time gave him the barest hint of a smile. He felt dizzy and gripped his chest as a particularly sharp stab of pain sliced through his lungs.

Barzani noted his guest's discomfort and motioned to his men. Two stood, grabbed Danson by the arms, and hoisted him into the air. The woman ran to the table at the edge of the carpet and gathered the fruit and utensils on it into the cloth covering. His carriers laid Danson carefully across the table on his stomach, his head and upper torso hanging over the edge, lower than the rest of his body, which was held securely in place by the two men.

"Altitude sickness," announced Barzani matter-of-factly. "As soon as the blood goes to your head, there will be an improvement." Despite the added pressure of the table on his lungs, Danson soon began to feel less lightheaded.

"I admire your freedom fighters as I do those of Afghanistan and elsewhere," he said between gasps. "Your mountain guerillas, the Pesh Mergas, have truly earned their proud name. . . ."

The mere mention of the mountain militia brought everyone in the tent to his feet with rapid, excited exclamations in the Kermanji dialect that Reg took for reverent awe. They crowded more closely about the man draped over their table and Barzani, crouching and peering intently up into Danson's now rapidly reddening face.

"What do you know of the bravest men the world has ever known?" he demanded excitedly.

Reg hurried on, "They are the Pesh Mergas—'We who face death.' The best of commandos, they daily risk torture, maiming, and certain death to secure an autonomous homeland for eight million of your people. Many thousands of Kurdish refugees, mostly women and children, have fled into Iran where they are tolerated as political pawns of the government. As long as you keep large numbers of Iraqi troops occupied in war, the Iranians have less to contend with in the future."

Barzani joyously clasped Danson's blood-gorged face in his hands and planted a sweaty kiss on his forehead. He motioned for the two attendants to return and up-end his guest, whereupon Danson sank gratefully back to the carpet.

"Better?" asked Barzani solicitously as another tray of fruit was set before them. This time the woman's eyes contained naked admiration for Danson.

"Better," Reg replied, the beginnings of a thudding headache replacing the dizziness. The irritability returned stronger than before. An annoying scriptural admonition to "Count it all joy . . ." joined the anvil chorus hammering at his cranium. "Why am I here?"

A smoldering resentment shoved the gaiety from Barzani's features. "Reg Danson, you are a most foolish man coming here with your Western notions, your fat funds, your little army of academics guarded only by a few tin soldiers—untested by fire— emissary of some distant kingdom whose sultans stupidly believe that at the push of a button or the scratching of pen on decree, they can have whatever they desire.

"How many days did you fast before you came? What spiritual preparation did you or your followers make for a holy quest such as this? How many rocks of Ararat have been wet with your tears? What kinship have you with us, Reg Danson?"

The pounding in his head was louder now, the blows coming seemingly from without and from within. Something told him the questions were fair ones, but by now the itch of irritation had become the rash of savage indignation. This Kurdish lowlife was not about to get in his way or to hold up the expedition a moment longer.

"You have no cause to speak of me or my benefactors with contempt, Barzani," he said too loudly, banging his tea glass onto the table. Instantly, Barzani's men snapped to attention at the changed tone of the conversation. Their commander stayed them with an upraised hand. He nodded curtly for Reg to continue.

The slamming in his temples threatened to send Danson screaming from the room. He gripped his knees until his knuckles turned white. "I will be joyful in God my Savior. The sovereign Lord is my strength. . . ." He had whispered it aloud.

"*That* is your answer?" The sarcasm in Barzani's voice ate the air between them like acid.

The joy of the Lord is my strength. Danson shook his head to clear it of these incessant biblicalities. What was it he'd meant to say? *Rejoice in the Lord always, and again I say rejoice!* Why wouldn't his thoughts cooperate? He shook his head again.

Reg felt a terrifying weariness settle in his bones. The pain in his head at least reminded him he was alive. The pain in his bones felt deathly. Perhaps, like Moses, like Arthur Bryce, he was not going to be allowed to claim the ultimate prize for which he had crossed the wilderness. Maybe this man with the dagger would slit his throat and toss him from the mountain stronghold like yesterday's compost.

The taste of panic coated his tongue.

"Our coming is not at odds with your agenda,"

he managed, wondering even as he said them where the words had originated. Not in his tortured skull. *God, clear my head, please, God.*

"Your people occupied this part of the world centuries before Christ," Reg plunged on, feeling oddly that he was not in control of his own vocal cords. "Being peaceable farming people, they were an easy conquest for the Romans. They plundered your treasury, taxed your people till they bled, and shipped your famous library off to Alexandria to replace the priceless collection that had burned there." A deeply puzzled look came over Barzani's face as the infidel from the U.S. told him things he had not heard since he was a small boy.

"By A.D. 43 your land had been completely integrated into the imperial system. Gradually, you were allowed prosperity and security under the mantle of Pax Romana. Your people formed government councils and sent delegates to provincial assemblies to advise Roman governors. But it was peace without contentment. Your ethnic complexity, your exotic otherness could not be denied.

"Constantinople became the seat of the Roman Empire. Paul, the apostle of Jesus Christ, brought Christianity and eternal hope to your people, but it was made the official state religion and corrupted. It did not reach out to your people in truth and love, it did not meet your hearts' need. Your estrangement grew, and even after the Christians were driven from the land by the Turks, you mothered your distinctives and became the largest ethnic minority in Turkey."

Reg paused for more tea. The room was deathly

quiet, the heat like thick wool blankets. He wanted more than anything to run from that tent back home to Seattle or D.C. or the little white cottage perched on the edge of the sea, bulging with evidence that the Ark was as real as rain.

The joy of the Lord . . . He gulped tea and spoke again. "You have two terrible strikes against you, Barzani. The Kurds are a threat to Turkish national unity, and you will not allow your clever minds to put genuine Christianity to the test. You need to send me on my way with your blessing, for we sit less than two kilometers from the Ark of Noah. For too long the Kurds have held to bits of paganism, Islam, Judaism, Zoroastrianism, and a perverted Christianity. The truth of God's salvation plan for the Kurds and all humankind will become clear when the Ark is reclaimed."

Barzani rose from the carpet and unsheathed his dagger. Pointing it first at Danson's nose, he threw it deep into the top of the table, smiling maniacally all the while.

"You have much to learn, Reg Danson. Jewish legend identifies the Kurds as the bastard offspring of a party of virgins raped by devils while on the way to King Solomon's court. Others say we are descended from the idolatrous Medes.

"Neither presents a very flattering portrait, certainly not the type of people to become the sheep of some crucified Messiah's pasture. Perhaps you're right, though. The Ark might provide a sorting out, a reaffirmation of the common root from which we all sprang. I hope you're right, for war and hatred are a wearisome business.

"For now, though, and for the sake of argument, let us suppose that my dagger cares little for your Jesus or the American who has supposedly come in His name. Suppose I want to cause the gutless Turks a portion of international grief by spilling your entrails all over this mountain? Suppose I were to tell you that a quarter of a million angry and heavily armed Kurds and their sympathizers are massed not eighty kilometers from here ready to take back what is rightfully theirs?

"But little matter. More than any slender hope of some eternal reward, Reg Danson, I want assurance now in this life that you will intercede for my people. When you reach the Ark, tell your President Pierce that one condition of its safe removal is that he extract a promise from Turkey, Iran, and Iraq that they will recognize and help establish a Kurdistani nation within the next three years. If he will not agree, *he* will be responsible for the largest high-altitude mass execution in history. When your children have been reduced to eating grass and insects, you become less particular about your image in the global community."

Reg felt sick at heart. Lieutenant Cayan saw the Ark as her passport to high command. Barzani viewed it as a bargaining chip for a united Kurdistan. For that matter, was he all that sure what Bascomb wanted it for? At least Reg knew that he himself wanted it for the right reasons. But trusting this cat with the canary—and the truth—was a risky business. His own safety mattered little, but Tony's? He sighed resignedly.

"That sounds like maybe you think it's up there," Reg said, stirring his tea with a melon wedge.

"Indeed."

Reg dropped the melon into the tea. "Where?"

"Two days ride from here. Three, by foot. You can trust Cevdet Demirkol's intelligence. It was my men who rode to tell him. Let's just say that Cevdet is one of our chief advocates. "

Danson forcibly calmed himself, suppressing the persistent throb in his brain that was making reason difficult. "You have seen it?"

"Indeed." Again that maniacal smile. "You are seventy-two hours from fame and, I daresay, fortune. Are we agreed, then, on your discussion with Pierce?"

What was Cevdet, a Christian, doing mixed up with these mongrel brigands? Still, with him in some kind of league with the Kurds, Reg had little to bargain with. They undoubtedly knew Agri Dagh like the backs of their hands. And there was no denying the Kurds had been cruelly misused for centuries.

"I will state your case as firmly as I can," Reg replied. "I cannot, however, guarantee the outcome."

Barzani nodded grimly. "Just as I cannot guarantee yours." He rose from the carpet as Reg stood shakily to his feet. "You must think purer thoughts, Reg Danson," he said mockingly. "I have never suffered pains in my head."

The donkey, rested and fed, waited at the tent opening. As one of Barzani's men boosted Danson to the saddle, Reg's eyes met Barzani's, and the grim agreement passed between them once more. The woman watched from the tent opening and said nothing.

The tall mountain commander again bowed low, the flash of the great knife sending daggers of light into Danson's thudding brain. Barzani straightened and slapped the flat of his blade hard against the donkey's flanks. The female animal bolted over the edge of the ridge without hesitation, and rider and mount plunged downward from the mountain.

As they descended ever more swiftly than they had come, Danson's pain began to subside. It did not leave, but neither did it split his mind in two.

With a clearer head came a riot of thoughts. He might have concerned himself with the expedition below, but the donkey seemed to know exactly where it was going. He would, of course, demand of Lieutenant Cayan why they hadn't come after him, but for now he had more tantalizing thoughts to consider.

Within three days the most wondrous sign under heaven would stand revealed before all mankind. It would be as if Noah himself were there and the testimony of the ages would ring forth. Danson remembered the description of those days in Scripture.

"The end of all flesh has come . . . for the earth is filled with violence through them. . . . Come into the ark, you and all your household, because I have seen that you are righteous before Me in this generation" (Gen. 6:13; 7:1), said the Lord God.

"Noah found grace in the eyes of the LORD. . . . Noah did . . . all that God commanded him" (Gen. 6:8, 22), said Moses.

"By faith Noah, being divinely warned of things not yet seen, moved with godly fear, prepared an ark for the saving of his household, by which he condemned the world and became heir of the righteousness which is according to faith," said Paul the Apostle to the Hebrews (11:7).

What will be written of Reg Danson? he wondered. Would his name be preserved one day in some sacred record book? It must be the rarified air, but suddenly he felt less an archaeological errand boy than an important link in a divine plan: *"He did go to Ararat as the Lord God instructed and at great personal risk did bring God's holy boat down from the mountain and it was accounted unto him for righteousness."* Reg could barely contain his joy at the thought. And was it too much to presume that Barbara might be there to share his honor, that God would transfigure her right there in front of the entire assembly to share the incredible moment with him?

Orange . . . did you forget something orange? . . . something important . . . Barbara, would you be here if I hadn't forgotten something important? . . . Nope, got the toothbrush right here . . . Hurry now, hurry . . .

Then it dawned on him that the donkey labored upward again, already well past the point where he had been abducted. But he still saw no one, and an unnamed dread gripped his stomach. The soldiers had made no attempt to rescue him. They had, in fact, gone on without him.

The pitiful donkey began to slow with fatigue and thirst when a smudge in the shimmering distance riveted Danson's attention. Dust! It was his loyal battalion carrying valiantly on without him. He spat in disgust and slammed his heels ferociously into the donkey's ribs.

Half an hour later he overtook them. From behind, the rear guards seemed unnaturally abject, their shoulders slumped, their footsteps erratic. Their weapons were nowhere near the ready even though there were Kurdish thieves about. Reg steamed.

To be able to confront the sluggards head-on, he urged his exhausted mount up a side draw and down a twisting gully one hundred yards ahead of the expedition.

GEORGE Lacey hated the prostitution of nature. Would it happen with Ararat?

Mark Twain once described the sprays of stringy crimson fire and brilliant white sparks of Kilauea Volcano in Hawaii as resembling an "unnatural mingling of gouts of blood and snowflakes."

That natural juxtaposition of raw beauty and gore haunted the volcanologist. He had seen it at Giant's Causeway in Antrim, Northern Ireland, where hundreds upon hundreds of elegant basalt columns march in hexagonal symmetry along the cliffs and the shore. How beautiful and awesome their natural regimental regularity; how terrifying the forces that vomited miles of thick basalt lava from the bowels of the earth to form them.

And how obscene were the volcanic ashtrays, key chains, and coffee mugs on sale at every gift shop within a hundred miles of Mount St. Helens in Washington state. How obscene were the obsidian knives used by Aztec priests to cut out the hearts of their living victims. Even obscene was the traffic in pumice prayer mats made from Jebel Marra Volcano and sold to the Muslim faithful in the Sudan. Make a buck if you can.

Lacey watched the seismic printouts and chided himself for begrudging the Muslims a soft place to kneel. It wasn't that. It was the horrific helplessness he always felt before an eruption. You could divert a river, seed a cloud, or tunnel under the sea, but to stop a volcano was impossible.

And to make of it a bauble in the marketplace was a little like handling poisonous snakes. Sooner or later, someone would be bitten and die.

Everything that was humanly possible to do was being done. The U.S. and Turkish authorities were executing a highly coordinated and so far efficient evacuation of every village within fifty miles of Ararat. The eastern highlands were emptying of people, who streamed westward in dark rivers of trucks and cars and wagons and carts, an orderly confusion of flocks and children and hastily assembled belongings. Little of value was left behind. There had been little enough to begin with.

Much of the provinces of Bitlis, Erzurum, Karaköse, Kars, Mus, and Van would soon be virtually devoid of human life except for those far back in the hills. And the stubborn Kurds, of course. No one could evacuate a Kurd. They would rather take their chances with the volcano than accept charity from a Turk.

Evacuation at night in winter was the worst. In

December 1939, the city of Erzincan was laid waste by a violent earthquake that left 160 thousand dead. Thank God it was summer now.

Lacey was handed the earthquake count for the previous day. 357. It was now three-fifteen and already 314 separate tremors had been recorded. Activity was building.

"Those poor Turks!" he said aloud. An eruption would leave them homeless and without a source of livelihood. Land recovery after an eruption is fairly rapid in wet tropical areas, but it would take centuries in a harsh climate like Ararat's. Those not killed by the blast could die of disease and famine if they were not quickly assimilated into the rest of Turkish society. But how does a government assimilate the countless thousands who have little or no education and are so different from the urban Turks?

"At least, God willing, no one will die on the mountain," he exclaimed under his breath. "Thank God everyone is off the mountain!"

17

EXCRUCIATING PAIN ROCKETED from the base of Danson's spine to the roof of his head. He cried out. The sickening ache and shortness of breath that had plagued him in Barzani the Kurd's tent returned more savagely than before. *Where are the others?*

Demon mountain. That's what some wizened old Turk in soiled turban had shouted repeatedly at the expedition in broken English as it had filed out of dirty little Dogubayazit well before dawn. Demon mountain. Demon seed. Spawn of Satan.

"Don't!" screamed Danson in defiance of the machetes of pain hacking at his mind. The donkey stumbled and threatened to go down, a racking bray caught in its pulsing neck. Its head whipped back and forth as it, too, sought to free itself of stabbing pain.

"Don't!" screamed Danson again. He lurched from the saddle and ran hunched over, low to the ground, to a little rock alcove and pressed his face up in the tiny cluster of shade. He panted his prayer. "My . . . God, why . . . have you . . . forsaken . . . me?"

A slender jet of fresher air coursed from the far recess of the alcove. He gulped and lapped at the nectar and felt his senses returning. From inside the demon mountain came sweet charity. Curse the heat—God would triumph!

The donkey lay on its side in the dirt. A low moan bubbled from its foam-rimmed lips, and then it was still.

Reg jerked away from the oasis of air and stood to face his forces. The heat was a blessing, for without it the Ark would remain out of reach. They would fight on, and with God's help, the devil would eat the heat.

Below him the expedition shuffled along wretchedly like a weary chain gang. Several of the men pressed dry cracked hands hard against their ears as if in imminent danger of losing their heads.

Danson started for them and nearly collided with Lieutenant Cayan's mount, and Tony's close behind. She stared at Reg with a confounding mixture of compassion and pained obstinacy. "I see Barzani left your hide intact," she said.

"No thanks to you!" Reg said icily. "The Turks send a score of protectors with enough fire power to blow up a tank division, and I get picked off by one man on foot with a dagger."

Tony silently dismounted and knelt beside the lifeless donkey. He gently stroked the sweat-soaked neck and waved away the gathering flies.

"That was no man who abducted you, Mr. Danson," Lieutenant Cayan said, half mockingly. "It was

Barzani the Deranged. He has roamed this mountain for years, pretending to be a great Kurdish freedom fighter, yet he seems unable to find his way to the front lines. I didn't think he would harm you, and we could make progress while you and he discussed the number of fleas in a Kurd's beard. No doubt he extracted some promise of aid from you, you bargained with your fingers crossed, and there has been no change in the price of tea in Ankara." Nilay Cayan saw Danson wince with pain, and it was as if she fought to keep from going to him.

"Atmospheric pressure. Particularly bothersome on Ararat. The men seem to be suffering. . . ." she said.

Danson ignored her. The expedition had halted. The men were sitting beside the trail, rocking from side to side, heads in their hands. A rising wail of torment made the hair stand up at the back of Danson's neck.

He started to go to them when Tony spoke in a sad and disbelieving tone. "Is the donkey just a pile of meat to you, Dad? You walked away from it without so much as a glance." Tears glistened in his eyes. "Don't you feel? Don't you care? It carried you here and died practically beneath you, and all you can do is look for another one? Is—is that how it was in Scot . . . ?" He trailed off without finishing the sentence. The expression in his father's eyes killed the rest of it.

"Don't you equate some lousy donkey with what happened to your mother!" Reg said with unmistakable venom. "You've gone too far."

It was a stupid blunder to bring Tony on this

trip. There's too much at stake, too much pressure to succeed. We need time with no distractions to make things right again. I've spent too much time ignoring him, hoping he would mature without me. Oh, God, will I get another chance, or is this the last?

He could not take time to answer the question now. The donkey was dead. His men needed him.

Reg hurried down the slope—whether to escape Tony's stricken look or to minister to his hurting men, he wasn't certain—and walked among the expedition members.

As his shadow fell on each one, the men looked up. Blood streamed from their noses and trickled from their ears. The fear in their faces made the crimson rivulets appear as cracks in their skin. The pack donkeys heaved, their flaring nostrils bleeding profusely.

It was terrible to see their anguish, but Reg steeled himself against any thoughts of retreat. He patted the shoulder of a groaning soldier whose blood-caked baby face seemed impossibly young for this assignment. Reg started to speak words of courage when Tony walked slowly past, leading his laboring donkey and looking neither to the left nor the right.

Reg said nothing and moved on. For the most part, the men were stalwart sons of the soil, hard-baked as the stark eastern plateaus from which they'd sprung. Were he given to friendly wagers, Danson would have placed his money on their deep desire to solve once and for all the mystery of Ararat. This trouble, too, would pass, and they would soon laugh at it. He felt like shouting, "Who's afraid of a bloody nose?"

A commotion at the head of the line tore Danson's attention from Anwar Farugi, the hydrologist from Cairo University. Tony rolled in the dirt with someone who shrieked unintelligibly. Though Tony outweighed his opponent by fifty pounds and soon had him pinned, the younger Danson was no match for the automatic rifle a Turkish soldier leveled at the back of his head.

Reg tackled the soldier, and the rifle clattered into the rocks. Others made for their weapons but stopped when a bullet grazed the back of one's hand. Lieutenant Cayan lowered her rifle, and Reg wondered at her marksmanship.

Danson separated the two combatants with difficulty. "Tony, stop!" The other man was Ahmed Kassem, the Iraqi demolitions expert. Both were covered in blood and sweat, the veins in their necks threatening to burst from the pressure.

"Kassem called you an idiot, Dad. He said you'd get us all killed with your insane march into hell. He says it's Satan's mountain, that werewolves inhabit the upper reaches. When I told him to shut up, he ordered this thug to keep his gun on me, said we'd all be better off if you weren't seen again." The two glared at each other and would have fought again had Reg not intervened.

"It's all right, all of you!" Danson shouted back up the line. "The atmospheric conditions and the heat are making us all a little crazy. Just past the head of the line of march is a stream of fresher air coming from a crack in the rocks. Each of you breathe a minute's worth and make the donkeys do the same. We should reach ice by early morning. Fresh water for all!"

The men grumbled, but hope returned as the bleeding and the pain began to subside. A few cast longing looks down the trail; some peered skyward at the moon visibly approaching the sun; their bloody kerchiefs blotted absentmindedly at drying blood. Most passed the message of fresh air along the line of march, and the rattle and clank of equipment marked the beginning of a rush.

Tony turned to leave, strong, dirt-smeared arms hanging limply at his sides.

"Son." Reg spoke the word with more emotion than he'd intended. "Why'd you stick up for me?"

Tony eyed his father dejectedly. "I don't know. Maybe because you're the guy who showed me how to ride a bike, bait a hook, multiply fractions. You were my walking encyclopedia. For the longest time, you were God to me. You taught me by example."

Reg choked back his sadness. "And now?"

Tony stared at the ground. "You teach by decree. The scales have fallen from my eyes, and you're not God at all. You are a bullheaded, opinionated, dogmatic man who makes me love him and hate him at the same time. Only Mom would let me think for myself. Who knows? I might even have come around to your way of thinking eventually. But no, you needed your little 'yes man' right now.

"And you've become, I don't know, kind of hardened to suffering and the very real limitations of people—and animals." He looked far off in the direction of the dead donkey and shuddered. The undertakers were here. Vultures were beginning a slow, lazy descent.

Reg sighed. "Tony, look at me. Please."

His son's hazel eyes met his own. "I'm sorry for all the times I've cut you off. It's just that once you were my biggest fan, you know? Then, when you became one of my biggest critics, I handled it badly. I took everything personally. But I've never stopped praying for you. Every day of my life I pray for you.

"As for the donkey, I guess I was seeing it as more of a tool of the job. Add to that my anger that no one tried to rescue me from the guy with the dagger, and I'm afraid I was as edgy as a cornered pit bull. Forgive me?"

Tony placed his hands on his hips, and at last a lopsided grin spread over his face—as if he were seeing his father for the first time.

"So you're the stir stick from the Smithsonian, huh? Man, Dad, you sure did knock a few of those test-tube jockeys on their collective backsides. Imagine, one of their own trusted insiders turns out to be a raving creationist and calls them intellectual pretenders to their faces!

"I never told you this before, but I always kind of admired your guts for standing up for what you believed. I just didn't think I believed it myself. And by the way, Lieutenant Cayan told us to keep moving, that Barzani the Kurd was nothing but a blowhard. Said he'd talk your leg off for a bit, then return you good as new. I didn't want to interrupt any high level discussions."

Reg grinned back, touching the knife nick on his

throat. "Yeah, well, maybe next time you would be so kind as to look in on me from time to time. But thanks for defending your old man's honor today. Just don't make a habit of beating the troops." He winked at Ahmed Kassem who glared in return, rubbing a sore spot on his knee.

Tony looked chagrined and wiped a sleeve across his nose. "No sweat, Dad. Makes me wonder, though, if I shouldn't have taken that lifeguard job for the summer."

"What? Give up this paradise for blue water and pretty girls?" Danson laughed. It felt good, normal, right to be joking with his boy.

Reg hated to spoil the moment of openness between them, but there was something he had to know. "You don't think I rushed into resigning the Smithsonian or going public the way I did?"

When Tony didn't answer right away, Reg added, "The way you think I rushed into—other things?"

The warm grin on Tony's face, the sweet taste of honesty they hadn't experienced in so long, fled like a startled crow, raucously accusing in its hasty flight.

"Yeah, it was too sudden." The sullenness in his son's tone came between them, granite tough and immovable. "You should've talked with Mom and me first. It was like we weren't part of your life, and then suddenly the media's on us for something we didn't decide."

Reg swallowed hard. "And what happened at Loch Ness? Did I charge in there without thinking too?"

His son jerked straight and dropped his hands.

Mouth ready to open fire on Reg again, Tony stopped when he saw his father's afflicted look. "Apparently Mom's case is closed in your books," Tony said glumly. "You know what happened and you have to live with it. What I think doesn't matter."

"It matters to me, son. The Lord wants us to confess our sins to each other and pray for each other so healing can take place. We used to pray together when you were little."

"If you have any sins to confess, Dad, I think you'd do better to talk to old Ibrahim Hasan. He seems a level head. My philosophy is, those who want things to happen, take action. Those who don't, pray."

Tony started to walk off in the direction of the fresh air grotto.

"Tony, wait!" Danson wasn't sure why he stopped him. "I, uh, just want you to know that whatever happens, I'll always love you."

An embarrassing silence ruled between them. Why had he said that? Why was everything on this mountain so monumental in importance?

Tony shifted his weight awkwardly, a boy-man so handsome, so healthy, so full of promise. How long had it been since they'd hugged?

"Go on and get your air, chum. Tell Cevdet to have a half dozen men tether the donkeys in that meadow we passed two hundred yards or so back and to leave two guards on watch."

Tony nodded. Something passed between them, unspoken to be sure, but no less palpable. Danson wanted desperately to grab his son and hold him, apologize for whatever mistakes he'd made as a father, and tell him God the Father wanted them back together again.

Reg was suddenly aware that Ahmed Kassem had been watching them appraisingly.

"Ahmed!" Reg shouted his irritation.

The man glowered at Danson and did not speak.

"I was assured you are one of the most able members of this expedition. How do you explain your actions?"

Ahmed spat blood. "You have eyes, Mr. Danson. We have no wounds, yet we bleed. We all began this journey in our right minds, yet before the first day is out our heads threaten to explode. And though we all bleed, you and Cayan do not. Evil forces are at work here, beyond the power of man to resist. We have trespassed on fiendish ground and ought to turn back."

"Nonsense," Danson said, clenching his teeth. "You are clinging to the tales of old women and cowardly men. Surely you do not determine your life goals on the basis of superstition. Otherwise, why have you come with us at all?"

Kassem would not meet Danson's gaze. Danson handed him a handkerchief to staunch the flow of blood from his nose, which had already begun to clot. The Iraqi watched the others scramble for air in the rock. Lieutenant Cayan rode up but stayed astride her donkey and said nothing.

"Do you recall our encountering scattered flocks of sheep and goats at the lower reaches earlier today?" Ahmed asked Reg.

Danson nodded.

"And did you not see a few pitiful sheep and goats at Barzani's encampment?"

Danson nodded again, his impatience growing at this seeming small talk.

"Have you seen any sheep or goats since?" Kassem looked at him, a look half fearful, half pleading.

Danson slowly shook his head no.

"It is because the sheep and goats of Ararat die above eight thousand feet. It is because the demons allow no life beyond here. They do not want us or anyone to enter the strongholds of the powers of the air.

"I came, Mr. Danson, because I did not want to believe the tales. All my life I have fought an enemy I could see, and ever since our ascent began, I have felt the power and presence of an enemy I cannot see. Can you not feel it?"

The uneasiness stole over Danson vicious as a bomb threat. Was he wrong to have come here? He glanced at Nilay and was shocked by the open physical interest he saw in her eyes.

"Of course the sheep die, Kassem," he said, shaking off that look and turning back to the dejected Iraqi. "The altitude is beyond their ability to endure. That is why we will make our base camp a little below here and leave the animals to graze.

"As for ourselves, we will become acclimated to the conditions with time. It is difficult, I agree, and troubling. But all the published reports from expeditions on Ararat show similar harrowing physical trials. As for the presence of an enemy, seen or unseen, I am not about to chock up the wild atmospheric fluctuations of Ararat to unchained devils. God is with us, and now is the time for the Ark to be revealed to all the world. You tell the men that there will be a nice bonus for all who remain loyal."

He saw the ugliness of the bribe as soon as it was out. Money, the great cure-all for the world's ills.

Kassem's shoulders slumped miserably. "I will come with you, Mr. Danson, but not for more money. The Ark legend is the greatest in the world and therefore worthy of pursuit. Ararat is the highest point and the first in all of Turkey to be struck by morning's light. It is therefore worthy of our veneration and perhaps I shall be able to blast the evil from it. But I warn you that I believe our chances are slim at best and that I am resigned to our deaths. Before leaving my home in Baghdad, I said my goodbyes and left written instructions for the dispensation of my earthly goods."

What an exasperating people, thought Danson. *What fatalists!* "Fine. I make only one request. Keep your gloom and doom to yourself. I'll not have you sowing discontent among the others."

Kassem nodded glumly and went off to get his ration of fresh air.

Nilay Cayan jumped to the ground, surrendered her donkey to one of her men, and stood watching as the mounts were led away to pasture. She was sorry to see them go. Willful as they could be, they were still in a better temper by far than the rest of the expedition members.

Reg went to her, and she turned at his approach, the spark in her eyes promising both danger and delight. Without thinking, he pulled her into the gully beside the trail, took her in his arms, and kissed her tenderly. She did not resist.

From the rock ledge above, Tony observed the two of them. He turned away, and there was Ahmed Kassem watching too. They stood motionless, staring at each other for a time before Kassem nodded curtly and moved on. His words roared through Tony's mind like a desert wind . . . *evil forces at work here beyond the power of man to resist. We have trespassed on fiendish ground and we ought to turn back. . . .*

R EG'S WATCH read twenty minutes to two in the afternoon—or "two, twenty there is" in Turkish reckoning—when he called a halt for a brief lunch break. A peculiar, thick fog below continued to obscure the plain as it had for most of the morning. How could intense heat and fog coexist like this?

The strain on the earth at the convergence of the African, Eurasian, and Indo-Australian seismic collision zones was tremendous. As distant as 250 miles from the epicentral activity beneath Lake Van near the Iranian border, herds of domestic animals stampeded and knocked into one another in mass confusion. Occasional sharp jolts dislodged objects from shelves, and in Ergani a man was killed when the ladder he was standing on to repair his roof was knocked over by a geologic convulsion.

Without warning, the rock table beneath the expedition began to rumble. "Look out!" Tony cried as a dozen large stones and a shower of gravel rained down on them from the rock overhang above. A sudden jet of hot steam blasted from a fissure near three men playing backgammon. One shrieked in agony as the steam hit him square in the face. He writhed on the ground, clawing at the blisters on his cheeks and forehead.

It was over in a blink, and some of the men rubbed their eyes as if to confirm it had happened. Tony and Dr. Norman Leagues attended to the injured man. Lieutenant Cayan strode determinedly over to Reg and planted herself inches from his face. Her beautiful face was smudged with concern.

"My people and I didn't bargain for earthquakes," she said firmly. "I suggest we make contact with Turkish Civil Defense. This region is notoriously unstable. You have heard of the ancient Armenian village of Arghuri?"

Reg shook his head no and she continued. "Arghuri was nestled at the mouth of Ahora Gorge, a stupendous black chasm nine thousand feet deep on the north side where we are bound. The village was said to be quiet and lovely with many grapevines, two hundred homes in all and the Monastery of St. Jacob. On the twentieth of June, 1840, there was a mighty roar, and a quake buried it all under tons of ice, rock, and debris. Hundreds of innocent ones were entombed forever.

"But for you, Mr. Danson, perhaps the greater tragedy was the loss of irreplaceable artifacts. Legend says the monastery was a treasure house of the Ark, that the monks were keepers of priceless evidence of the Flood and its aftermath, including some of Noah's personal belongings." She studied his face for signs of emotion, but the handsome features were immovable.

"Our current situation does not escape me, Lieutenant," he responded, meeting her gaze. "We could very well be in some earthquake danger. But I'm certain that the authorities would contact us at once if they knew the situation to be dangerous."

He looked at her critically. "With all due respect, Lieutenant, it seems to me that commitment to the task at hand is not one of your strong suits." He was getting angry again and began to wonder if there wasn't a streak of hotheadedness ethnically entrenched in his lineage. But if this woman forced him to pull rank, he would do just that.

"With all due respect to you, Mr. Danson, you lack a certain appreciation for the safety of your people and the sensitivities involved in hosting a multinational expeditionary team. You are the guest of a sovereign state not your own, and I would suggest that you start to behave like one!"

Reg smiled disarmingly, sat down on a boulder, and offered her a chunk of trail mix. She shook her head in annoyance. "Nilay Cayan," he said, his words thickened by a great bite of mix, "there once was a very wise man in America by the name of Grover Cleveland. When he became president, he said that sensible and responsible women did not want to vote. Then he proceeded to seal his coffin by adding that the relative positions to be assumed by man and woman in the working out of civilization were assigned long ago by a higher intelligence than ours."

She looked at him as one might look at a mass

murderer. She said, her voice tight, "Your Grover Cleveland is a *hamam bocegi!*"

"And just what is that in English?" he inquired innocently.

"A cockroach!" she replied.

CHAPTER 19

RELENTLESSLY THE SHADOWS raced toward the man where he lay, belly-flat against the granite slab. Though not of this world, they normally would not have worried him. On Ararat, however, nothing was normal.

He refused to blink and miss the moment. As the shadows closed at forty feet per second, the afternoon was silver molten, the heat shriveling. It would soon be three o'clock and dark.

Even now the dragon was devouring the sun. The Chinese, however inscrutable, did have a way with words. He was surprised to find himself trembling slightly, despite the temperature.

The dusk was unnatural. The shadows arrived. Darkness fell.

The man looked up.

The last of Bailey's Beads cast a diamond ring about the moon as it obliterated the sun. A faint reddish glow appeared along the moon's leading edge, a result of the sun's chromosphere. His face bathed in the eerie gleam of the sun's corona, the man envisioned the screaming ancients fleeing in terror from a total solar eclipse.

He imagined himself viewing the spectacle through cosmic sunglasses from the summit of the Leibnitz Mountain Range highest on the moon, half again as tall as the Himalayas.

In two minutes it would be over. Just 120 seconds to record the chromium splendor for a lifetime, a tiny disc in the heavens blotting out a sun four hundred times its size.

The beads appeared again, this time on the opposite side of the sun. The shadows moved on. Shafts of ultraviolet rays ten thousand times brighter than the moon spotlighted the man on the stone.

Lieutenant General Nikolai Shkidchenko watched the one-hundred-man remnant of the former Red Army resume its struggle up the north face of Mount Ararat. The other 2,333 remained bivouacked by the river below. He despaired for them. No sooner had they found surcease in the river than they discovered that their campground was the haven for multitudes of scorpions. Their truckloads of Russian-made AK-47 machine guns afforded little fortification against Ararat and her vermin.

A feral snarl and an answering whinny of challenge attracted his attention to a rock outcrop two hundred feet below. A malnourished black wolf was circling an equally deprived wild mountain mustang. The black beast lunged repeatedly, wearing down its prey. The mustang's hooves scored several telling lashes, one resulting in a ribbon of scarlet spray from its antagonist's eye. But the wolf would not be deterred and gathered itself for one mighty leap. It hurtled at the throat of the mustang and attached its fangs to the horse's jugular. The dying mustang groaned in pain, using its remaining energy to whirl madly in a circular dance of death. The wolf flew outward from its victim like a black flag of piracy, but the death grip held. Hunter and hunted crashed to earth, the breath loudly knocked from the fallen horse. Its hind hooves flailed their last even as the wolf tore away its meal.

Shkidchenko had debated saving the horse but decided instead to watch the killing in gruesome fascination. Now he peered through the sights of his rifle at the ravenous wolf, which was feeding frenziedly. The ground around the nearly decapitated mustang was soaked with its blood. Shkidchenko whistled. The wolf's head snapped up and the gore-covered creature looked wildly over its shoulder straight into the rifle's sights. Shkidchenko squeezed the trigger, and the shattered wolf somersaulted over the side of the mountain.

The lieutenant general stood and motioned to his men that all was well. They would soon be too close to the Ark hunters to so carelessly signal their presence, but for now the shot was excusable.

Shkidchenko's bowels had ceased their warring at last. Now an unsettling knot, untraceable to bad food or ulcers, lodged itself in his gut. It was the reason he hadn't saved the horse, that he no longer resented this mad march up a godforsaken mountain.

An irresistible magnetism had begun its pull when he awakened that morning. The little drama of the wolf and the horse underscored a heightening

sense of something inconceivable about to happen.
While the world clawed and killed and raped its own,
while the gruesome Hitlers and Stalins and Turkish
potentates of the ages had spilled the blood of innocent victims by the untold millions, the astonishing
great vessel of condemnation and salvation known as
the Ark of Noah had remained, a symbol of both
damnation and redemption, a silent hulk locked in
glacial depths.

Shkidchenko had sat bolt upright this morning,
the stomach knot as insistent as a three-pound tu-
mor. He'd rushed from the tent and looked up at the
hoary Mother of the Earth and he could clearly see
the blunt prow of the Ark jutting defiantly from its
ancient trap. Like the cold, expressionless face of a
medieval black knight, it bulged malignantly from
the side of Ararat. As tall as the onion domes in Red
Square, it yawned impossibly wide, and its length
stretched from sight. He thought of the ancients felling the timber, hauling, milling, and hoisting it into
place with massive block and tackle, a forest of scaf-
folding beneath their feet.

A new understanding outraced the beating of his
heart, shrieked louder than the throb in his head. His
new insight reduced to insignificance the crusted
blood on his nose, chin, and neck, the stiff dark stain
on the shirt of his uniform. He had bled in the night;
they had all bled in the night. It was nothing.

What mattered was that Lenin's minions had for
too long bled the church, had reduced it from nearly
fifty-five thousand holy sanctuaries before the Revolution to fewer than seven thousand state "shells" at
the time of the communist fall. Puny and powerless,

these modern churches were peopled largely with women, old people, and puppet priests. Ritual and homily had become thinly disguised party propaganda, and crossing oneself was as much a sign of good luck as of good religion. The real church, the church of power, the church that would not die, had met in the woods, in dingy apartments and cottage kitchens, and praised the divine architect of the Ark with hand-copied psalms and hymns passed on from cradle memories. A few of these true believers had gathered about an old porcelain bathtub while a mother scrubbed the soil from her little boy's ears and a father in faded military regalia sang of heavenly places in a booming voice that dared discovery.

Shkidchenko fingered the little medallion at his neck, picking away the scab of blood that had formed on the likeness of St. Seraphim. For thirty-one years, long before the Marxist dogs came sniffing, the monk lived in total seclusion and prayer. Then eight years before his death, he broke silence and ministered to thousands upon thousands who sought his counsel, encouragement, and healing. He told them that all his ritual good works—and theirs—were nothing compared to their real purpose in life: to acquire the Spirit of God.

Shkidchenko whispered aloud the words his father had taught him at the age of ten. "The joy which the Epicureans in their superficial philosophy sought in vain . . . is a joy known only to the innocent heart united with Christ, and through Christ to God." He smiled bitterly at the words first uttered by a seventeen-year-old Karl Marx. It took that young man less than nine years to exchange union with Christ for melding with godless atheism.

It had taken Nikolai Shkidchenko these forty-five years to gain his revenge on Marx and his ideological progeny. They had made man the "highest divinity," with submission to anything remotely religious the basest form of cowardice. Now in their bloated ignorance, they had sent the wrong man to do their dirty work. Oh! He'd blow the American off the mountain, all right. Pop religionists made in the U.S.A. were no better than pop atheists made in the U.S.S.R.

The holy Ark was another matter. It would not be destroyed. He would stand on its roof and declare to the world via satellite that he, Nikolai Shkidchenko, had made the discovery of the century. In the name of Mother Russia, a Soviet Mafia hit man would return the Ark to humankind at long last. Then he would smile and place a gun to his head, his last thoughts those of a porcelain bathtub, Mother and Father, and the Muslim-Christian hordes storming atheist strongholds and making believers of the worst of them.

Lieutenant Shkidchenko made his way rapidly down from the granite perch, a new energy and urgency lengthening his stride. He rubbed the medallion at his throat. He would lead this charge, with St. Seraphim by his side.

REG Danson swallowed the prednisone capsules and had Tony distribute more to the others. A synthetic derivative of cortisone, prednisone was a steroid that would reduce the swelling of the respiratory passages and allow for greater oxygen intake. It was also a favorite of high-altitude climbers because it both heightened and prolonged wakefulness and aided in fighting off the lethargy common above six thousand feet. Fatigue would catch up with them at last, but by then, he hoped, the expedition would be at a successful end.

Only the old priest refused the drug. "I have spiritual medicine to give me energy," he assured. "I have simply to repeat the ninety-nine beautiful names of Allah and soon I am skipping along like a child."

"Why just ninety-nine names?" Tony asked.

"Ah! We have a popular saying that the one hundredth name was revealed only to the camel, which accounts for his haughty bearing," Ibrahim replied with a sunny smile. "I hope to discover that name on this mountain—it is said that he who calls upon God by that exalted one hundredth name will receive all he desires."

"And what do you desire, Mr. Hasan?"

The priest soberly contemplated Tony's question. "I desire to know my destiny," he said at last. "Islam teaches that no one can know his or her end in advance since Allah has predestined some people to paradise and some to perdition. On the Judgment Day, each will be presented a Book of Destiny. If it is placed in your right hand, you are saved; if in the left, you are lost."

A cloud of concern passed over the priest's face. Then he said brightly, "But I feel in my bones that we can know in this life. I want to be able to dance on a razor's edge!"

When Tony looked puzzled at that, Hasan hastened to explain. "To reach paradise, believers will easily cross a bridge as narrow as a hair and as sharp as a razor; unbelievers, as soon as they mount the bridge, will fall into hell."

Tony grinned. "I know some dances that'll get you across that bridge without ever touching down!" They laughed together and promised to meet for an exchange of dance steps at the campfire. Hasan would show Tony a version of the dervish that he was certain would become all the rage in American colleges.

Reg listened to their laughter from his seat on a boulder fifty yards uphill. He wished he could smile and be lighthearted, too, but he could not. Something was not right here on the steeply rising slopes of Agri Dagh. He'd said nothing, but he'd seen other jets of steam that day besides the one that had blistered a man's face. Even now, from where he sat, he had a panoramic view of a football-field's length of terrain and possibly fifteen or twenty geysers of steam spouting at random intervals from cracks and clefts. The ground seemed to be heating up, not cooling off, as night fell.

He knew there had been plenty of thermal activity in the mountains of Ararat over time. Bound to be, given one of the most earthquake-prone regions on earth. But a display such as this was highly irregular. And as still as he sat, he felt periodic vibrations in the rock. A build-up to something bigger or a mere subterranean burp? Ararat was geologically unstable at the best of times without—

"Steam vents," said Nilay Cayan from farther down the slope. Dusk was settling fast, and he could barely make her out in the gloom.

"Just what I was thinking," he hedged.

Cayan moved upslope, then stopped and pointed. "South and west of here on the plain, the gypsies camp by the hundreds at a place of many geysers and hot springs. Limestone covers the basalt, but the lava beneath is still hot. When groundwater trickles down through the rocks, it is returned to the surface as steam and hot water. These must be part of that system and evidence of a sub—"

"There is no groundwater," Danson interrupted. "This is the worst drought of the century. Have the gypsies been seen this summer?"

Cayan sighed in exasperation. "No, they have not," she replied sharply. "Tell me, Mr. Danson, what will it be tonight? Truth or fiction?"

"I don't know what you mean."

"I mean that when I say there may be danger on the wind, you belittle my theories. When I opt for a more benign explanation, you prefer raw truth. It is difficult to know exactly what you want!"

Danson laughed apologetically and threw a stone down the mountain. Its bump and rattle could be heard for a long time on the night air. Tony and Ibrahim Hasan began their battle of the dance, and the merriment punctuated the night stillness.

"You're right," Danson said. "I have been acting like a sunstroke victim. Truth is, I don't know how much I want to know. Part of me'd like to turn tail and run, and part of me is quite ready to die here. But neither a militarist nor a chaser of mysteries ought to be too quick to call off as important a journey as this one. If we can show Noah's Ark to a dying world, they will be without excuse for rejecting God and His plan for every man, woman, and child on the planet."

Silent for a long time, Cayan peered into the vast inky blackness as if searching for signs of life on the plain.

"What would it take to turn you around?" she asked, her tone strangely tight.

"Irrefutable proof that this mountain is about to cave in and swallow us whole," he said, trying to keep his tone light.

"Then take a good look out there," she said, again pointing to the distant plain. "What do you see?"

"Nothing," he said patiently. "Exactly what I'd expect to see in the dark."

"There is your evidence of coming disaster, my city-bred explorer. There are numerous shepherd encampments, towns, and cities there on the plain—people by the thousands, and yet there are no lights in the night. That is unnatural."

Danson jumped to his feet and strained to find signs of light. He saw none save moonrise and the expedition campfires.

The plain was empty, and they were alone on a volcano.

CHAPTER

THE HEADACHES were brutal. Before dawn the camp resounded with the banshee wail of tortured men. Squeezing the sides of his skull in an effort to contain the sledgehammer, Danson prayed for respite.

Though . . . the fields yield no
    food;
Though the flock be cut off
    from the fold,
And there be no herd in the
    stalls—
Yet I will rejoice in the LORD,
I will joy in the God of my
    salvation.

The LORD God is my strength;
He will make my feet like
    deer's feet,

And He will make me walk on
my high hills. (Hab. 3:17–19)

The words of the prophet Habakkuk anesthetized the pain a little.

Despite his own torment, Ibrahim Hasan passed from tent to tent, administering Koranic curatives. Reg felt such a wave of love for the man, he would have hugged him had he been able to stand without assistance.

Twelve men had defected in the night. Half were military personnel; the others, expedition civilians. The only great loss was Norman Leagues, a British surgeon and expert in mountain medicine. Besides attending to the minor scrapes and sprains of the expedition and any major mishaps that might occur, his particular charge was that of bleeding Reg, Tony, Cevdet, and Ibrahim Hasan and administering the air-oxygen mixture. But while they were hooked to the nasal hoses, Leagues and the others had departed. They took nothing but their own gear, and oddly none of the guards posted at that end of the camp reported the defectors.

At Reg's insistence, Lieutenant Cayan had ordered three of the guards to pursue Leagues on the fastest donkeys in the party. They had overtaken him at four in the morning nursing his ankle, twisted in his haste to get down the mountain. He gave his newly arrived escorts no difficulty—his former companions in escape had abandoned him to his fate.

When Leagues stood before him, unable to look him in the eye, Reg reminded him how highly recommended he came from the British high command, how distinguished the service to Her Majesty he had rendered in the Falkland Islands conflict. Would such a man flee in terror from a nosebleed?

As long as he lived, Danson would not forget Leagues' reply. With trembling lips, he said, "I would gladly lay down my life for my God, my queen, or my allies. But please, sir, do not ask me to do so for the devil!"

Though Danson had tried to reassure him, the words carried little conviction. The ominous eclipse the day before, Barzani's and Kassem's dire predictions, the wretched head strain, the deserted plain, a growing sense that others were climbing the mountain, even the eerie fog bank—all contributed to a dull foreboding that was intensifying in Danson's own heart. These were not just drunken superstitions told around campfires a safe distance from Ararat. The accumulated weight of experience was tipping in favor of forces darker than he cared to contemplate.

Nilay was a maddening bright spot. Her kisses had reignited a long-dormant flame within him, one that had seemed to freeze with Barbara's death. But surely it was only the flesh stirring; he could never love anyone with the inner core that Barbara alone had tapped. Why, then, was he always checking Nilay's location, wondering where she was and if he was on her mind?

The beautiful lieutenant had resumed a strictly officious exterior since they had kissed on the trail. There could have been no mistaking the fervor in her embrace, and yet she treated him now as if it all had been a mirage.

The bleeding and oxygenation had invigorated him from the neck down. Some of the men had downed sleeping pills to gain some relief from the head pain, but he had not. He wanted to stay clear-minded, alert to further desertions. Too, they would reach the snowline by eight in the morning, and he had heard ample reports of killer avalanches and crevasse falls on this perverse peak.

A dim glow lit the eastern sky as the expedition broke camp. With the coming of dawn the headache intensity lessened, and the men were anxious to bring the expedition to as early an end as possible. Few believed they would ever see an Ark, let alone send it sailing over the clouds slung from cables attached to the underbellies of giant helicopters. Over the years, several had accompanied other Ark expeditions with legendary eccentricities. As far back as 1887, one John Joseph, prince of Nouri, archbishop and apostolic ambassador of Malabar, India, and Persia, had proposed disassembling the Ark for ease of transportation and reassembling it at the Chicago World's Fair. Schemers!

The sun rose a sliver above the horizon, driving a shaft of brilliant light into the camp. The scene was instantly transformed from the disgruntled packing of a wounded expedition to a glorious paradise exploding in orange and yellow and amber. The breaking of camp ceased, every man riveted to the startling rise of the sun.

As soon as Reg Danson could stand again, he went to the edge of camp to pray. He sank to his knees and cried, "Lord God, forgive me my sin, and make your servant triumphant this day. Grant us all speed, that nothing will prevent the rescue of the Ark. Slay any enemy that would get in our—" The sun flung its shocking shard of light, and Danson looked behind him and above.

The mountain peak was obliterated in a churning caldron of black cloud. The writhing mass festered with stabbing jolts of lightning, a confusion of whirlwinds whipping the frenzied tempest. Little crackles of electric explosions charged the inferno.

Scores of the devout looked up then and saw the meeting of the anointed golden dawn and the midnight black of the mountain. They prostrated themselves amongst the duffle bags and climbing apparatus spread on the ground. Booted men in khaki uniforms and olive green climbing apparel laced their fingers behind their heads and buried their faces deep in nylon and canvas. A Koranic mantra rose to greet the clash of the holy and the profane: *"Estagfurullah!* . . . *Estagfurullah!* May God forgive me! . . . May God forgive me!"

"May God forgive us all!" Cevdet Demirkol dropped to his knees beside Danson and repeated his version of the sacred formula. Danson was grateful for the company.

"Discover a way to deliver them of superstition, my friend, and you could conquer the world with such a handful as these." Demirkol smiled broadly.

Danson smiled, too, thankful for this strong Turkish soldier of fortune with whom he felt he could secure the Ark, whether the others came or not. "Will they desert in the end?"

Cevdet looked thoughtful. "An ancient Chinese

parable tells of a male traveler leaving a great city. On the road he meets two fearsome persons traveling in the other direction. The man nervously asks one of the travelers his identity. The reply? 'I am Plague, and I am headed for the city.' Shaking, the man asks, 'Will you kill many in the city?' Whereupon Plague answers, 'No, but my traveling companion, Panic, will kill thousands.' That is perhaps the greatest enemy to this effort, Mr. Danson. Fear of the dark." He peered at the boiling storm on Ararat's peak.

Reg stared at the ground, searching his own thoughts. "Are you afraid, Cevdet?" He half expected this descendant of the mighty Janissaries, a man who had risked his very life and hidden underground for the sake of the Ark, to scoff at such a notion.

Instead, the reply came slowly, carefully. "I have told you before that the Evil One is severely outclassed by the One we serve. I am convinced of that. I am equally convinced that some among us will die in His service, our bodies to be piled with lava rocks to keep the wolves of Ararat from dismembering us. Who that will be, I do not know. I do not welcome it, but was it not the apostle Paul who said, 'Death is gain'? We have left the trivialities of earth behind and ascended the great spire of God. Whatever happens, none of us shall ever be the same again!"

Reg nodded somberly and watched Lieutenant Cayan marshal the troops to finish packing. Camp broke slowly at first, each man glancing nervously at the dark maelstrom above. The soldiers, crisscrossed ammunition belts dissecting their chests, moved into guard position like X's on a tic-tac-toe board. Then a figure in rough cloth began to stride among them at the far side of the camp, hurrying purposefully from man to man and pack team to pack team, working his way towards Reg and Cevdet. He withdrew a small object from beneath his arm, pointed to it, gesticulated excitedly, and spoke rapidly before moving on to the next group. Each one who heard the news seemed to come alive and begin to pack quickly and with purpose.

At last, beaming from ear to ear, Ibrahim Hasan walked briskly over to Reg and Cevdet, his elation barely contained.

"Ah, Reg Danson, Cevdet Demirkol! How blessed is the sunrise! It is the caress of God upon our little band!"

"A blessed morning to you, Ibrahim," Reg replied. "Tell us, what spell have you placed the men under to make them so enthusiastic about resuming the march?"

Hasan swelled up like a rooster on a fence post. "I merely applied the healing and motivating words of Allah Himself!" He pulled a small, battered book from beneath his arm. Clearing his throat dramatically, he read:

"Blessed be the name of God forever and ever,
For wisdom and might are His. . . .
He gives wisdom to the wise
And knowledge to those who have
     understanding.
He reveals deep and secret things;
He knows what is in the darkness,
And light dwells with Him."

We climb to a brilliant darkness—He knows all and will not allow us to be devoured by it. He will grant us wisdom to triumph!"

The little *hoca* rushed off to finish his ministrations. Reg called after him, "Good for you, Ibrahim! Smart man to bring your Koran along!"

Ibrahim did not slow down. "What Koran, Mr. Danson?" he shouted breathlessly over his shoulder. "It is the Bible, second chapter of Daniel, beginning at the twentieth verse. Our little secret, yes, Mr. Danson?"

THE RUMBLINGS continued with unnerving frequency. The intense, air-sucking heat from above combined with the steamy wet heat from inside the mountain to create a sauna effect that made breathing difficult and progress agonizingly slow. The Noah's Ark expedition hallucinated cool, limpid pools of sweet water into which they would plunge and drink their fill, and oceans of fresh air bathing their lungs with an extravagance of oxygen.

A particularly jarring tremor caused two men to stumble and fall to their knees. After Reg hurried forward and helped them up, he turned and faced them all

"Stop and rest for a quarter of an hour. I'll attempt radio contact to determine the nature and severity of these tremors." Seeing the strain in their dirty, sweaty faces, he mustered a smile. "Two days more at most and you'll all be international heroes." He paused, panting. "Trust in God, men, and"—three quick breaths—"you'll not be disappointed."

Ahmed Kassem moaned. "More sunny platitudes!"—breathe, swallow, breathe—"Tomorrow's archaeologists will find our petrified bodies"—gasp, swallow, breathe—"beneath a mountain of ash." He took a long pause to collect air and check his pulse. "But the cause of our passing will be found to be death by an overdose of glad tidings!"

Reg didn't know whether to kill Kassem or hug him. "That's the spirit, Ahmed. Just for that, I will radio for bed pillows for all!" While Ahmed and the others tried to make sense of that, Reg took six shallow breaths and held the last. "Pillows to tie to our heads as protection against falling lumps." Several men smiled despite the effort, but Kassem and Lieutenant Cayan glowered. Well, it had worked for Pliny the Elder when Vesuvius rained rocks. With torches in hand and pillows lashed to their heads, Pliny and company had made their way safely to the sea under the darkness of a thick ash cloud and falling rock. His companions fled, and three days later his body was found by the shore in peaceful repose. Heart attack.

Even in times of volcanic upheaval, heart disease is the number one killer, thought Reg, setting up the radio to transmit. *My gallows humor is getting pretty bad.*

He switched on the radio and gathered breath for the transmission. Words from the book of Proverbs gave him courage:

My son, if you receive my words,
And treasure my commands within you,
So that you incline your ear to wisdom,

And apply your heart to understanding;
Yes, if you cry out for discernment
And lift up your voice for understanding,
If you seek her as silver
And search for her as for hidden treasures;
Then you will understand the fear of the LORD,
And find the knowledge of God. (2:1–5)

Reg loved Proverbs. His search for historical treasure must never outweigh his lifelong search for wisdom. But surely the finding of the Ark and the finding of truth were inseparable. To abandon either expedition was unthinkable.

"Massis One to Uncle, Massis One to Uncle—come in Uncle." Static sizzled and snapped; then a distortion whine sounded as if it were coming from the bottom of a hollow tube.

"Come on baby," Danson coaxed. "Massis One to Uncle, Massis One to Uncle, how do you read? Over."

The whine rose to a strangled whistle and then ceased. "Uncle to Massis One, Uncle to One. Roger One. We copy you clear. Hope all is *ship*shape, if you Noah what I mean. Over!"

Reg rolled his eyes. Where'd they get this satellite jockey? He couldn't resist. "Roger, Uncle. We've got a boat to float, but the earth keeps moving under our feet. What's the long-range volcanic forecast? Over."

The jocular code recalled space shuttle transmissions to Reg. It was serious business with the ears of friend and foe listening in. No reason, though, not to lighten the conversation.

"Stand by, Massis, stand by. Over."

Uncle remained silent for several moments. Reg tried to imagine the technology, the amount of hardware required to send his voice bounding through space. But the wheel was not invented in man's ability to manage natural phenomena. In an age when sunspots could scramble the North American Early Warning defense system, human knowledge was still at the preschool level.

"Massis One, Massis One, this is Uncle. Do you read?"

"Affirmative, Uncle. Over."

"Officials keeping a tight watch on seismic activity. Appears to have leveled out indica—" the last of the word lost in an atmospheric squeal "a weakening of the event. Over."

"Roger, Uncle, that's a comfort. Has there been an evacuation of Anato—" The radio emitted a piercing wail, and Danson jammed a hand forward to turn down the volume. The wail subsided, and he quickly turned the volume up again.

"—n't say. Tur—ment on the plain is—uing at this time. The presi—ous for you to cont—dition with all reas—aste. We will—you—any—lopments—"

"Negative, negative, Uncle!" Reg fumbled to adjust the reception. No good. "Repeat, Uncle, repeat. Over."

The return garble was impossible to decipher, and after a few futile tries to restore contact, Reg switched the radio off.

What had Uncle been trying to say about evacuation from the plain below? At least they felt the tremors were subsiding. That had to be a good sign. He prayed, "Heavenly Father, You are Lord of the lava, Lord of Ararat, Lord of my heartbeat and my breath. See us through this hell to the heaven beyond. Let there be no revolt or turning back. If evil does not wish the Ark to be found, please, Lord, let good find it anyway. Let Your will be done and make me content with whatever Your will is."

Meanwhile, a job needed doing. Reg slung the radio over his shoulder and went to inform the team. As they resumed the climb, Danson was in the lead and he was literally whistling Dixie.

THE bear seemingly materialized out of the mountain itself. It was emaciated and half-spent, its stringy, matted coat a dullish gray-black in the midday sun. Its gait was an odd sideways shuffle, and its left front leg and paw were stiff and never quite touched the ground. It was half dead when it fell upon Hayri Erbakan's goats.

If the goats had not panicked, the bear might not have been swift enough to catch one. But they bolted, bleating in terror, stepping on one another. A fawn-colored dam, Hayri's favorite, tumbled back into the bear's clumsy paws and lay quivering while its pink belly was ripped open with a single swipe of claws.

The goatherd bellowed and charged the bruin. Its crazed face was covered in fresh blood. The man drew a crude bone knife and ached to plunge it deep into the attacker's chest.

With a distant roar and a mighty shaking from deep underground, the earth parted beneath Hayri and he dropped into night. The jagged jaws of earth gyrated open for a moment, then slammed shut, overfolding one another like breaking waves.

The roaring ceased, and the bleating of the terrified goats receded into the distance. The bear continued to feed on the little dam, oblivious to the grinding of the earth.

I

T DID NOT grow warm the next day. The sun came and went, and the temperature steadily dropped. At ten thousand feet, it was nearly freezing.

But they could breathe freely again. Thank God, they could breathe!

The expedition members had donned their climbing parkas and snow pants. The crunch of snow beneath their boots had become a familiar sound. Crampons and ice axes reassured them, but many still had altitude sickness, despite bleeding and oxygenation.

Reg hated the bleeding, the oxygen tube in his nose, the interminable delay. But because Tony, Cevdet, and Hasan took it stoically, he gritted his teeth and said nothing. Dr. Norman Leagues was gentle, and Reg did feel stronger after each ordeal.

Water, salt, and sugar loss from exertion were among their greatest enemies. Antacid tablets helped mitigate the increased indigestion and vomiting. Trail mix, high in chocolate and honey, kept sugar levels up, and such "nibble rations" were distributed liberally. Kidney function was enhanced by chopping "ice cubes" and sucking them in addition to limited bottled water, which they alternated with the trail mix. The security forces and carriers, who had not undergone the oxygenation procedure, remained at Base Camp B with some supplies. The relief in the faces of these men at being spared what lay beyond, was difficult to conceal.

The climbers numbered thirty now, with Demirkol, Cayan, and Danson in the lead, Tony and Kassem at the rear. Hasan, the old priest, fancied himself a roving encourager and was allowed to roam ahead or behind at will. He carried no pack, and his surprisingly nimble antics and well-timed verbal prods seemed to keep the party's mind off the growing darkness and cold.

IBRAHIM Hasan watched the climbers ahead diminish in size, the farther they pulled away. He had allowed the expedition to move far ahead of him. It would be safe now.

Hasan sat down on a stone and removed the miniature radio from inside his rough gown. For two days the Pieps 2 transceiver, elsewhere in his gown, had beamed their exact position to the military climbing party led by Lieutenant General Nikolai Shkidchenko. It was necessary now to speak directly with Shkidchenko, though he'd been told never to use the radio except in the most dire of circumstances.

Did what he have to say qualify?

Beyond doubt.

The Soviet Mafia had made him an offer the obsolete, broken holy man found difficult to refuse. Die destitute and shamed in that stinking hole at the back of Adnan's tea shop in Istanbul, or supply intelligence on the American's expedition in exchange for a nicely furnished little cell in a converted monastery fifty miles inside the Armenian republic—a safe, secluded haven where he could live out his days on bread and water in search of a return of Allah's favor.

He liked Reg Danson and his son, Tony, and truly had taken hope in the American's kindness. But what of the end of the Ark hunt? Find it or not, Danson would return to the United States with some measure of fame while Hasan remained behind unwanted, unneeded, and unable to make peace with Allah. It was a fate worse than death, or collusion with the Soviet infidels, to waste away in disgrace and uselessness.

Still . . .

"Massis One to Red Star One, Massis One to Red Star One, come in Red Star One. Over!" Hasan waited while the little handset crackled and snapped static.

His mind raced with a confusion of thoughts. Was this betrayal worse than the stillbirth of the coffee vendor's child in Istanbul? He still felt responsible for not being able to pray a live child into existence. Could he redeem the first transgression through the second sin of treachery? What did it take to escape the spittle of angry Allah?

"Massis One to Red Star One, are you receiving?

Over." The crackle and hiss answered, and Hasan moved closer to the edge of the mountain.

What would seeing the Ark of Noah with his own eyes mean exactly? Was Danson right that Jesus Christ was the Messiah foretold in the ancient writings, the holy One of God who spoke of the wicked days of Noah's age as paralleling the days of His own future return? Was he, Hasan, fleeing the heat of the torch, only to fall utterly into the fires of eternal hell?

The radio squawked feebly. "—One . . . Massis One . . . read you . . . say again. . . ." Hasan squeezed the radio tightly. The last climber ahead disappeared from sight.

He hesitated, riffling the thin pages of the old Bible he'd been given by the wild-eyed Lord Onouphirius in the catacombs at Cappadocia. "He reveals deep and secret things . . ." Daniel's words in exile rang in his mind. "He gives wisdom to the wise."

Hasan pressed the transmit switch. "Red Star One, Red Star One. Massis One receives you. Over!"

The immediate response was so clear and loud that Hasan jumped. "Red Star One reads you, Massis One. Repeat. Red Star One reads you. Go ahead."

Hasan sucked in the bracing air, bent over the radio, and began his message.

MIDAFTERNOON, death came on the wind.

Reg had kept a wary eye on the altimeter. As the party plodded its way ever closer to the ice cap, locked in the seething nest of black cloud, the altimeter recorded twice the normal drop in barometric pressure for the thousand feet in altitude they'd gained. Under normal climbing conditions, a plunge of that magnitude would have precipitated a swift retreat down the mountain from the impending storm.

Nothing was normal on Ararat. Although the temperature hovered at twenty degrees Fahrenheit and their faces felt the air's bite, their backs experienced a lingering warmth from the searing heat on the lower slopes.

A silent alarm buzzed in the recesses of Danson's mind, but he suppressed it. The party had settled into a steady, methodical gait that was stripping away the gulf between the twentieth century and eight thousand B.C. Had Noah passed this way on the descent? Had elephants and hummingbirds?

At the last rest break, Nilay had given him a smile that rivaled the rising of the sun. With her love, Bascomb's backing, and God's help, he would rock the world with electrifying news—by late tomorrow if their fortunes held. This was not cockiness; this was the invincibility of David, the shepherd boy, facing a nine-foot giant. Precedence? He'd show them precedence!

Tony tried not to notice the two of them—the looks, the way his father seemed to straighten under Nilay's gaze, to laugh louder and longer whatever she whispered to him as they rested together. He guessed he wanted his father to be happy, but not this way. He wanted his mother back; he wanted her to laugh once again at his "notions" of social order; he wanted to be a family. His parents hadn't been very tolerant when he'd tested the spiritual waters, but his mother, at least, hadn't taken personal offense at his questions.

With his father, everything was black and white and hallowed all over.

Then Dad had taken her to Loch Ness and she'd drowned. If Tony had been three, he would have searched the murky depths until he found his mother. He would have died there with her if all else failed. He would not have come back without her, as Dad had.

THE expedition, refreshed, had been under way for half an hour. The twenty-nine men and one woman formed a line three hundred feet long. Each carried a light food and clothing pack of thirty pounds, an ice axe in one hand, and an aluminum probe pole in the other. Several men and Lieutenant Cayan also carried lightweight dome tents. The only sounds in the high altitude stillness were the measured "huffs" of their breathing, the rustle of blue nylon pantlegs brushing together, and the crunch of boots on snow. The cowls of their yellow parkas emitted little white puffs of condensed breath. Slowly and methodically, so as not to gulp air and become quickly winded, they drew ever closer to the now invisible summit of Ararat.

They were passing beneath a fantastic cornice of ice, snow sculpted into a monstrous standing wave twenty feet tall by currents of air flowing across a sharp ridge above. Danson would have gone around the other side of the ridge rather than risk the collapse of the snow mass, but it would have meant another hour of meticulous backtracking to regain the trail, just a hundred yards beyond the cornice. Eons of time had hidden the Ark. God would not bury them now.

With a fiendish shriek, a cancerous black blizzard hurtled down from the ice cap and a howling wind roared through the cornice like a runaway train. The bulk of the party, picking its way gingerly along beneath the intimidating overhang, was slammed flat to the wall of ice. Stinging slivers of ice lashed them with a terrible ferocity.

Reg, Tony, and Lieutenant Cayan had stationed themselves equidistantly along the wall to make certain the others passed safely. Reg, closest to the end of the cornice, turned to shout a warning to the three soldiers who had passed beyond into the open. The words froze in his throat.

The three soldiers were lifted by the wind and flung off the edge of the mountain like dead flies flicked from a window sill. So swiftly did they vanish, it was as if they had not existed at all. Their cries were swallowed whole by the bestial wind.

Hail fell on the Ark expedition, pounding with icy fists the size of baseballs. Danson shouted at his team to kneel, facing the wall, and to double over, presenting as little body surface as possible to the relentless pounding. The ice balls landed with dull thuds on the backs of the twenty-seven who remained. If anyone cried out, no one heard in the shrieking of the wind. The space-age material of their mountaineer clothing kept them warm while allowing greater freedom of movement, but against the hail, it provided painfully little protection.

Danson prayed with a fierce intensity. "Lord

God, my strength, protect us from evil—" Yet he knew their misfortune was due to his own haste and poor judgment. Men's lives, he now realized—too late—were more important than hours or days saved. *Barbara, sweet Barbara, if only I'd insisted on life jackets. You trusted my judgment—and now you're gone!*

A pound of hail smashed into the base of his spine and for a moment the world faded from white to gray to black. He fought unconsciousness. His back went numb; then all feeling returned with a sickening intensity. *Is this what stoning feels like? This pulverizing of the flesh into mush? This slow sledging of the features into unrecognizable pulp? Stephen, Christian martyr, dear Stephen, what agony did you know before God let you sleep?*

What is Nilay experiencing? Can her tender body endure? What was it she said: "I do not bruise like a woman"? Tony is tough, isn't he?

"Am I alone, my Lord?" he gasped, nearly toppling over from the hail's force. "Are You no longer with me?" Tears and mucus flowed from his eyes and nose and froze in stringy tendrils before they could hit the ground.

Unconsciousness threatened again, but he fought, desperately combing his memory for Scripture, a promise to cling to, sanity.

A picture of Elijah on Horeb, the mountain of God, filled Reg's mind. Elijah, one of God's greats, told Jehovah how very faithful he'd been when everyone else had deserted or been killed, how, in fact, he was the only faithful warrior left and he was in imminent danger of dying by the enemy's sword . . .

God's answer was to command Elijah to stand out in the open, for the Lord Almighty Himself was about to pass by. . . .

Reg attempted to stand and looked to his right to see how the others were faring. A hailstone struck his temple a vicious, glancing blow. Quickly, burrowing his chin back into the neck of his parka and covering the back of his head with his gloved hands, he gasped for air. It was suddenly hard to come by oxygen, as if the demon wind was sucking it away.

"*. . . a great and powerful wind tore the mountains apart and shattered the rocks before the Lord, but the Lord was not in the wind."* Elijah, how did you handle that? Did you bury your face in the dirt? Did you nearly lose consciousness?*

Despite the maelstrom, Reg raged against his own cowardice. He could almost hear the sniveling skid row wino promising God never to touch another drop as long as he lived if only the Lord would be so kind as to keep those hoodlums from sticking a shiv between his ribs and rolling him for his welfare check. Perhaps he could write a book one day. He'd call it *Dickering with Deity.*

"After the earthquake came a fire, but the Lord was not in the fire." So where are You, Lord? The icy assault was beginning to penetrate Danson's core. He was going cold inside. He had to find God or die.

"And after the fire came a gentle whisper." The Lord was in the whisper.

Danson sobbed softly and asked the Lord to forgive his unbelief. It was several minutes before he realized the hail had stopped and the wind died out.

CHAPTER
23

THOSE WHO could stand were huddled about the propane stoves; those who could not were placed in sleeping bags, a generous amount of muscle-heating ointment slathered on their battered flesh. Nilay coolly refused Reg's ministrations, but accepted treatment from Dr. Leagues, the camp doctor. Reg felt slighted but appreciated her modesty. He stole a glance at the ugly purpling mass beneath the smooth olive skin when her back was laid bare and wondered at her uncomplaining silence.

Three had died—twenty-seven remained. One was critical.

The old priest, despite his recent nimbleness, had suffered most among the survivors. Worse than the bruising, which seemed less on his aged body, perhaps because of the quantity of coarse material in his worn robes, was the onset of hypothermia. A tremendous loss of body heat was a silent killer. Hasan was comatose, his breathing shallow, almost nonexistent.

Lieutenant Cayan gave Danson a look that said, "I told you he would prove a burden."

Dr. Leagues immediately ordered a small amount of honey to be placed under the priest's lower lip to furnish energy as it was absorbed. He called for a volunteer to strip naked and snuggle against Hasan's nude body inside the sleeping bag where he was encased. The transfer of body heat between humans was the swiftest hope for recovery.

Tony did not hesitate. He undressed quickly and slid down behind the priest, pressing against the cold, pitiful thinness. He wrapped his arms tenderly around Hasan and hugged him tightly.

Within minutes the color began to return to the holy man. The lips, thin lines of blue rimmed with deathly white, pinkened; the scrawny chest visibly rose and fell so that Tony had to loosen his grip. He could feel heat, feeble at first, then definite, returning to the old man's skin. In half an hour, Hasan's eyelids fluttered open and shut, his vision cleared, and he looked into the relieved eyes of Reg Danson.

"Just—thought I would—inspect the hinges . . . on the gates of heaven," he said softly, smiling a little. Reg smoothed some melted snow on Hasan's cracked lips. The priest raised his head and hungrily licked the moistened fingers. His head fell back with a contented smile. "I must report that they are well oiled and all is in readiness!"

Reg smiled at Tony and squeezed his arm. His son had climbed into that sleeping bag and embraced this priest back from another world without a moment's thought. Tony returned his father's smile with an odd look of irritation as if saving another's life was a simple matter, requiring little time—or courage.

"You blame me for the deaths of those men, don't you?" Reg asked his son, fearing the answer.

"Shouldn't I?" Tony responded testily.

"No. I consulted with the men beforehand, gave them the choice to go around or take the shorter route. They opted for the cornice."

Tony studied him curiously. "This is no Boy Scout outing where you vote to ford the stream or use the bridge. This is one of the deadliest mountains on earth. You err on the side of caution."

Reg snorted derisively. "That's rich coming from a guy who loves to dive off cliffs and not pull the cord until he can smell the daisies under him!"

"At least it's just me risking me," Tony shot back. "I don't grab somebody at the last minute and take them down with me."

They were interrupted by a shout from the trailhead announcing the return of Cevdet Demirkol. Twelve hours before he had gone ahead to determine the Ark's accessibility. One disturbing common factor in all previous expeditions was the unsettling notion that the Ark never showed up in the same place twice. Lost maps, failed memories, shifting landscape, giant storms, and avalanches—a conspiracy of nature and human folly lent impressive variety to the accounts of the ship's exact locale.

Understandably, Demirkol had been anxious to confirm the validity of his own intelligence since they'd first set foot on the mountain.

Now he came down the slope towards Danson with determined strides. Everyone gathered about

Tony and Ibrahim Hasan and looked towards the handsome Janissary for a sign. Maddeningly, he stopped a dozen yards away, arms folded, staring dispassionately out to the far boundaries of the Anatolian plateau.

Danson joined him, fighting the desire to grab the man and wring the news from him. Found or lost still? Amazing grace or empty lava? But he did not push. He waited silently, staring too at the Anatolian plateau above which the Ark had once floated.

Cevdet's head slowly turned until his eyes met Danson's. The eyes of deepest ocher had seen the Holy of Holies. There was an unmistakable light there that spanned centuries of time and timelessness. God was in the whisper of Elijah. He was in the silence of Cevdet.

A single teardrop slid down the tanned cheek of God's warrior. He turned and placed his hands on Danson's shoulders. A tremor passed between them.

"Yes!" was all he said.

The news raced among them. They were less than a kilometer away from Ahora Gorge, the awesome scar on the face of Ararat created by the earthquake of 1840. Black Glacier, named after the pulverized lava dust that coated its face, hung six hundred feet thick over the gorge like the dreadful hood of an executioner. Immense beds of boulders and ice and other avalanche debris rendered the bottom of the chasm impenetrable to living things. It was like a wrecking yard of contorted metal remains, sharp and sinister and not a healthy place to play.

The glacial ice cap ringing the gorge advanced to the edge of the precipice and sheered off in great chunks that fell with a deafening roar into the wrecking yard. The one antidote to the horror of the gorge was a 450-foot waterfall that dropped majestically onto the head of the blackened glacier from the melting snow fields above.

High up on the side of the gorge in a crotch of rock and protruding from a small glacial finger of ice was the Landing Place of Noah's Ark.

Cevdet walked up to it, the hulk looming four and a half stories above his head. Almost all the ice was gone from around it, and so dark was the wood that it almost appeared burned. Many small and large pieces were missing from the hull, including a tremendous gaping hole on the port side near the protruding end. Cevdet had hurled a stone into the interior and heard movement. Alone, armed only with a rifle, he had not wanted to confront any wild beasts. He knelt, prayed swiftly, and returned.

The mood was one of stunned anticipation. Not many had dared believe in the existence of the Ark, and now that it had been confirmed to be less than a day's march from them, they searched their own thoughts for what it meant, less to the world than to themselves.

Danson felt a fresh surge of adrenalin. When Lieutenant Cayan had ordered two men to make arrangements to transport Ibrahim Hasan back to Base Camp B, he had intervened and said the choice whether to continue on or to return was the priest's to make. Hasan said that he had been spared for a purpose and that no one had to bow toward Mecca to know what that purpose was. The lieutenant had turned on her heel and ordered the others to eat a double dose of rations; they would break camp within the hour.

No one saw the dog at first. It trotted timidly up the trail the way they'd come and slowly approached two men packing their stove and other supplies for the last leg of what all now felt was the archaeological coup of the age.

It was a female. Ears flat against its skull, it simpered and sidled submissively toward the men. Gray and black, chunky and thick-limbed, ugly, it was a survivor of unforgiving Ararat.

One of the men pointed at the dog and laughed and continued on his way to the far side of camp to relieve himself. His partner knelt, held out a small piece of jerky, and called to the dog with kissing sounds.

It was Danson, a hundred feet further up the slope, who noticed the saddle of cloth encircling the dog's chest and belly. It appeared lumpy on top. The dog whined and licked the jerky.

"*Merhaba!* Hello!" said the man, gently scratching the dog's ears. When the dog snatched the dried meat and wolfed it down, the man laughed. "*Guzel, guzel!* Good, beautiful!"

Danson shaded his eyes from the snow's glare to see two little spots of red protruding from the middle of the cloth saddle. He started forward; then something deep in his brain ordered him to freeze.

"Don't touch that dog!" Reg screamed. "*Dikkat! Dikkat!* Danger! Danger! Everyone get down, *Get down!*"

The explosion sent two orange fireballs rocketing across the clearing. Danson felt the heat of the blast, and bits of debris pelted his climbing jacket. He looked up but saw no man or dog, only a blackened crater where they had been.

A frightful roar filled the clearing, the deranged bellow of a thousand cornered lions. The concussion ripped through his body and soul and ricocheted off the mountain above like the boom of an elephant gun. Ancient boulders, wrenched from sockets of volcanic rock, began a downward slide undermining untold years of delicately balanced winter accumulations.

A massive rumble forced him to jerk his body around. It seemed as if half the mountain high above and to their right was collapsing, great slabs of sun-weakened snow and ice sheering off Ararat's craggy face. Mesmerized, Reg could only watch as incredible tons of Ararat's mantle rushed to the brink, then exploded into the air and dropped into nothingness, detonated from centuries of sleep.

As the reverberations gradually subsided, other avalanches unseen could be heard in the distance, many probably filling Ahora Gorge with their snowy discharge. What of the Ark?

After a quarter of an hour of lying flat and praying more "Elijah" prayers, the loudest sound Danson could hear was the thudding of his own heart against the snow. He leapt to his feet and found Tony and Cevdet a short distance away. Together, they ran throughout the camp counting heads. All, save the unfortunate one who had offered a bit of food to a wayward dog, were accounted for.

Now they numbered twenty-six.

Lieutenant Cayan ordered six of her remaining

ten troops to fan out and explore the surrounding terrain and shoot on sight anyone not of the Ark expedition. With special silencers, manufactured for
avalanche country, affixed to their weapons, they
moved off.

Eyes blazing, Cayan planted herself squarely in
front of Reg Danson. She was tough; she was beautiful; she was furious.

She waved a two-way radio and a Pieps 2 transceiver under his nose. "Your priest is a traitor! These
were found in his gown while you and your son were
so busily bringing the rancid vulture to life! We don't
have a chance, Mr. Danson, not when those you
seem to have the fondest affection for are spies and
cutthroats."

Present company excluded, he wanted to say,
but didn't dare.

Cayan's four other soldiers had their rifles leveled at Hasan's forehead. The murderous look in
their eyes said that little more than a sneeze on the
priest's part would place him back at heaven's gate—
for real.

"Put up your rifles!" Reg ordered. The soldiers
looked to Cayan, who took her time but finally gave
a curt nod for them to comply.

Danson knelt and helped the priest to sit up.
"You are my friend, Ibrahim," he whispered fiercely
into the *hoca's* ear. "What is the meaning of this?"

Tony, putting on his clothes after restoring Hasan's normal body temperature, had accidentally discovered the radio equipment in the priest's gown.
Had he brought warmth and life to an assassin?

There was both terror and hope in the old man's

eyes. He kept looking at the charred spot where a living human being had stood, minutes before laughing and petting a dog.

Hasan began to weep. "I told them just this morning that I could not continue to be their agent any longer, that betrayal in the face of such kindness and regard from the American was unthinkable. I would no longer be party to it. I am a stupid man, Mr. Danson, and I beg your forgiveness."

Cayan snorted in disgust. Reg looked questioningly at his son.

Tony nodded. "The transceiver was off when I found it."

"Start at the beginning, my friend," Reg said, "and leave nothing out."

When Ibrahim Hasan finished, Danson looked down over the snow and ice over which they'd come. The path had been scoured clean by the avalanche; the cornice where they'd clung for their lives was gone. It would take some careful picking of their path to return after they'd found the Ark and had it transported to safety. Perhaps it was futile. "One thing's certain," Danson said firmly. "They had contact with the transceiver long enough to get a rather accurate fix on our location. The dog was a calling card meant to kill many more than it did.

"The odds now, according to Hasan, are 101 fully armed men to twenty-six of us—assorted geologists, archaeologists, university students, and adventurers, and a handful of armed soldiers."

Hasan moaned miserably at the accounting.

"So we take this as a sign from God that we are not to meddle with sacred things!" Ahmed Kassem, the Iraqi munitions expert, shook as he spoke. "We must return down this mountain without delay." He picked up his backpack and walked off.

A bullet snapped into the rifle chamber. Ahmed did not stop. Reg Danson, who had never aimed a rifle at anyone in his life, took careful aim and squeezed the trigger.

The silencer did its job and the bullet kicked up a plume of snow three feet in front of Ahmed. He stopped, turned, and looked at Danson with hatred. "An army marching at gunpoint is worse than useless," he spat out. "Better you should attempt to reach the Ark alone!"

And though we all bleed, you and Cayan do not. Ahmed's words echoed accusingly in Danson's mind.

Reg held the rifle steady until Ahmed resignedly moved up the trail. *Dear God, what do You require of me to get this job done?* Before anyone could see the barrel shake, he quickly lowered it. *Once they've seen the Ark for themselves, the victory is won! Just a few more hours, Lord, just a few more hours . . .*

Ibrahim Hasan wobbled to his feet and brushed the snow from his gown. He reached out and grabbed Danson's hand as he passed by. Reg stopped, handed the rifle to Tony, and gripped the knotted old hand in both of his. "Shh, don't speak, my friend," he said. Tears spilled from the priest's eyes. "Christ is waiting for you at the Ark. Believe it!"

Danson left the old man, whose hands were clasped in prayer, and went to the edge of the world and looked down. Clouds obscured his view, and he wondered how many enemy had died in the avalanche. At least some had surely sealed their own fates with the wired dog.

Reg Danson lifted the radio handset to his lips. *The bath house thief has struck again.* He felt his neck and spoke. "Massis One to Red Star One, come in Red Star One. Over!"

He waited. Nothing. "Massis One to Red Star One, do you read me? Over."

"Red Star One reads you, Massis One. Come in. Over!"

It was a moment before Reg could summon the words. When they came, they were just four: "In the beginning, God."

He switched off the radio. The clouds were boiling again, coming up from below, white and pillowy, to join the tempestuous black of the storm mass above. The black consumed the white, changing its victims to black without resistance. It reminded him of something silly Barbara would say when predicting an argument: "Uh oh! Looks like rain!"

If she were here right now, she could take the lead, and I would follow.

Something else was wrong. Though the avalanche and its reverberations had subsided, the mountain continued to rumble beneath their feet. The sound was coming from deep inside and could be felt up the backs of the legs. The vibrations left goose bumps on Danson's arms. Dr. Leagues was making tea on his portable stove to calm jittery nerves, and the thin metal water pot rattled rapidly as if about to take flight.

Cevdet Demirkol cleared his throat and came alongside Danson on the ledge. "What vibrations?" he said with forced cheerfulness. Then he saw Danson's sober expression. "How does it look, captain?" A melancholy smile, but no hint of retreat.

Danson relaxed a little. "My wife had a saying that covers it, I think. 'If you have to eat a frog, don't look at it too long!'"

Cevdet nodded solemnly. "My people have a similar saying. 'If maggots are all you have to eat, eat them all at once and get it over with.'"

The two men looked at one another. The excitement at what the one had seen that day in the gorge beyond and the other had conceived a thousand times over in his heart was their bond. The loss of four men was a terrible blow, the warning tremors were frightening, but to dwell on their fears would be to cripple the mission, exactly what the enemy wanted. They were committed to the end. Each knew the danger, the legends, before starting out. Each had signed a death waiver.

Cevdet and Reg made their way back to the head of the expedition. A thick, globular mass of doubt and exhilaration coated Reg's emotions. Turning back from this quest was not as simple as canceling a fishing trip due to inclement weather. The stakes here were much higher than a mess of trout.

Had he taken unnecessary risks? Was he developing a callous disregard for human life? He did not know; he knew only that there had to be some causes worth the cost.

Four men had died, true, and he prayed God

might show favor upon them for dying in this cause. But how many more would live for eternity because of the sign of the Ark?

Probably the whole state of Missouri, for starters.

24

THE OVAL OFFICE *has to be one of the most desolate rooms on the face of the earth* decided President Thurston Pierce. He hated to come to this room alone. He acutely felt the accusing presence of his dead predecessors. When he'd entered alone this time, it was like walking into a thick spider's web. The more he fought it, the tighter and stickier it clung to his face.

He did not measure up in this room. Anywhere else he could fake it, but not here. Unimaginably difficult decisions had been made here. Untold millions of trusting ears and eyes had tuned into this room via radio and television. Fortunes and futures turned on every word and every nuance of body language that issued from this chamber.

Thank God the media were not present when he decided to keep Reg Danson and the Noah's Ark expedition in the dark. The chances of Mount Ararat blowing were better than fifteen to one. The shocks were no longer of the "swarm" variety—hundreds of

buzzing individuals posing little danger. The quakes
coming now were singular and sharply defined. The
last had gone 3.9 on the Richter. Deep muffled explosions like underground artillery fire were reported
throughout eastern Turkey and northwestern Iran.

At least he'd evacuated the civilian population.
As long as radio contact with Massis One remained
atmospherically "impossible," he could not be
blamed for what happened to them. It was simply too
dangerous to send a rescue team in there now even if
he wanted to. Things were well beyond that point.
Quite frankly, Danson and his team were in the
hands of God.

Bascomb had been a bear to deal with. He'd
wanted to stop short of nothing to go after the expedition. Just like him to want to bulldoze the mountain
flat if necessary. He told the president in no uncertain terms that Mount St. Helens had blasted open a
valley one-fortieth the size of the Grand Canyon, and
St. Helens was a hill compared to Ararat. So what
was Thurston Pierce going to do about it?

At least Freddy Delaney, the ex-secretary of
state, was no longer moping about, his every look
dripping with pathos. Sad how the secretary's plane
went down over the Bermuda Triangle without a
trace. Strange. But give it a couple of years, and the
tabloids will have him on that island where Elvis and
JFK are spotted from time to time. Freddy'd been a
likable enough guy when he wasn't out saving the
world.

Delaney's survivors would be well cared for.
Thirsty Pierce owed him that.

Pierce nibbled at a hangnail on his left thumb,

then turned to a stack of legislative research his aides had been nagging him for weeks to read. *They say there's a million earthquakes a year on Mother Earth* he mused. Most went unnoticed. Ararat would settle down tomorrow.

He'd play the odds.

CHAPTER
25

LIEUTENANT GENERAL NIKOLAI SHKIDCHENKO lowered the binoculars and spat into the snow. *Massis, Mother of the World, you have swallowed forty of my men whole . . .*

He spat again. The taste of hell was upon his tongue so strong not even vodka could erase it. That scurvy old priest had been a stupid gamble.

"In the beginning, God" might make a fitting epitaph on the American's tomb. He would share the golden chalice of death, that was certain, just as instant death awaited those who drank from the golden chalice of exquisite craftsmanship in Tokapi Palace in Istanbul. When full of the fairest of wines, it was exceedingly beautiful to behold, a vessel fit for royalty, a burnished symbol of political mastery.

But as the cup is tipped and the ambrosia within consumed, an evil quite unexpected lies revealed: a golden serpent with cold ruby eyes coiled in the bottom of the cup, its open maw and glittering fangs poised to deal a death blow.

So it is with sin, thought Shkidchenko sorrowfully. Not a popular topic back home, rarely acknowledged, certainly not publicly. But how many of the party faithful had ever witnessed two score of the cream of Russian youth plowed under tons of ice and snow?

The hidden serpent had struck a vicious blow and would strike again. *Two will drink from this cup!*

And better his men should die here and perhaps make believers of those who survived than for them to return to the living death of an unemployed, "liberated" atheist in Moscow or Kiev.

Shkidchenko watched the last of the Ark expedition disappear behind a lava outcropping on its way to Ahora Gorge. He stood in a huge cave that had provided life for the men able to scramble into it before the frozen wall had thundered past. The monstrous sound of it had sent shock waves pulsating into the cave for what seemed like half an hour, and the men who huddled there had waited for the ceiling to collapse.

It held, but the horrifying image of bodies hurtling past the cave mouth left them all numb.

But Shkidchenko had seen something else. At the far back of the cave in a thick, diagonal vein running right to left, floor to ceiling, were the countless splintered bones of animals entombed in stone. The incredible jumble included one fantastic bone running the width of the cave and continuing on into the stony depths of the mountain.

The famed mammoths of the Lyakoff Islands of

Northern Siberia had received widespread notoriety in the newspapers and scientific journals of the world. So incredibly well preserved were they that for thousands of years the inhabitants of Siberia had made carvings from their ivory tusks and dined on mammoth steaks.

What was less publicized he knew was that the Lyakoff Islands were first known as the Bone Islands. The sheer mass of bones found there indicated that the mammoths had crowded onto the islands in a frantic last effort to escape the Flood.

Shkidchenko had studied the writings of Dr. Immanuel Velikovsky, a foremost Russian scientist. It was he who had made the startling statement on the suddenness of catastrophic animal deaths several thousand years ago:

> In many places on earth—on all continents—bones of sea animals and polar land animals and tropical animals have been found in great melees; so also in the Cumberland Cave in Maryland, in the Chou Kou Tien fissure in China, and also in Germany and Denmark. Hippopotami and ostriches were found together with seals and reindeer. . . . from the Arctic to the Antarctic . . . in the high mountains and in the deep seas—we find innumerable signs of great upheavals.

Ah, but to *touch* them!

The lieutenant general caressed the bones at the back of the cave and ordered others to stay away. This was his private moment, he alone with the bones of animals too fantastic to imagine, hurled together in a timeless zoological stew.

In the ravine below, the bones of his men mingled with them. There was no need to search for survivors.

NIGHT was a long time in coming at the top of the world. The Ark expedition crested the lip of Ahora Gorge just as the sun sent its last wave of gold washing over them.

To peer into a grand canyon contained within a single mountain forced them all to silence. The glaciers, the vertical rock wall, the snarl of avalanche debris deep within its throat gave the appearance of another planet. The titanic forces that tore this gash in mighty Ararat were too fearsome to contemplate.

This was earthquake country. No one had to announce that it could happen again. It had in 1883, burying numerous villages. Mosul, Ahak, and Bayazid destroyed. Countless others lesser known buried for eternity. As late as the 1970s, an earthquake had taken two thousand lives in the immediate region.

But a Turkish government relief team sent to investigate the magnitude of the nineteenth-century disaster encountered more than death and destruction. They found the Ark. Because of the humanist skepticism of the day, most newspapers in the U.S. reported the incident with ridicule. But the original news release from Constantinople reported a gigantic dark wooden structure protruding from the ice at the foot of the glacier, strongly constructed, painted over with a deep brown pigment, the interior partitioned into stalls.

That was the end of it as the cynical world moved on and winter's grip reclaimed the Ark.

Now twenty-six people strained to see what for so long had eluded conclusive verification. Cevdet pointed to a shadowy cleft, carving a fan-shaped ditch in the northeast portion of the gorge, but last light was winking out, and nothing could be singled out in dusk's gloom. In its final hurrah, light illuminated the wispy translucence of the waterfall so that it sparkled and shimmered and called to them to join in its fairy dance.

Shadows claimed the depths of Ahora, but the expedition's position high above remained bathed in light for another forty-five minutes. Camp was established, each tent erected as much as possible in the lee of stone outcroppings and lava walls. The weather generated by Ararat had seethed above them since the hailstorm earlier in the day, the temperature hovering just below freezing. With nightfall, the black lid above began to descend and, when the lamps came on at last, was tight upon them.

Danson took one last look at the world they were leaving, for it did seem as if they had reached a significant border crossing. Two thousand feet below, the peak of Lesser Ararat faded into the primordial swirl of cloud. The Anatolian plateau had long since disappeared in the first dark of the flatlands.

August 13, eight o'clock. It seemed ludicrous to mark time in this eternal place. Marco Polo had passed by Ararat in the fifteenth century, commenting incorrectly in his journal, but in keeping with

popular opinion, that the "snow [on Ararat] is so constant that no one can ascend; for the snow never melts and it is constantly added to by new falls . . ."
Oh, Marco, if only you could see me now!

The snow *had* melted. Evidence of the melt was everywhere. Massive patches of exposed stone and rock declensions turned the landscape into a giant black and white checkerboard. Though the temperature was falling, it was still shirt-sleeve weather for Montreal, Helsinki, and Nome.

Even breathing seemed less strenuous on the lip of Ahora. Tea glasses brimming with hot cinnamon and apple cider from Seattle clinked in celebration. A bottle of fermented raisin juice made the rounds, just a sip each to dream warmly of tomorrow's great deeds.

It was a pleasant enough camp except that Tony had retreated into a depressed silence. He refused to speak more than a cursory yes or no to his father. What little ground they'd gained in their relationship seemed all but lost again.

The time had come for Reg to radio their position to Karaköse where four huge S-64 Sky Crane helicopters waited. Lieutenant Nilay Cayan posted all ten of her troops around the camp and then entered the command tent to lead the planning session of the actual removal of the Ark.

"Massis One to Dragonfly One. Come in, Dragonfly. Over."

The radio crackled and whined. The signal was being relayed by Magnum Star, a top-secret communications spy satellite reputed to make short work of the distance between mountaintop and plain.

"Massis One to Dragonfly One, how do you read? Over."

The static popped for a few seconds more. "—Fine . . . Clear, Massis One. Your order, please? Over."

Danson smiled and winked at Nilay who could not resist a smile in return. "Dragonfly One, this is Massis One. The order is to go, order to go. Meet me in St. Louie, Louie. Will have red carpet out for all. Bring candy, cookies, punch, and streamers. 814, maybe. Hold the catsup. Over."

In code, St. Louie was Ahora Gorge, red carpet was red plastic ribbon marked on the ground. Candy, cookies, punch, and streamers referred to the expedition's geographic reference point on the U.S. Defense Mapping Agency's Aviation Navigation Chart: two intersecting quadrants, one minute left of their location longitude, one minute below their location latitude, or QJQK1843. That would guide the air team to the 175-foot in diameter helipad near the present campsite. The next day's date was "814," and "hold the catsup" meant wait for exact roll-out time.

When the Sky Cranes arrived, one of the trickiest balancing acts ever attempted would begin. The crack Israeli flyboys had practiced the carefully orchestrated lift procedure with a specially constructed cargo container. It was actually several reinforced standard cargo containers welded together into a colossal rectangular box the dimensions of the Ark and approximating its weight. Structural engineers derived the dead-weight tonnage by feeding a computer the facts: according to the Bible: the volume of the Ark was approximately 450 feet long by 75 feet wide by 45 feet high or 1.52 by ten to the sixth power cubic feet. Using the weight and dimensions of wooden beams found on Ararat by French explorer Fernand Navarra, allowing for three levels of decking, it was calculated that 22.5 percent of the total volume of the Ark was actually the wooden structure itself. That translated to a total weight of just over 800 thousand pounds or 400 tons.

Among them, the immense Sky Cranes had a maximum payload lift capacity of a million pounds. Maximum cruising speed in formation would be 125 mph, for a maximum distance of six hundred miles before refueling.

The Ark's two ends rested on alluvial deposits of glacial silt, as if it were a riverboat stuck fast on two sandbars. The extremely warm Omega Blockbuster had melted most of the ice from the hull, and it was now possible with low-charge explosives to loosen and remove the remainder from beneath the hull and the two ends. A harness, ten-foot-wide tungsten steel straps hardened by a special alloy created by Bascomb's research team, would form an aerial hammock to protect the Ark in flight. Thick leather pads lined the straps to protect the wood itself. The ends of these straps would be passed beneath the Ark and connected to six-inch-thick double steel cables of the same metal alloys and threaded through the floors of the helicopters to hydraulic winches inside. Each chopper would be attached in turn to one of the side, stern, or bow cables of the Ark. Each would fly clear of the launch area once connected, playing out the cable to its maximum length. Once all four Sky Cranes were so connected, they would winch up the four corners of the cradle straps like a giant diaper and, in radio-guided unison, lift their "baby" clear of the peak.

The pilots, all veterans of precision aerial acrobatic teams, had flown houses, oil derricks, and train locomotives to their destinations in the past. All had responded to the collision of two huge vehicle ferries in the English Channel. In raging storm conditions they had righted the capsized vessels and received medallions of honor for their bravery.

In formation, the Sky Crane quartet would transport the Ark to the Black Sea port of Samsun and lower it gently into the hold of a special container ship operated by the Turkish Maritime Lines and taken to New York under the protection of U.S. Naval destroyer escorts. From there it would be transported by Sky Crane again to Washington, D.C., for permanent display at the Smithsonian.

The scientists with the expedition had been collecting small samples and conducting various experiments all along the way and would be able to give a more complete geologic dossier on Mother Ararat than ever before gathered on the mystery mountain. The photogrammetrist and archaeologists were poring over rough sketches with Ahmed Kassem, discussing the placement and force of the several explosives necessary to rapidly melt and dislodge any ice and rocks refusing to relinquish their hold on the Ark.

Reg shook his head and marveled at the ways of God. In the morning they would look upon the Ark of Noah, an imposing vessel. A ship longer than the Ark was not constructed until the 1880s. And the Ark was fourteen thousand feet above sea level!

They would fly it out in the afternoon.

"Roger, Massis One. Looking forward to party. Dragonfly One over and out."

Reg should have asked for an update on the volcanic disturbances that were now constant companions of the expedition. But somehow he could not bring himself to spoil the moment.

THE bloated carcasses of people and animals banged incessantly against the side of the ship. The reek of death made breathing difficult. A great mastodon, its fur matted and soaked, floated past with what had once been a man impaled on its great curved tusk. He must have been a powerful man, for the muscles glistened and bulged, but they were a grayish-green from putrefaction. When the body banged against the hull, hunks of flesh broke off and drifted away trailing oil.

Thud, thud, thud—the bodies banged and slapped and crowded against the hull, louder and louder, more and more until the ship could no longer make headway. The bodies began to cry and wail so that soon it was impossible to hear or breathe or go forward or back. *Got to get low . . . to the ground . . . or die . . . more air down low . . .*

Reg awoke on the ground, sucking hungrily at the air at the tent flap. His head felt like a lead weight, a sledgehammer of pain attempting to smash a hole through the top of his skull.

He struggled to sit upright, but a crushing doubt engulfed him as if pinning him to the spot.

Demons of doubt . . . demons of doubt . . . He'd

heard that somewhere. But hadn't the expedition toasted success just an hour before, the grandest archaeological rescue in human history?

Not everyone was thrilled, to be sure. Several kept nervous watch for snipers and falling ice. Ahmed stole a furtive snatch of conversation now and then but seemed at last resigned to completing what he'd started.

Snow was falling along with the temperature. The wind swirled little clouds of it into Reg's face. He felt so alone, so devoid of companionship. When Barbara died, he had felt terribly lonely but not this abandoned orphan feeling. Always before, God, his deliverer, Christ, his burden bearer, had intervened.

Look what they'd come through to get here. God had to be with them. They'd escaped death itself to reach the rim of Ahora Gorge.

Some had not escaped. Some had died. He tried to think of their names. Halka Iliskiler had shown kindness to the dog. Turgut Suley . . . something had been one of those blown off the mountain. The others?

Dear God, I can't remember all their names. Did I ever know them?

He stood to his feet and felt a peculiar charge in the air. His whiskers and the hair on his arms prickled. The hair on his head stood on end. The tent poles hummed, and the air smelled of burnt insulation.

He had to get away. To pray, to find God. Turning back now was unthinkable, but could it be that the Lord no longer wanted the Ark found?

Preposterous. He'd seen them through fire and flood, melted the unmeltable and peeled back the layers of time—for what? To have them turn tail and run when with light and a telephoto they could take the Ark's picture from here?

"No-o!" he cried into the night. Cinching the bindings on his parka, Danson made for the helicopter clearing.

He passed the orange dome tents with their three or four occupants each, fluorescent toadstools sprinkled with powdered sugar. . . . *orange is the color of my true love's . . . life jacket . . . there safe on the shore safe from all sea serpents . . . and it's all my fault, Barbara . . . hey, won't you play another somebody done somebody wrong song . . . please, honey, don't go. . . .*

There were rustlings and angry, distressed snatches of conversation coming from the tents as others struggled with the pain and the weird, crackling air. Reg hurried past, not wanting to be spotted and stopped.

He rounded a ten-foot wall of basalt bordering the clearing. Snow fell heavily here and long stalactites of ice hung eerily from the stone outcroppings like the teeth of prehistoric tigers. A little alcove of rock beneath afforded some protection from the wind, and Danson knelt at a step of stone beneath the frozen fangs of ice.

"Oh Lord, my Lord, how majestic is Your name in all the earth. You, and You alone, are Creator of all I survey. As securely as You redeemed me from sin, attend me now. Let me depart in peace and conclude this task that You—"

A clap of thunder whacked the shoulder of

Ararat with a reverberation that knocked Danson sprawling into the clearing. He stood for a moment, disoriented, until two cymbals of thunder crashed together overhead. It was as if Danson was caught in the middle, then released and hurled flat, ears ringing with the resounding concussion.

Electricity crackled and snapped the air, and hideous, searing bolts of it struck the basalt wall, then formed a jolting ring of electrical fire around the jutting stone perimeter.

Danson crawled and stumbled for the center of the clearing, scrambling as far from the big rocks as possible to avoid being struck by lightning. The blinding snow and fury of sound were disorienting. The next lightning bolt showed he had crawled too near the basalt wall.

Before he could fully rise to his feet, a weight fell on his shoulders and drove him face-first into the snow. He felt the skin rip away from his nose as he skidded in the ice. Knees on his back ground into his spine. Hands tore at his hood, then gripped his hair, and repeatedly pulled back his head and pounded it into the ground.

My Lord, do not forsake me now!

A deafening clap of thunder sounded just as Danson reared up on his knees and flung his assailant to one side. He strained to see in the inky blackness. The attacker came hurtling back, knife blade glinting in a flash of lightning.

Barzani? No, too light.

Reg kicked the legs out from under his adversary. He snapped off a sharp stalactite and lunged after the dark figure. They circled warily in the clearing's center, the staccato lightning flashes illuminating them in a jerking black-light marionette show.

His attacker wore a black ski mask and dark sweater, but Reg was convinced it had to be a commando sent by the Soviets. If Reg could be dispatched by night at the hands of a secret raider, the Kurds were as likely suspects as their Moscow benefactors should his death become international news.

A brilliant streak of lightning smashed the rocks behind the attacker, and Reg was momentarily blinded. His assailant hit him with a flying tackle, and they landed with a shattering crash against a column of crystal stalactites. Ice flew every direction in a thousand tinkling fragments. Before the enemy could slash with his knife, Danson swung the stalactite in his hand with a roundhouse arc that ended in a shattering of ice against the side of the masked one's head.

The attacker fell back stunned, his feet flailing the air. The boots! They were not Russian military issue. They were the climbing boots required for every member of the Ark expedition.

Ahmed Kassem! Reg Danson would have bet the farm that's who he would find beneath the ski mask.

Reg snapped off another stalactite and came roaring after his opponent with great swinging slices of icy dagger. The masked one neatly danced away from each swipe until his back was against a large rock that had already been struck by lightning several times.

"I'd get away from that rock if I were you, my

friend!" Reg shouted, the wind a bedlam of cross-currents.

The assailant pushed his foot against the base of the rock to launch himself at Danson. At that instant a searing white bolt of lightning struck the rock with such force that incredible jolts of electricity pulsed through Reg's body ten feet away.

Nailed to the rock as if sculpted from it, the attacker was helpless as a newborn. His arms and legs were flung out straight in midair as if he were a recharged Frankenstein monster; he quivered and bucked as if skewered alive.

Reg begged God to turn the man loose so that he might be helped, kept from dying so gruesomely. *I didn't want this—I didn't want anyone to die!*

The masked one forced a leg to the ground. The electrical circuit completed, he was catapulted off the rock by the surging force. He lay hunched and quivering, whimpering unintelligibly.

He recognized that voice. Danson crumpled to the ground, legs numb with paralysis. *It can't be. Dear Son of God, don't let it be.* He used the thick end of the stalactite as a pick to pull himself along the ground.

The storm quieted and moved on, the wind dying as suddenly as it had struck. Sheets of bone-chilling rain began to fall. Reg reached the man and pried the knife from his gloved hand before rolling him onto his back. He ripped the mask away and groaned.

Tony's face was scorched and blistered. At first, he looked at his father as if he had never seen him before. When the confusion cleared, he began to sob.

"You were jeopardizing everyone like maybe they didn't matter to you. All you cared about was the Ark and that woman, Cayan. Didn't seem like Mom mattered to you anymore." He stopped.

Reg said nothing. He could not make sense of—

"I never meant to harm you, Dad. I thought maybe if you believed you would die, that you'd never make it off this mountain alive, you'd quit and go down. I—I just planned to knock you out or something. I—"

"Shut up!" The viciousness in his own voice startled Reg.

Tony looked stupefied. Never had his father spoken to him in that voice.

Reg grabbed fistfuls of his son's sweater and pulled him off the ground. His eyes bulged from their sockets, the veins on his neck knotted in fury. "You sniveling little brat! Who made you judge and jury over me? How can you place so little value on the recovery of the Ark? Why would you deny me happiness with someone else now that Mom is gone?

"And what about the misery you gave her with your petty rebellions and sulks? And wouldn't she have just loved to live to see you attacking your father with a knife!"

"She would have just loved to *live!*" Tony shouted, and the words drove deeper into his father's heart than the knife ever could have. Reg let the sweater slide through his fingers and turned away.

"So that's what this is. Oh, Tony, when did we slip away from one another?"

Tony swayed to his feet. "When you left Mom in that lake to die!"

The numbness in Reg's legs subsided. Now it paralyzed his heart and soul. "As God is my witness, Tony, I searched, we searched, that lake as thoroughly as we could for Mom. I prayed more than I ever—"

"Don't! Don't tell me you sat there and prayed while she drowned. Look how you parade your affection for that Turkish gunner, never giving a thought for Mom. I thought you pledged yourself to her for eternity—or was it just until something more exciting came along?"

Reg leaped on his son and slapped him hard, then backhanded him across the other cheek. He stared in disbelief at the trickle of blood at the corner of Tony's mouth, then wrapped his son in a bear hug. "My God, what am I doing? Please deliver me! Forgive me, Tony—forgive me!"

The dull, lifeless reply tore at them. "I don't know how."

Tony looked stricken, homeless, hunched, and defeated like an abused animal. He began to cry again, tears and rain streaking his face. He looked fifteen again, and desolate beyond words.

When his father stretched his arms pleadingly toward him, Tony stepped back. Reg looked with utter loss at his son, his only child. Tony was all he had left of Barbara, and Tony didn't want him.

"I'm sorry!" gasped Reg, feeling that same terrible loss of breath and hope that had seized him every time he dove beneath the waters for Barbara. "I'd give anything, I'd give Noah's Ark, to bring your mother back. Just don't reject me, Tony. Don't leave me to die inside. Jesus knows I loved her and never meant to gamble her life away like that. I wasn't careful. I was in too big a rush, too cocksure, too blasted proud of myself as a big-shot adventurer who didn't need to follow precautions. . . ."

"Dad?"

Reg looked up. Without knowing it, he had fallen to his knees in front of his son. Tony reached out and touched his father's cheek. "Say it, Dad. Say exactly what you mean."

Reg clutched Tony's wrist as if grabbing for a life preserver. "I'm responsible. Because of me—your mother died!" he groaned loudly, the barrenness in the sound making the night darker still. Tony bent and placed his cheek on his father's head. They clung to one another in the night, their tears mingling with the rain.

After some time had passed, they parted without a word. Tony walked shakily toward camp, the incessant rain swallowing him within seconds after he left his father.

Reg followed him as far as the little basalt alcove on the far edge of the clearing where he had been praying when the storm hit. The ice fangs hanging from the rock overhead ran with water, forming a curtain of rain. He dashed through and went to his knees before the rock shelf, ignoring the downpour, defying the lightning to strike him dead.

"My God, my God, I feel so alone!" he cried. "Please won't You send me someone who believes in tomorrow as much as I do? Don't take everyone from me."

The rain fell more heavily. God was not in the rain.

"God of our fathers, where are You?

"Where two or three are gathered in Your name, there are You in the midst of them. I need another person here with me now, Lord Jesus. You calmed the storm, please now favor me with someone to keep me from sinking!"

He wanted in the worst way for that someone to be Nilay. He desired her warmth, her beauty, her touch; he wanted her to hold him and kiss him and tell him that he was brave and considerate and had not forsaken his beloved Barbara. He wanted her to tell him of God among the Armenians, of ancient miracles, of a little girl running across the roof of Noah's Ark.

"The Lord is my shepherd, I shall not want . . ." Someone slipped down beside Danson at the small altar of stone.

". . . He restoreth my soul. He leadeth me in the paths of righteousness . . ." An arm in a rough cloth sleeve slipped around Reg and kept him from falling.

". . . and I walk through the valley of the shadow of death, I will fear no evil . . ."

At the last verse of the psalm of David, two voices joined as one. "Surely goodness and mercy shall follow me all the days of my life and I will dwell in the house of the Lord forever."

Danson turned to Ibrahim Hasan with tears in his eyes and clasped the *hoca's* arms. "Tell me, dear friend, is there some place that God is not?"

Hasan pulled the old Bible part way from the folds of his gown and tapped the cover. "It says no," he replied, a gentle smile wreathing his bearded lips. "And I have seen it proven."

A mental picture of Adnan's dilapidated tea shop off a dirty Istanbul alley strengthened Hasan as it had many times over the preceding days. A destitute old priest in a dim and squalid closet, terrified of having lost all eternal hope and glory, of having angered Allah beyond the possibility of reconciliation. In walked an American covered in dust, chicken feathers, and worse to share his burden.

Hasan tightened his grip on Reg's shoulders. In a strong voice, he called out above the pouring rain, "Welcome, thou, moon and sun of God's salvation, Welcome, who knowest from Truth no deviation. . . ."

"Welcome, the rebel's only place of hiding," said Danson, his voice choked with emotion. "Welcome, the poor man's only sure confiding!"

Hasan patted his friend's back and said nothing for a time. Then he whispered, "*Selamunaleykum.* Peace be to you, Mr. Danson."

Reg Danson did not look up. "*Teşekkür ederim,*" he said. "Thank you, my friend."

Hasan was silent a moment longer. Then he laughed joyously. "Ah, Mr. Danson," he chuckled. "Such predicaments as we fabricate for ourselves! You ask if there is any place that God is not, the God who made heaven and earth, the Keeper of the Mysteries of the Universe. Knowing all that, I have asked the same question myself, more than once."

The priest turned stiffly and sat with a sigh, back against the stone. "There have been two best answers to that question for me. Both are no, and both involve signs from America.

"The first sign involves an American businessman, a friend of my father's. He was a God-fearing

Christian pentecostal. This man quit his lucrative job in Detroit and moved his family to a filthy slum in Surabaya, Indonesia. He built his pitiful little home of wooden packing crates like all the devout Muslims who lived about him. He tapped his wealthy friends for donations and they responded with much.

"Then our Christian from Detroit called all the Muslim men of the community together and announced that his wealthy Christian friends wanted them to collect the money to build a mosque. He worked alongside them for six months to build that mosque. By then, he was such good friends with his coworkers that he held a Bible study and they came.

"Eventually thirty adults became baptized Christians, and another thirty teenagers came to hear the Bible taught. News of such faith and love travel fast even among more aggressive peoples." Hasan smiled and lifted his face to the rain. It was much warmer now.

"The second sign is you, Mr. Danson!" He clasped Reg's hand tightly in his own. "I thought God had left me when you walked into Adnan's. Never before had you seen me, yet you wept with me and joined in my grief and sustained me."

Hasan was silent for a long while, looking at Danson with a wistful sadness. "Do not place too much importance on the Ark, Mr. Danson. It is a valuable find, to be sure, but nothing compared to the arm of a friend or the prayers of the faithful."

The rain fell, softer, warmer now, rivulets of melted snow and dislodged ice swirling away down the mountain, disappearing through rock fissures, exposing fantastic spires and long-hidden formations, denuding the mountain of its great cloak.

Intense exhaustion overpowered Danson. He slipped from the stone step of prayer and stretched prone along the base of the basalt cliff. The soothing rain gurgling down the rocks and around his form bathed him in soft reassurances.

Were the lives of the few people in his party of more eternal significance than the great Ark of Noah? To guide one Ibrahim Hasan into the arms of Christ of more value than to parade an ancient wooden boat before a Super Bowl world?

These were not the feelings he had expected on the eve of reaching the Landing Place. Champagne and roses had given way to introspection and self-doubt. *Holy Spirit, comfort me, please. Make me strong for the task at hand. We will bring the world to its knees before the throne of God by showing it the indisputable evidence of the Ark. Won't we?*

He stretched, the warm water soothing away the stiffness, the bone-chill, the headaches. He momentarily forgot Hasan and allowed the delicious sensations to carry him far away from the harrowing fight in the storm—and its aftermath. His fingers stretched across the world of stone and ice and touched wood.

Danson's head shot up. He sighted along his arm to where his fingers scrabbled in the gravel and melting ice. A dark object with unmistakably hand-hewn right angles lay along the base of the rock. Five or six feet of it was exposed.

"Hasan!" he whispered hoarsely. "I've found wood. Wood, man, wood!"

He groped in his parka for a flashlight and turned its beam on the object. Together he and Hasan marched carefully forward on their knees, almost not believing what they saw.

The heavy wooden beam was nearly entirely exposed, about six inches square and composed of thick fibers. Danson touched the rough surface reverently. A tingle of discovery and awe more powerful than the surge of lightning shot the length of his arm.

He grabbed Hasan and hugged him wildly. The Ark, the precious, priceless Ark! They had done it! They had spanned the ages and made a liar of every scoffer and heretic and depraved one who had ever lived!

He swept the holy man to his feet and danced him about the clearing in a swooping reel, shouting and hopping with glee. He bent and flung snow and slush at Hasan, laughing deliriously when the old man responded in kind, the two of them splashing and gasping like kids in a pond.

"I must tell the others, Ibrahim. No, I must!" He raced across the clearing, disappearing through the rocks with a last wild whoop.

The smile vanished from Hasan's face. He made his way to the stone step in the wall. Grateful of heart, yes, yet heavy. Why did God's treasures have to be found? What would people, who had trampled every other sacred thing under their feet, do with this precious find?

What perhaps worried Hasan most, however, was the look in Reg Danson's eyes. Discovery aside, the look said that nothing else mattered. This one archaeological bonanza would save them all and cure the world.

Hasan was not so sure. Danson's question kept turning in his mind. "Is there some place that God is not?" Had he answered too quickly? Might God not be in this place, in these ambitions, among these disparate people? Was the God of triumph, victory, and salvation the same God in heartache, misery, and grief? When we are most bereft, is God most visible?

The Bible said it was so.

A shiver passed through him, and he pulled his soaking gown closer about himself.

He knelt before the wood and placed a weathered hand upon it. He looked to the sky and then to the earth and began his prayer. "Our Father, which art in heaven and hell . . ."

26

THE EXPEDITION prepared to leave before dawn, wishing to allow as much daylight as possible for the actual rescue and assorted scientific examinations. Reg decided the day would be spent preparing the Ark for actual removal on the next day. To risk destruction of the priceless artifact through haste would be foolish. Besides, the team had earned some rest and recovery time before being flown from Ararat into the jaws of media attention.

It had been a relatively sleepless night with repeated trips to the basalt wall to view the wooden beam and to ponder excitedly where it would all lead.

First light revealed a world very different from the one the night before. The warm, heavy rains had washed away a great deal of the snow covering, and water was everywhere.

Before breaking camp, Danson ordered the team to assemble in the helicopter clearing where he and Cevdet had stretched several scarlet lengths of plastic ribbon well anchored with stones to signal the chopper crews.

He felt he had neglected his spiritual duty as expedition leader. He should have been more solicitous of everyone's needs and at least have prayed with them at day's beginning and end. Several of them never failed to bow in the snow five times a day in obeisance to Islamic duty. It mattered not how precipitous the slope or if they had to run uphill to catch up to the rest of the party, prayer toward Mecca five times a day was essential.

The Noah's Ark team looked rumpled but eager this morning. With the coming of the rain, their headaches had subsided. Sleep was a serious and blessed possibility at last. Then Danson returned. Little sleep was possible after he came bellering through camp proclaiming the presence of a hand-tooled wooden beam at fourteen thousand feet. Their faces looked younger with the news, an air of light-hearted summer camp expectancy revitalizing their drawn expressions.

"Friends, and you are friends of mine and friends of the ultimate goal of this expedition, I celebrate with you our proximity to success in this endeavor!" It was probably a pretentious beginning, but he felt the need to lend some dignity to the final assault. "I also must ask your pardon for failing to treat you more like family and less like hired workmen." Lieutenant Nilay Cayan smiled warmly, and Danson was elated.

"Whether you call Him God or Allah, the Lord of us all has provided abundantly for our needs. He has most assuredly given and most swiftly and definitely taken away."

To a restless shuffling of feet and questioning glances, Danson continued. "I refer, of course, to those brave men whose lives have been lost in our effort to retrieve the Ark. We were together but a short time, and I confess that I did not get to know them before they perished. To some of you, however, they were friends. I am told by Lieutenant Cayan that there were a father of four, a top-ranked wrestler, a portrait artist, and a ruthless backgammon player." The ripple of collective laughter was good to hear. Turgut Suleyman had challenged everyone to a game on his mobile magnetic backgammon board, which was strapped to the outside of his pack. His intended victims could walk behind him and study their moves before he buried them at rest stops and lunch breaks.

Danson attempted to clear his throat, but a lump remained.

Others were having trouble too. "In memory of those men, I'd like to share some words with you from God's written word, the Holy Bible." He winked at Hasan. "Please don't take me wrong. I don't mean to preach at you. One holy man per team is plenty." Laughter again, Hasan's the loudest.

"This is something I should have done long before now. In his letter to the believers in Christ at Corinth, across the Aegean Sea from Turkey, St. Paul wrote, 'For as in Adam all die, even so in Christ all shall be made alive. . . . Then comes the end, when He delivers the kingdom to God the Father, when He puts an end to all rule and all authority and power. For He must reign till He has put all enemies under His feet. The last enemy that will be destroyed is death.'

"Christ is different from all the other 'prophets,' the term I've heard you use. Only He said we must believe in Him alone for salvation. Then, and only then, does death have no hold over us.

"My prayer for each of you is that you might learn from the deaths of your friends that life is fleeting and you must be spiritually ready at a moment's notice. I pray, too, that in the Ark, so surely referred to by Christ Himself, you will find the courage to take Christ at His word and make that full commitment to Allah, the commitment that means death cannot separate you from the love of God."

Ahmed Kassem stepped forward, scowling. "I have never pretended to be a devout man," he said, "but of all the highly esteemed prophets, including Christ and Noah, Mohammed was the final and greatest. Our submission is to Allah alone, without equal or partner. A Muslim submits to the will of Allah. To convert from Islam is a capital offence." He glared defiantly.

Reg looked at Kassem with unexpected kindness. "Ahmed, the *hoca* tells me Islamic tradition says 124 thousand prophets have been sent to humankind. The Koran calls Adam 'the chosen of Allah,' Noah 'the preacher of Allah,' Abraham 'the friend of Allah,' Moses 'the speaker of Allah,' and Mohammed 'the apostle of Allah.' But do you know what title the Koran reserves for Jesus Christ? Do you?"

Kassem shifted uncomfortably. The others were looking at him, waiting for his reply.

"Jesus is called 'the word and spirit of Allah,'" he mumbled.

Reg allowed that to sink in a moment before continuing. "Only Christ has power over death," he said, trying to look into each face. "Only He by the force of His own divinity was able to conquer the grave. That, I believe, is the lesson to be learned from the deaths of these four men.

"Each of you has my personal gratitude for bringing this mission to the brink of success. To Lieutenant Cayan and the men of the Third Army, my special thanks, for you have lost the most. Your normal charge is patrolling the trans-Caucasian border, a critically important post to Turkey's national security. Thank you for giving yourselves for our benefit. Were it not for your presence, we might have suffered a full scale attack by now.

"To you men of science and medicine and other specialized skills"—he looked at Ahmed Kassem knowingly—"I say that what you accomplish on this mountain will benefit mankind in valuable ways the full extent of which we may never know.

"So thank you all for your extraordinary efforts. With your help, we can now cross over and reveal for all humanity what has so long been hidden. *Mukafat alacaksin!* You shall be rewarded! Let us be off."

The party hesitated a moment, still pondering Danson's words. Then, as if by prearranged signal, they shook hands, clapped one another's shoulders, and teasingly questioned the contribution each had made, delivering exaggerated compliments and playing "keep away" with a hat or a sleeping bag. Several pointed *dogru* or straight ahead up the mountain, excitedly speculating on what lay just ahead. The expedition hoisted its gear and broke camp amid noisy cries of *"Ugurlu olsun!* Good luck!"

Cevdet hung back and took Danson aside. "You have spoken holy words of truth. Christ the Conqueror is indeed our only hope. But we have probably five or six dozen Soviet Mafia infantry at our heels that we cannot wish away. They have kept out of sight for the most part to allow us to pinpoint the Ark. We must not be caught thinking they have no intention of risking an international incident. After all, there are 'accidents.' They could shoot us all and throw our bodies down a crevasse without trace. They could lay our disappearance to wild beasts or Barzani's roving bands. And worse than that, they could hack the Ark to pieces and stuff it down a crevasse. Why don't we take it slower and allow me to flank them and see if I can't instill the fear of God in those atheists?"

Reg admired the man's earnest bravery. But he didn't share the crusader's zealous approach to settling disputes. Mideastern Christians could be every bit as headstrong and spill as much blood as their Muslim counterparts. Reg felt an overwhelming sense of protection as if nothing, certainly not a few Soviet soldiers, could scuttle the expedition's sacred assignment.

"Cevdet, there is a prayer among the Irish that goes something like this: 'O Lord, turn the hearts of our enemies; and if You can't turn their hearts, then turn their ankles and we shall know them by their limp! God will hobble the adversary. We must forge on with you in the lead to take us there!"

"I will, of course, accede to your wishes, Mr. Danson, but I do not believe you understand the nature of the enemy. You have spent your growth in God, studying His beneficence and magnificence. I, on the other hand, while reveling in what the Lord has done, have kept one eye on the enemy's malevolence."

Reg felt a flash of irritation. He wanted to be gone, not to linger discoursing on an enemy that for all they knew might well be at the bottom of a canyon beneath a million tons of snow. "Last night, I asked the Holy Spirit, the Comforter, to reconfirm that we were in the Lord's will. It was then I touched wood, holy wood; salvation wood, cut and shaped by Noah the Patriarch; wood for cages for thirty-five thousand animals; wood that kept them safe and dry for 371 days; blessed, precious wood that meant death to maybe three billion unrepentant people and kept eight righteous people safe and sound. That wood is our sign on this day to lay hold of the treasure of the ages. The enemy is defeated, Cevdet. We have nothing more to fear from him in any form."

Before the sound of the declaration faded, the shaking began. Rock and ice formations jumped and lurched like wooden blocks tossed in a shoe box. Without being told, the expedition members hit the ground or fell, gripping the earth as if afraid of sliding off. A geyser of steam erupted from a crevice with the piercing shriek of a Fourth of July skyrocket.

Other volcanic shrieks sounded at a distance, followed by the rumble of a fleet of jumbo jets in takeoff. Stones and chunks of rock-hard ice bounded over the clearing, thumping bodies in their path and coming to rest with a rattle and thud against a wall of basalt.

It was over in eight or nine seconds. *Thank God nothing really big came down,* Reg thought. He lifted his head and felt hot ash against his cheek. A small cloud of it drifted down and coated everything a gray-white. "Anyone injured?" he called out. The others got to their feet, checking for damage. Bruises, sore muscles, but nothing broken. *Thank You, Lord.*

They must proceed with all speed, Reg knew. No telling how much more time there was left to borrow. That jolt was a 5.0 on the Richter or he was Shirley Temple.

Cevdet was looking at him again. The drilling gaze of the young warrior left Danson wondering if he himself was the man for this job. Then he straightened and returned the gaze steadily and without concession. He was not the same man who had entered the catacombs of Cappadocia and questioned his fitness for the task. He remembered Cevdet's words that day in the catacombs when Reg had touched the roughly hewn cross of gopher wood around Demirkol's neck. "You yourself have now touched the Ark, and there is no turning back!"

Without speaking, Cevdet removed that same cross and placed it over Danson's head. It came to rest on his chest and burned there like a hot ember. "In the name of God, let us be gone!"

With that, Cevdet Demirkol strode past Danson to lead the way to the Landing Place.

THEY dug out of their snow caves just before dawn, sixty grim-faced recruits of an obsolete army. The heavy rains had caused the ceilings of their temporary abodes to collapse but they had stoically remained in place, breathing sparingly from warm pockets of air, their parka-clad backs forming makeshift protection against the elements.

Miserably wet, they emerged from the frosty crypts, their stiffened limbs unfolding with cracks of protest. Lieutenant General Shkidchenko ordered no stoves, no lamps, no bright tent cloth, nothing to betray their position to the Ark expedition.

Much of their food was entombed with their fallen comrades. Six ration sledges! They would have to overtake the American and "appropriate" his supplies as well as the ultimate prize.

Shkidchenko paced restlessly while his troops readied themselves for the march. The morning rations were cut by two-thirds, and those who dared, grumbled.

The bone fragments from the Deluge in the Russian commander's pocket were a smooth augury of triumph. No shortage of food or men or strength would prevent Shkidchenko from this day giving Mother Russia the supreme relic of hope. The Christian devout would be proven correct, their icons, their liturgy, their musty, ancient faith vindicated on a mountaintop a scant eighteen miles from the decaying gun towers and border wire of a bygone captivity. A millennium of ritual had not been wasted motion. The plotting remnants of communist tyranny would have the devil's own time of it factoring the Ark into their comeback equation.

Shkidchenko distractedly picked his teeth with a sliver of rhinoceros femur and contemplated the rancid political intrigues that had for untold centuries made peace and prosperity impossible anywhere near Mount Ararat. It was no accident that the Ottoman ruler Selim II was nicknamed Selim the Sot or that his successor, Murad III, sired one hundred offspring.

Fratricide had been legalized by ordinance as early as 1451. Elimination of male rivals—often including dozens of brothers—was accomplished when possible by strangulation with a silken bowstring so as not to shed exalted blood.

By 1600, members of the dynasty were at last fed up with the sultans' murderous excesses and substituted what was considered the more humane practice of "caging." All heirs to the throne were confined to the seraglio in luxury, literally cut off from the outside world and deprived of effective training for office. Abdul Hamid I took the throne in the late eighteenth century after forty-three years of confinement to a life of perpetual pleasure. Mentally deranged by the experience, he nonetheless ruled for sixteen years in insanity.

The sliver of bone snapped in two under Shkidchenko's relentless probing. He tossed it to the ground and chose a fragment of crocodile jaw as a replacement.

It was Russia's own Czar Nicholas I who in 1833 was astute enough to call the declining Ottoman Empire "the sick man of Europe." But how to divide the corpse so that no one European power would gain an advantage at the expense of the others? Several armed conflicts ensued between Russia and the Ottoman Turks, the Crimean and Balkan wars among them. Eventually, Ottoman territorial holdings crumbled, including the loss of the Bulgarian and Romanian Principalities.

But for all their moral dissipation and bloody rule, the Turks retained a certain residual toughness that made them still a force to be reckoned with in the twentieth century. And what of Russia? She had yet to rise above a third-rate economic status and feed—let alone exalt—her people.

Shkidchenko flung the bone pick away and sighed heavily. He must change all that. He, a Russian, must announce the incredible to an incredulous world. Those living human relics in the Kremlin, suspended in their own kind of "caging," would understand in an instant that they had bought a lie. He predicted that the suicide rate in Moscow would soar.

All was ready. His chief advisors had been briefed to begin stealth maneuvers to pick off the remaining military escort of the Ark expedition. That would isolate the more scientific and less armed members of the group—including the American—all of whom he wanted to witness his grand announcement.

The Russian troops began to move in the direction of Ahora Gorge, colder, wetter, and fewer now than when they had burrowed out of the morning snow. Sixty groaned and swore under their breath at their leader's wake-up call; just fifty-five stretched along the trail for the final assault on Ararat. More would have defected but for decades of conditioned obedience.

Shkidchenko licked his teeth and did not know of the deserters. No one bothered to tell him.

27

CREVASSES YAWNED deep and broad along the direct route to the Ark. Some gaped in sinister secret beneath a thin crust of rotten ice, ready to swallow whole the unwary. The expedition was forced to backtrack in search of alternate approaches. Footing proved treacherous, and team members were securely roped together in groups of four and one of five for maximum safety. Ice axes and crampons were mandatory.

Several tall rock outcroppings had been struck by lightning in the night and reduced to rubble. The resulting slag piles also required careful negotiation.

Danson led the line, Cevdet having been sent ahead to scout the most direct route. It was dangerous for him to go alone but the proud Janissary would have it no other way. Lieutenant Nilay Cayan followed Danson with Ahmed Kassem immediately behind her and Ibrahim Hasan behind him. The rest of the party followed Hasan; the last seven in line were

Tony Danson and six of Cayan's crack shots, who covered the rear.

They began a gradual descent down a long, narrow rocky passage climbers called a defile. Its high walls prevented them from seeing the glacial cleft where the Ark lay caught. It did not stop them from stretching and straining every few yards to be the first to lay eyes on the ancient craft.

The mild descent was enjoyable and placed most of the party in a jovial mood. The nosebleeds, the headaches, the shortness of breath, even the loss of life seemed momentarily forgotten as they took long plunging steps down the slope like a team of romping St. Bernards. At the bottom, a glacial melt plain a hundred yards broad formed what looked like a wide skating rink before another ascending defile on the far side.

Reg studied the glacial melt, searching for Cevdet's footprints. It appeared that he had done a kind of deer hop across, something they could not do in one move safely, roped together as they were with 120-foot lengths.

"Wait here at this boulder, Lieutenant," he ordered, trying to sound as nonthreatening as possible. "I will match Cevdet's steps as far as the length between us. You follow suit, catch up to me, and then I will move on while Ahmed catches up to you and so on. Please pass those instructions to the others."

He did not wait for a reaction from Nilay Cayan, but started across the glistening field of sludge ice in quick steps, careful to match his stride to that of Cevdet.

Lieutenant Cayan had no intention of hanging

back with an old priest and Ahmed the Sullen and began her own crossing two leaps behind Danson.

A sharp crack like a pistol shot ricocheted off the brooding sides of the defile. Two jaws of ice split apart in a hideous grin to gulp Nilay Cayan whole.

Reg whirled about and watched her vanish. He swiftly wrapped the rope twice about his right forearm, vaulted around a finger of rock jutting vertically from the ice, and prayed the rock would take the brunt of the fall-and-hold.

Ahmed Kassem had no rock to brace the rope against and was jerked off his feet when the slack was gone. He slid headfirst for the brink of the chasm, managing to thrust his legs around and forward when he was ten yards from the edge. He dug in his heels and halted his slide.

"Ah—med, can—" panted Danson, "can you—hang—on?"

To his horror he watched Kassem extract a short-bladed gutting knife from a sheath at his side and begin to saw and hack frantically at the taut rope.

"Stop!" Danson roared, visions of Barbara sinking from sight in the unforgiving waters of Loch Ness flashing in his mind. *He could not lose another!*

With a cry to the almighty, Ibrahim Hasan plunged forward, a small boulder raised high above his head. He brought it down hard on Kassem's skull.

The knife flew from the Iraqi's hand. The limp body twisted and slid backward toward the gaping chasm. Hasan quickly grabbed the retreating rope, jammed his feet into the depressions left by Hasan's heels, wrapped the rope around his forearm, and prayed like a condemned man.

The strength of his past youth surged along Hasan's arms, and the unconscious man skidded to a halt at the edge of the crevasse. The expedition team behind raced to the priest's side and pulled Kassem to safety.

While Reg hauled on the rope, hand over hand, an agonizing burning shot the length of his arms. His joints felt as if they were parting, never to be joined again.

You are my strength, my high tower. I will lean forever on your everlasting arms . . .

Nilay was conscious! She struggled for toeholds, gasping and fighting her way out of the crevasse. The top of her head barely showed, and it looked as if she would win.

But she found no secure purchase and began to slip back. Her head disappeared, and then with a sickening jerk, the line snapped taut again, brutally wrenching Reg's shoulder sockets. He cried out in pain and felt as if his back was on fire.

Chewing his lip until it bled, Reg hauled again on the rope, praying it would not fray against the rock. He shouted joyously when there was again a lessening of tension on the rope, a sign Nilay was once more trying to make her way out.

After what seemed an eternity, the little knot of climbers on the far side of the crevasse cheered when they caught sight of Lieutenant Cayan nearing the top of what had almost become her tomb.

Her hair was wet and stringy, and a bloody gash on her chin flashed red. She threw an arm over the edge of the crevasse, then a leg, and then she seal-flopped the rest of her body onto safe ground. With effort, she got to her knees beside Danson, who had collapsed behind the finger of rock. Cayan panted and swayed weakly, trying to regain her faculties. Danson saw her wound and reached out to her. She caught his hand and held it to her cheek. They stayed like that until their heads cleared.

"Thank you for hanging on," she whispered, diamond ice crystals sparkling in her hair. "There are rewards for the valiant beyond ribbons and medals. I could come to your tent tonight and bestow such honor upon you."

For one moment, more frightening and delicious in its power than any he had ever experienced, he wanted her in every way. She pressed the back of his hand to her lips.

The crevasse, Nilay vanishing, the dread of loving again, of losing again, of killing everyone he ever loved . . . *Barbara, sweet Barbara, did I lose you because the quest was more important than us?*

"Yours is a dance of many veils, Lieutenant," Reg said quietly.

"Meaning?"

"Meaning you have blown hot and cold all the way up this mountain. That is often the sign of someone baiting a trap. I am attracted to you—how much, I don't know—but you took that ambivalence and toyed with it in case my commitment to this project should waver. For someone who can take the Ark or leave it, you certainly haven't allowed anything to stall the mission. You've lost good soldiers. I watched you after the dog bomb killed one of your best. I detected no regret, but I do recall you winked at me. Strange behavior for a military commander, agreed?"

Lieutenant Cayan stood up and turned her back to him. She appeared to be studying the peak of Ararat, rarely visible, but clearly etched in the cobalt blue of the morning sky. Should he take the gamble? He had to know where she stood.

Reg sighed. "I have no right to jeopardize yours or anyone else's life for some prize antique. Too many have lost their lives over it already. I was blind, too ambitious to see straight." He glanced at her from the corner of his eye, gauging her response. "There are things more important than finding the Ark—things like love and caring more for someone than to use them up in some ill-fated search for something God prefers remain hidden. For you, Nilay, and for God, I'm terminating the expedition."

She was upon him like a whirlwind. "You stupid American! Because they had placed this, the greatest of all missions, in the hands of a weak-willed Westerner, I knew it would take some extraordinary measures to get you to lay hold of the Ark.

"I knew the minute you insisted upon bringing that traitor priest up the mountain that you were far too driven by heart. I saw the shaky relationship with your son, the way your wife haunts your every step. Anyone with that kind of sensitive baggage is doomed to failure.

"So, yes, I played the flirt. I took advantage of your vulnerability to keep you climbing. Why? Because I saw the way you looked when those men were torn from the mountain in the wind. It was an act of God that could all too easily have made you quit. And you needed a correspondingly harsh hu-

man act to spur you on, to remind you that evil is
hoarding the Ark, not God. So I gave it to you!"

Reg pushed her away and stood. "How do you
mean?"

The emerald drill bits of her eyes cut through his
soul like butter. "Barzani the Kurd has been following us for insurance. He provided the dog. I wired it."

Reg stared at her in repulsion. For a ruse, she had
destroyed a man with little more thought than that
reserved for taking out the garbage. Both necessary, if
mundane functions.

"Your idea of shed blood again?" His throat felt
tight. It was difficult to speak at all. "That Turks, the
people entrusted to your care, are expendable because their ancestors plowed your ancestors under? It
has to end somewhere, Lieutenant. Your Armenian
Christian faith should have told you that it ends at
the cross!"

She shook her head, and he was amazed to see
tears. "No one hunted your wife down, raped, tortured, and mutilated her body and left her barely
alive to bleed slowly to death. The Turks did that to
my grandmother. My grandfather they impaled on a
stake. With or without you, I must go on!"

Danson's emotions raged. How could he want to
hold her again after her terrible confession? She was
less a woman than a viper.

A shout from across the crevasse drew his attention. They were pointing up the defile behind him.
He turned to watch Cevdet approach. There was no
energy in his stride. His shoulders drooped, and he
stared dumbly ahead.

He stopped ten feet from them and was silent.

"What, man, what?" Danson shouted.

For a moment Cevdet swayed as if he would topple face forward at their feet. Then he turned and fixed Danson with eyes brimming with terror.

"It is not there," he said numbly, his voice tinged with awful fear. "My God, it is not there!"

28

UNITED STATES President Thurston Pierce held the six-foot gold-plated shovel poised above the freshly graded dirt. He smiled toothsomely into a bank of cameras that whirred and clicked and flashed, then dug a hefty shovelful and held it while the cameras captured the image.

"I hereby declare the ground officially broken for the new Hall of Mid-Eastern Antiquities!" said Pierce with feeling. The huge crowd pressing in on three sides broke into loud and enthusiastic applause and whistles.

A secret service agent spoke into his cuff. "All secure at Ground Zero." In his ear he heard, "We copy. All secure at Skyview." The agent responded, "Copy." He looked to the roof of the Smithsonian Institution's National Air and Space Museum adjacent and saw the sharpshooters at their posts, and Skyview scanned the crowd with his high-powered binoculars.

Pierce chafed in a charcoal gray suit. The heat

was intense, and nearly every one of the spectators was dressed minimally. Capitol Hill wags said it was so hot that Woodward and Bernstein would be able to pin it on the president within forty-eight hours. Those less inclined to joking predicted the most disastrous power failure in the city's history if Washingtonians didn't cut back energy consumption by at least twenty-five percent.

Pierce didn't care. It would always be sixty-eight degrees in the ten-story building soon to occupy this space. Twenty-four times each day the air would be cleansed to pristine quality. White-coveralled workers would move noiselessly on crepe soles, the muted *whir* of climate-controlled technology accompanying their movements as ethereally as cicadas serenading fly fishermen on some forgotten lake.

The newest and largest of the Smithsonian exhibit halls would rise by presidential fiat and would house but a single precious treasure, the most valuable artifact ever found—Noah's Ark!

All regular television programming would be interrupted during prime time on the most-watched day of the week—Thursday. The president, speaking with just the right blend of forcefulness and awe, would come to the nation from the Oval Office and make his stunning announcement. For now, it was enough for the public to know that the building would house priceless ancient workmanship.

NASA experts would oversee around-the-clock construction of the massive facility. Their experience with gigantic rocket assembly hangars made them indispensable. Experts in launch control consoles would install the most sophisticated monitoring systems. TPS, Total Processing System, the multimillion-dollar gadgetry, regulated every conceivable aspect of the building's operation. Anyone entering the structure would automatically be scanned for prohibited items preprogrammed into the computer. Admission after the grand unveiling was to be by ticket only—excess body heat generated by too many visitors would raise temperatures and humidity and endanger the Ark.

It was a balanced trade-off. While they would ensure the visitor's comfort by not maintaining the Ark in its decay-inhibiting frozen environment, neither would the Ark be exposed to the harsh, eroding elements of wind, rain, and lightning that it had suffered on Ararat.

A bulletproof glass retaining wall 75 feet tall by 550 feet long would further protect—and divide—the Ark from the people.

Television cameras trained on every square inch of the building's interior and exterior would relay the images to command posts located at each of four strategic locations on the main floor. Highly paid screeners would do nothing all day but watch the parade of visitors, on guard for anything suspicious.

Elaborate alarms and warning lights would inform not on saboteurs alone but on everything from dangerous humidity levels to a malfunctioning vending machine. A staff of twenty-five hand-picked security guards had been intensively trained to read the equipment, including rehearsal for endless hours of how to deal specifically with thirty-four potentially threatening scenarios. Any errors were likely to be human, not mechanical.

Unknown to the guards was a specialist unit of ten U.S. Marines schooled in the deadliest anti-terrorist tactics. Among their obligations was surveillance of the guards for the slightest indication of incompetence, insubordination, or human frailty that could in any way jeopardize the exhibit. None of the Marines was married or permitted to date. They had been conditioned to hunt, to hurt, to remain acutely suspicious of anything that moved. They had not been permitted to love.

President Pierce was up for reelection November 5, and Democratic challenger Matthew Handford was stiff competition indeed. Going into summer it was anybody's horse race, though Pierce's hawkish stance vis-à-vis nuclear proliferation both militarily and domestically was beginning to cloy with the electorate. Voters in droves were wowed and wooed by Handford's boyish good looks and sincere rhetoric on the need for peace now. Despite his junior status in Congress, increasing numbers of voters were finding the challenger's inexperience somehow disarming and not a little refreshing.

It had not taken the president long to see the handwriting on the wall. The mood in America had become decidedly wary of old-guard politicians. A scant 40 percent of eligible voters had gone to the polls to elect him over the "tried and true" Republican incumbent who had shown signs of boredom with the job. There was a distinct and frightening probability that those former supporters were too apathetic (or outright angry) over his Social Security cuts to back him again while the young were certain to turn out in favor of Handford, one of their own.

Yet President Pierce was a survivor. He'd nearly died three times in World War II and had narrowly escaped assassination by a knife-wielding White House maid his first year in office. The Ark was his ace in the hole. Bringing it to America would captivate the people's attention, and Handford would be lecturing on failed domestic policy to an empty house.

And while it awaited the completion of its new berth, the Ark would be safe in the hold of its Turkish transport vessel at an undisclosed moorage somewhere in New York's Hudson River maze of freight terminals.

Pierce put an arm around Del Ranheim, the chief curator of the new hall, and they grinned for the cameras like Cheshire twins. Microphones sprouted thick as weeds and Pierce obliged them with stirring platitudes and slogans. He stopped short of flashing a "V" for victory but did evoke Teddy Roosevelt's charge up San Juan Hill. Then he put down the prepared script and looked America in the eye.

"I know that some of you in recent months have questioned my priorities and wondered at my leadership style. I don't fault you for that. When you care as deeply for America as you and I do, you keep your eye on the hen house.

"Just don't be fooled by the debonair fox who'd like to bust in. His arguments are smooth, his coat neat and sleek, but no matter how he dresses or how persuasive his tongue, he is still a fox. Clever, devious, and oh, those teeth!" The crowd laughed. They liked sly, folksy innuendo. When they quieted, Pierce grew sober.

"What you want—what America needs—is a guardian who will not throw the door wide and invite predators, however smooth, to spend the night. Whatever else I've done these four years, I have not slept through the watch. The hen house is secure. The hens are all present and accounted for.

"Now I am not at liberty just yet to tell you what astonishing thing will soon be on display here where we celebrate today. Within forty-eight hours, though, I hope to come to you again with wonderful news. Until then, I value your continued trust and confidence. When again we gather in two days, I want to reward your trust and compensate your confidence far beyond a tax cut here or lower interest rates there. I want to give you a national treasure that will revive your spirits and captivate your imagination. For America is far more than crime bills and foreign trade; America is an ideal to which the world aspires."

The ovation was louder and more prolonged than Pierce had enjoyed in a long while. He drank it in and beamed. He looked at Del Ranheim, who was clapping vigorously. Ranheim looked back in open admiration.

The president relaxed inside. The itchy suit, the 101-degree heat, pretty boy Matthew Handford—none of it mattered in the face of adulation. Playing God had its benefits.

NOAH'S ARK was not there. Cevdet's distress made it abundantly apparent.

The rage building inside Danson was a scalding mass. Were the periodic earth tremors that dogged them, ever growing in severity, God's laughter? Was Reg but the latest in a long line of sappy, deluded men to be lured to this spot under heaven only to have their spindly little dreams flung back in their faces?

The godfather had predicted Danson's death. More like professional suicide. Once the sage good ol' boys in charge of bones and shards at the Smithsonian got wind of this, he'd have to build a grass hut in Outer Mauritania to escape their scathing ridicule.

What had Barbara said in her note to Tony a gallivorous insect was? One that "feeds on gall tissue." Reg's stomach was manufacturing enough gall to support the whole gallivorous population.

Noah's Ark was the most important find in the whole misbegotten span of man. Why, why, *why* would God snatch it back like this after so cruelly leading Reg on, giving him so much cause to hope and dream?

When he thought how many souls he could persuade by the evidence of the Ark, Reg clenched and unclenched his fists at the sheer unfairness of it all.

He had planned to include Arthur Boyce in an international lecture series with selected members of the discovery and removal teams. In his head, he had run and rerun a hundred times what he would say to the blind guides at the Smithsonian, who had so arrogantly dismissed the truth. And most delicious of ironies, when he was asked to return to the Institution, he would laugh in their faces and tell them he did not work for frauds.

And Tony, dear Tony, how he would look up to his father, the acclaimed finder of cryptoantiquities; he would commit his life to Christ. They would be a family again, the two of them, and roam the world together just as Barbara would have wanted. Tony would love his dad and brag about him among the academics and archaeologists of higher learning. Oh, the discoveries they would make together, the unseen worlds they would explore!

Reg Danson wanted the Ark of Noah more than anything else life could offer.

He paced like a frantic bull, kicking at the earth, and savagely tossed lava stones and chunks of ice at the faceless devils that had deprived him of his finest hour. It was not right, it was not just, it was not good of God to lead him into an empty cul-de-sac. For what? God, the Creator of matter itself, had no need of a lousy, used boat you couldn't even steer. But to

Reg, it would mean so much. And to the world, it might mean everything.

What a stupid fool he had been. He had put all his eggs in this basket, and in one brief moment they were squashed flat by God the Omnipotent. Was God so bored that He had to amuse Himself at Reg's expense? Maybe the Muslims were right. Maybe God *was* a hard-edged taskmaster who demanded total allegiance and meted out good things sparingly.

Reg knew full well what the others were thinking. Tony must consider him a joke of a father. Ibrahim Hasan would declare an Islamic holiday on the spot to commemorate this triumph over Christian folklore. Ahmed Kassem could ill afford to say anything given how close he came to sending Lieutenant Cayan to her death. He wouldn't have to. His annoying, brooding silence and curled lip would be accusation aplenty. And what of Nilay Cayan herself? She had a whole other agenda, and this would only confirm her opinion that he lacked the ability to complete anything worth completing. Would they have found the Ark had she led the charge?

Trust and obey . . . for there's no other way . . . to be happy . . . Reg cursed the bit of old hymn that penetrated his rage. "Not this time," he said aloud, pacing in circles, fists hitting fists like a boxer awaiting an opening. This was no Sunday school picnic rained out. This was Satan victorious; if the mountain had erupted right then, Reg would have lain down like Pliny the Elder and gladly pulled the ash blanket over his head for a good long sleep.

Moses played and lost, Arthur Bryce played and lost, Reg Danson played and lost. Reg wondered if God kept adding a notch to His cosmic belt every time another naive fool went down.

Well, he'd not sit here and take it. He'd hitch up the team and ride until they fell on their faces from exhaustion. Let God pick up the pieces.

The ensuing march was a forbidding, joyless onslaught to the place where Cevdet's map and his memory said the Ark should be.

He had been to the rocky nest on the side of Ahora just two days previous. The Ark had loomed above him, virtually unattached from its glacial vault, sparkling ethereally beneath a thin skin of hoarfrost.

He should have touched it, for now he agonized over whether it had really been there at all.

And now the very path he had followed just hours, minutes, before, seemed alien, uncharted. A sudden fierce blizzard condition called "white out" had obliterated familiar signs. A sharp wind-whipped spray made him shield his eyes and perpetually wipe them clear. Left turns became right turns, and right ones were now left. Landmarks he'd counted on had switched places or vanished altogether, and the temperature rose and fell half a dozen times within the hour.

Reg cared little for this world gone mad. They would go until there was nowhere else to go.

When at last they reached the farthest place Cevdet remembered having gone, he stood weeping before them. Nothing was the same; north and south had lost their meaning.

The members of the expedition unroped upon reaching the rocky clefts of Ahora's north wall. The first few minutes they stood about, listlessly, with no more purpose for being there. They willed the Ark to appear in the craggy contours of the gash in Ararat's side. After that, they slumped in the snow, cheated, rescuers with nothing to rescue.

Reg went apart to rant at God. Instead, he fell to his knees and threw a handful of powdery crystals into the air. He thought of prophets in the Bible who had flung dirt in their worst "sackcloth and ashes" moments. He hurt all over. But it was a wounded pride kind of hurt. For was he all that much different from Arthur Bryce who had withheld information, hoarded insight, built a personal legend as carefully and with all the shrewd calculation of a snake-oil salesman? He was no different, and he knew it. He wouldn't even be able to get his swelled head into the David Livingstone jungle helmet Barbara had bought him.

The Ark, whether theory or reality, stood between Reg Danson and God. The gulf fixed between God and unrepentant man looked an awful lot like the black depths of Ahora Gorge. Reg had built an altar to the Ark god and sacrificed all manner of people and things upon it. God had meant the Ark for good. Reg Danson had twisted it into something bad. Human life became less important; prayer became more expediency than devotion; love turned from loyalty to seduction. Reg's quest had been no different from that of a sunken treasure seeker who says, "Hang the historical value! What's my cut of the booty?"

Reg Danson had become an archaeological mercenary. Worse, he had done it in God's name.

"Father," he prayed, "forgive my anger, take away my self-glorification, grant me spiritual balance. I have sinned against You and I ask You to pardon me. How dark is the mind and heart of man! What will I tell the world? Can I still bear witness of Your mighty redemption without the Ark? Not in my strength, but in Yours alone will I trust. Thank You for bringing us here for Your own good purpose. Bless Tony and help us to find the love we once had, and may it be a love rooted in You.

"And, Lord, I didn't mean it about the cosmic belt. You are sovereign, and I do not question what in Your good providence You choose to do. I love You, Lord, and praise You for Your undying love toward me. In Your Son's name I pray. Amen."

Danson suddenly felt as if he were not alone. He looked up and saw Tony and Barbara a little above, heads together, studying a square rock with great interest. Reg rubbed his eyes, and Tony and Barbara became one. Tony brushed the snow and ice from the stone.

"Dad? Dad, come here, quick!"

Reg scrambled to a place beside his son. A thrill rippled through him. The rock was covered in pictorial and cuneiform inscriptions. He'd brought Bryce's collection of cuneiform photos, including those taken high up on Ararat by Russian Colonel Alexander Koor. Included were sheets of corresponding translations. Father and son nearly collided in their excitement to match one to the stone at hand.

"Here—here, this is the one!"

The translation leapt at them from across the span of time. "God sowed the seeds of the word into the waters . . . the waters filled the earth, descending from above. . . . His children came to rest on the mountain peak."

Reg turned to Tony with eyes glistening. Tony grinned back.

There, near the center of the geographical land masses of the world, Reg Danson reverently traced the strange inscription from another dawn with a trembling finger.

He stood suddenly and climbed up between rocks jammed together by time into misshapen, arthritic fingers pointing to the sky. He could not shake the feeling that if only he climbed high enough, things would come clear. A dozen or so feet higher was the top of a narrow ridge of mountain, dusted with white fog, as if two opposing rock slabs had been clapped together like chalkboard erasers.

Danson crested the ridge and looked down upon the Ark.

The dusky, looming immensity of it was staggering. One and a half football fields long, nearly five stories tall, it was deposited in a long, moraine shelf at the end of a river of ice. The two ends rested on land, but the space beneath the great belly of the Ark, once filled with ice, was now melted open. It was as if the Ark had slid to a gentle grounding as easily as a beached canoe.

It was a box, a gigantic, rectangular, dark brown box, flat on bottom and top save for a narrow row of raised windows extending the length of the roof. There was neither bow nor stern, but a gaping hole in the top and another in the side of the near end. The right side perched near the edge of a sheer precipice, plunging to the invisible, misty depths of the gorge.

All about the base of the craft were tumbled altars of stone where worshipers had bowed the knee. Against the side of the mountain rift was a ten-foot cross made of the vessel's timbers.

Danson's throat constricted, his mouth as dry as ash. His legs were of no use; he could do nothing but fall before it and utter a strangled cry.

". . . and on the seventeenth day of the seventh month the ark came to rest on the mountains of Ararat."

He felt lightheaded, disoriented. Smell, sight, sound ebbed and flowed in the supreme wonder of the diluvian shrine. He sensed, rather than saw, the flow of bodies rushing past and descending the decline. When they did take form, they were as fairies floating in cotton vapors, their joyous clamor filtered through a pillowy daze.

The Muslims stripped off their parkas and shirts and plunged into the powdery snow. In a rite of spiritual cleansing, they vigorously rubbed their skin with the icy crystals and flung it wildly into the air with exuberant shouts. Nuh had disembarked on *Al Judi*, the heights, just as it had been told them in the Koran. The hills of *Mahser*, doomsday, had given back the hostage Ark.

Cevdet, smiling incredulously as if he and the Ark had been raised from the dead together, knelt at the base of the mighty boat, arms outstretched, and placed both hands flat against her prehistoric side. His head dropped in prayer.

Ibrahim Hasan stretched his arms toward heaven. Bearded lips moved in silent recitation of Mohammed's vivid account of the flooding waters. When it ended, his eyes fell upon the rugged cross of gopher wood and he, too, could no longer stand. He fell to his knees a little way from Danson.

Tony knelt beside his father. He surveyed the inconceivable scene below, then squeezed his eyes tightly shut. He slung an arm over his father's back, and together they prayed.

"As the days of Noah were, so also will the coming of the Son of Man be," Reg spoke the words of Christ from the book of Matthew. "For as in the days before the flood, they were eating and drinking, marrying and giving in marriage, until the day Noah entered the ark, and did not know until the flood came and took them all away, so also will the coming of the Son of Man be" (24:37–39).

Lieutenant Cayan watched the two Americans, the younger cradling the elder before the amazing tableau. The arms of the cross spread just above their heads, stark black against the milky whiteness. She thought of the One who had hung there, mentioned ninety-three times in the Koran, Jesus the Christ. She thought of her people, her ambitions, her treacheries. Her shoulders sagged. She turned away and walked back down the hill.

SHKIDCHENKO focused the rifle scope until the crosshairs met crisply at the base of the American's spine. The Russian commander adjusted his position in the glacial blind fifty yards above the Landing

Place, resting his elbows more comfortably on a smoother portion of ice.

They'd been slow to overtake the expedition; not a single Turkish soldier had they been able to eliminate. Shkidchenko would waste no time.

At first he'd weighed killing the younger Danson first, then the elder. But he thought it kinder to let the son live to perhaps explore another day in a place far away from the scene of his father's death.

Shkidchenko would accomplish the necessary with one shot.

His blind was not in the path of an avalanche should the shot trigger one. His men were similarly stationed about the perimeter of the bowl containing the Ark, all instructed to hold their fire and allow any mass of falling snow and ice to do its work before they moved in for the spoils.

Patiently he waited for Reg Danson to straighten and allow a clean shot at the base of his skull, bloody visions of the wolf spinning to its death still fresh in the Russian's mind.

Shortly, Lieutenant General Nikolai Shkidchenko would climb to the roof of the Ark and proclaim to the fools in Moscow—the fools everywhere, for that matter—that while they'd spent so much time and guile on rising to the paltry top of humanity, the Grand Design had been working its own inexorable way toward the climax. The revolver in his pocket would place him well beyond their scurvy reach.

Suddenly, the American straightened, and the Russian's heart beat faster. The crosshairs found their mark, and the gunman began a slow squeeze on the trigger.

Father and son embraced, and the side of Tony's face filled Shkidchenko's view. He cursed and eased off the trigger, barely noticing the tears streaking the son's handsome features.

Then father and son released each other and turned back to the brooding Ark, the men splashing in its shadow. Again the crosshairs found the mark. The finger began the slow squeeze that would explode a shell from the chamber. The target did not move.

Neither did Shkidchenko. Cold steel slid silently across his throat to form a necklace of certain death. He had no desire to die like a gutted deer.

"Slowly release the trigger, my besotted friend," hissed a voice in his ear. The smell of campfires and a body unwashed filled the space between them. "Should the gun fire, you will not enjoy the close attention you will receive from this blade!"

The Russian general carefully relaxed his trigger finger, and the rifle was wrenched from his hands. He was unceremoniously hauled to his feet and smartly backhanded across the face.

"Introductions!" bawled his turbaned captor. "You have fallen into the capable hands of Muhammed Barzani, son of General Dara Mustafa Barzani, supreme commander of all Kurdish freedom fighters! And who are you besides the son of a withered she-wolf?"

Behind the Kurd stood a relieved Lieutenant Nilay Cayan. Their prisoner smiled ingratiatingly

and saluted sarcastically. "Lieutenant General Nikolai Ivan Shkidchenko, son of Major Peter Vladimir
Alexei Shkidchenko, supreme commander of the
czar's commission to find Noah's Ark. And these—"
he shouted, with an expansive sweep of his arm,
"—are my men!"

The smile drained from the general's face when
all fifty-five of Barzani's men stood, each with a
Kurdish warrior and a dagger at his throat.

The ringing shout of Barzani the Kurd reverberated around the Landing Place and seemed to rise in
volume. The frolicking Turkish soldiers froze in
their tracks, then dashed madly for their weapons.
Barzani roared at the abashed Turks. It was im-
mensely satisfying to catch them with their rifles
down.

Reg raised a hand to stay them. Barzani grinned.
"Allah sends kindest regards, Mr. Danson. How is the
throat?"

"Healed nicely, thank you," Reg responded.
"When I return to America, I intend to continue
shaving with the dagger of the Pesh Mergas. It seems
to shave closer somehow."

Barzani's rollicking guffaws threatened to bring
the mountain down on top of them, but soon Danson's men nervously returned the laughter.

A MERRY and busy camp bivouacked that
afternoon with the Ark of Noah at its center.

Inside and out, the vessel was inspected, photo-
graphed, tested, and recorded. Most of the animal
stalls were missing, having long ago become relics

for the faithful, but the hull of the Ark was incredibly sound, except for the two manmade wounds in its structure. The one in the ceiling was probably an enlargement of the open window through which Noah sent a raven and a dove to find dry land. The one in the side was most likely an extension of the door through which the animals and humans passed on their way to replenish the earth.

Ahmed, having recovered from the blow the priest delivered to his head and threatened with criminal prosecution for attempted murder, was placed under guard. Tony and a Turkish munitions man made sure that Kassem set the explosive charges honestly and precisely. They would free the far end of the Ark from the last remnant of glacier still holding on and loosen the moraine wherever the Ark touched ground. The Russian captives were set to work clearing the snow and debris from the Ark's interior.

A fire made of the captured Russian equipment sleds burned brightly in the center of camp as the sun at last slid from sight. Barzani's men took turns guarding the Russian soldiers and sang and danced about the fire with verve and passion, seeming never to tire of leaping and whirling and making the canyons ring with florid love songs of heart-wrenching intensity.

Tony joined in the merriment, flinging himself about the encampment with the best of them. He wished he knew the Kurdish tongue so that Lieutenant Cayan did not have to keep interpreting and he could sing along. The two of them had taken tentative steps towards friendship. When he tried the only

Turkish phrase he could remember, overheard at the door of a crumbling garage in Istanbul, she laughed until she very nearly fell into the fire.

"What? What's it mean?" Tony feigned anxiety.

"*Otomobil yaglar mos miz*. Please grease my car!" She laughed again, and he saw at last what his father found so captivating.

Reg did not join in the gaiety. For the eighth or ninth time he climbed the rope ladder to the top of the Ark and walked on its petrified surface. Every time he felt the elemental fires of creation burning through the soles of his boots. *How many living beings had ever been this close to the origins of man?*

Still, the thought was oddly unsatisfying. Though he did not share the hilarity of the party, he did not begrudge celebration. This was the zenith of human discovery, and they deserved to rejoice and savor it. Yet the revelry below reminded him of the Israelites romping before the golden calf.

In a few moments he would radio President Thurston Pierce and announce the impossible. It would be another shot heard around the world, only this time the repercussions ought to rock the very soul of humankind. Bombastic Bascomb would be there in the White House with Laura and Thurston Pierce and others whose stars would rise with the announcement. For that matter, Reg contemplated, his own star stood to rise a constellation or two.

Had God heard his prayer of confession when it seemed the Ark had been taken away? Was this God's answer? Unsettling tendrils of doubt, somber and haggard from overuse, crept unbidden into his thoughts. They'd come when he'd looked up that afternoon and saw daggers and rifles—the Russian soldiers, young and scared like kids, fearing for their very lives. Was God pleased that men were fighting and killing over the Ark?

ARTHUR Bryce might have said it best: "There's something very sad in the solving of a mystery." After all, the Ark was only made of wood. To be sure, it was an awe-inspiring ancient engineering marvel, but so were the pyramids. And what had the quest for this wooden box done to his relationship with God? As soon as God pulled back this carrot of Reg's own making, Reg had cursed God and doubted his Creator and Savior. The Ark had not deepened Danson's faith in God; it had threatened to destroy it.

The sun departed and the flicker of firelight licked sensuously over the surfaces of the Ark. Danson's skin crawled. The partying group below—he—had made the Ark an idol.

And something else . . . A change had come that afternoon when they'd come to Cevdet's "dead-end." A new stillness in the air, a hush, had transcended their dejection and sense of loss.

The periodic rumblings of ice sheering off the face of Black Glacier and crashing into Ahora's throat had abruptly ceased. The wildly fluctuating temperature had as suddenly stabilized and dropped. No longer did water run; they had melted ice in buckets for supper for the first time in two days.

The temperature was falling, and Danson skidded on the ice forming on the Ark's roof. This freeze was deep and irreversible.

Ice was also forming about his heart. He had known hatred for his son on this mountain. A woman he knew little about had easily stolen his love for his wife, and even when she had proven herself a Mata Hari, he yearned for her embrace. Kurdish, Armenian, Russian, and Turkish interests collided at every bend in the path, and what was so noble in America's interest? An election coup?

Violence, death, murderers on every side—a pretty place for salvation's boat to harbor! "As the days of Noah were, so also will the coming of the Son of Man be." The days of Noah had broken God's heart. "The LORD saw that the wickedness of man was great in the earth, and that every intent of the thoughts of his heart was only evil continually" (Gen. 6:5). Reg had believed the Ark was the answer to all the questions. Instead, it seemed the source.

Would plastic ashtrays with slivers of Ark embedded in them one day be given as service station premiums?

The boys of Dragonfly One, the Sky Crane command post, had informed him that transmission space was cleared for one in the morning on Baby Huey, the powerful Titan VII communications satellite that would beam the announcement to the eager ears in Washington. It was now two minutes after one. Reg switched on the radio transmitter that would connect him to the White House.

"Massis One to Uncle. Massis One to Uncle, do you copy?"

A celestial hum, static, hum was all he heard.

"Massis One to Uncle, come in Uncle, over," he repeated.

The hum intensified, then cut out altogether. A male voice from across the continents spoke clearly. "Uncle to Massis One, Uncle to One, we copy clear and sweet. The president is here. Go ahead, Massis One, go ahead. Over."

Reg took a deep breath, looked over the quieting camp, and pressed the transmission switch. "Uncle, Massis One has claimed the prize. It is pure gold and ready for lift-off at 0900 our time this morning. Dragonflies alerted, all systems go. Over."

He could hear whistles and cheers as the White House crowd toasted the news and the radio operator excitedly responded. "Roger, One! Thumbs up for all! President Pierce standing by!"

The radio spit static in short spurts as the president took the microphone. "Congratulations, Massis One! You have brought news of great joy to many hearts this day. A parade awaits your return, a commemorative medallion is being struck in honor of you all, and we've broken ground for a Noah's Ark exhibit hall at the Smithsonian. You have our gratitude and our prayers. Over!"

Reg's throat tightened, and it was a long moment before he could respond.

"Massis One, Massis One, are you reading okay? Over?"

"Roger, Uncle. Let's talk again when Noah's on the ground. Over."

"Roger, One. You—" The radio operator sounded as if he'd been interrupted by someone loud and nearby. The familiar boom of his employer's voice echoed in the Landing Place. "Reg, lad, are you there? Are you okay? This is Bascomb. No, don't say anything; just listen. We should have gotten you off that mountain the minute the quakes started. We will now—you can bank on it. Bring the Ark back without a hitch and you're reinstated at the Smithsonian—no loss of tenure, and apologies from the bimbos who are now parking cars for a living. They'll have to wait in line, though. I've got another mystery or two I want you to check out. In two weeks I'm flying you to the Ubangi-Congo basin of central Africa. Pygmies in the Likouala Swamp are terrified of Mokele-Mbembe, a thirty-five-foot creature that rises out of the river and kills them. I believe it's a living dinosaur, and I want you to bring one back alive. The way I've got it figured —"

"Massis One, Massis One, this is Uncle. Mr. Bascomb sends his thanks for a job superbly done and will discuss details with you upon your return. You need your rest, and we've got serious celebrating to attend to. Good night, good flying, and Godspeed. This is Uncle going off channel. Over and out!"

"Massis One, out."

Reg sat still on the roof of the Ark for a long while, the radio transmitter dangling limply from his fingers.

He would have prayed had there been anything more to say.

30

L IGHT BEGAN to seep back into the world, a pale, milky film shot with gray and smutty black.

August 15. The freeze had returned.

The combination of plummeting temperatures and exhausting celebration had narcotized most of the camp to the coming dawn.

Let them sleep while they can.

At gunpoint the Russian troops had cleared away the blocking debris from inside and beneath the Ark. A man could stand crouched over under the massive bulk. The aerial harness would pass underneath easily. Ahmed Kassem had detonated low-intensity explosives, and all was ready for the immense Sky Cranes with their 75-foot wingspans and vertical lift capacities of 250 tons.

That had been the plan. But now the plan would have to be changed.

The Great Melt was over. An ash plume from twelve-thousand-foot Lesser Ararat to the east towered upward two thousand feet into the air. The tremors had died down, and there was an eerie calm. That's when volcanoes liked to erupt.

Reg hadn't eaten much in the last twenty-four hours, and he felt light-headed, feverish. He had spent the hours before first light wondering how many of the animals that set foot, hoof, and paw on the ground outside the Ark and flowed down onto the great Anatolian plain in a mighty zoological din of whistles, squawks, peeps, and roars, still walked the earth. The grand parade of furry, scaly, leathery, and feathery beasts had departed Ararat fifty thousand strong. Today, a dwindling fraction endured in the face of ever-increasing innovative methods for their destruction. Even the days of those who romped in the sea while the Ark rolled the swells above were likewise numbered.

August 15. The earth was a dangerous place, and he and his crew were fools to be where they were not wanted, not really, rescuing an object better left buried.

No one else stirred, no one to see him remove the batteries from the radio to prevent long distance hysterics—and interference. No one saw him place the stiff lumps of blasting gelatin along the walls inside the Ark. The explosives were a product of Nitro Nobel, Sweden, and though invented in 1875 by Alfred Nobel himself, few more powerful explosives had been manufactured. They had been included in the supplies manifest in case some portion of the Ark proved strongly captive to the surrounding geology. The gelatin had been mixed with implosive and incendiary agents to apply maximum force with minimum noise and concussion.

Into the center of each lump he placed a tiny remote detonator. He took one last look about the cavernous interior of the Ark, so ingeniously
illuminated by the double row of skylights fifty feet
above. He thought of Noah and his family tending to
the precious breeding stock for the restoration of life
on earth.

The Ark existed; the Flood occurred; God was
faithful as recorded in the Bible, the Koran, the cuneiform stones. They had documented, recorded, and
pinpointed it from every conceivable angle. More
than one hundred credible eyewitnesses of six nationalities could verify the discovery. Photographs,
measurements, wood samples—they had it all.

But the Ark itself must be destroyed. It was far
better hidden than found. People would worship it,
kill for it, mock again the God who commanded it
built. It was an idol, a stumbling block to true
belief—a sideshow Ark for an admission fee. What of
the throngs of humanity who saw the Ark, watched
it being built, *before* the Flood? How many of them
had believed and were saved? *Not one!*

*Blessed are those who have not seen and yet
have believed.*

The air was biting, swirling patches of black fog
hovering over the camp like ugly hags. Stinging snow
sprayed the camp with buckshot, yet no one moved.

He had made certain none slept near the Ark.
The prisoners and their Kurdish keepers had removed themselves to a wide snow field halfway back
to the helipad. The sentries could see nothing of the
Ark from there.

Danson's hands shook; the trembling made it

difficult to locate the detonator control pack. To reduce the great Ark of Noah to powder and kindling was . . . unthinkable? Humankind would revile him; believers would forsake him. And God? He believed now that God had brought him to this cleft in the rock of Ararat to eliminate Noah's Ark before it spiritually and physically ruined others as it had very nearly ruined him.

He walked to a little rise beyond the camp and turned to look upon the great hulk for the last time. Was it constructed of an extinct wood? Would they discover upon further analysis that it contained properties critical to human survival? He snorted at such childish fantasies. Human survival *had* depended upon that wood once before. A pitiful few had staked their future on its spiritual properties then; few, if any, would take eternal stock in its physical properties now.

God would not be mocked by the vessel used for salvation. Satan had used for ill the Ark that God had meant for good.

God would forgive.

Reg Danson aimed the control pack at the Ark. His finger quivered over the fire button and froze.

Tony Danson stood on the edge of the roof of the Ark.

"Get down from there, Tony!" Reg cried, memories of Barbara scolding their four-year-old son standing on a stack of books piled on a chair, stretching for the forbidden cookies on the top shelf. "Get down!"

"Mornin', Dad!" Tony sang out. "A little overcast here at Six Flags over Ararat, but otherwise a great day for riding the Ark into the sky!"

"I'm still in command, Tony!" Reg shouted across at him. "It would be a mistake to expose the Ark to this generation. They'd spit on it or treat it like a direct-mail miracle prayer cloth. Look how crazy and unfeeling I became. I wanted the Ark for my personal trophy. How many more would feel that way? No, Son, the thing to do is to destroy it, hide it for all time, remove the risk of its ever becoming an historical sideshow, a plaything of the rich and powerful. Believe me, Tony—it's best this way."

Tony sat down on the edge of the roof, dangling his feet over the side, rubbing the timeless wood affectionately. Then he cupped his hands and yelled back, "Remember that stinking whale skeleton you, me, and Mom put together? Being the brilliant kid I was, I tried to get your goat about God because I knew how dear He was to you. I coughed up all that stuff about whales walking on land because I couldn't see how you could risk your reputation over a creation flap. Compromise couldn't be that bad a thing if it doubled the number of cars in the garage. What I didn't tell you was how incredibly moved I was by working, *standing,* inside the ribcage of leviathan!"

Reg said nothing, his tears falling on the remote control pack.

"I've seen the Ark, Dad," said Tony, choking back his own emotion, "and I believe!"

Reg thought of another mountain in another time. How a father and his son had climbed together, the son in obedience, the father in a quest for faith sorely tried and found true. It was for the best that a sacrifice be made, for the best that the son become that sacrifice. The son bound to the altar, the knife in the father's hand, the weapon raised to kill. The Lord would provide. God spoke; a sacrificial ram struggled in a thicket nearby; the son was spared. Faith won out.

Tony was a test. The Lord would provide. Tears streamed down Reg's face; his heart threatened to explode. He squeezed his eyes shut, steadied his outstretched arm, and felt for the button.

"*Selamunaleykum*, peace be to you, gentlemen," came a cheery voice from Reg's left. "*Masallah!* Glory be to God!"

With a swirling of brown robes bound in a bright yellow parka, Hasan, the holy man, chattering like a magpie, strode into the clearing between Reg and the Ark. He waved his tattered Bible at Tony, paused, breathed deeply of the crisp air, and looked deeply into the tortured eyes of his American friend. "Ah, such a discovery, Noah's Ark. Still, I have found one greater, Mr. Danson! Jesus Christ!"

Reg looked dumbly from Hasan to his son and back to the beaming *hoca. Provision, thy name is Ibrahim Hasan.*

"Truly, Mr. Danson, this extraordinary borning-again business is quite unlike the first time. I understand that I, Hasan the infant, greeted the world hindquarters first. This second time, I greet the world full-faced, declaring He is Lord!"

He looked to the sky, a sweet smile wreathing his face, the old made young again. "This is eternal life, that we may know You, the only true God, and Jesus Christ whom You have sent."

He gently took the control pack from Reg, then clasped his rough hands around Reg's, steadying them.

"The Ark is different things to different people, Mr. Danson. Look at the multitudes who had the law and the prophets and Christ Himself, and did not believe. Yet many did. You and I and your son are legacies of those believers. Leave Noah's Ark to God, and He will work in men according to His own good will."

Reg smiled and grasped Hasan's forearms. "I don't know, Ibrahim—perhaps you're right. I guess this bears further . . . research!" They looked to the murky sky and laughed joyously at large wet flakes floating into their mouths and eyes. Tony joined them and the three embraced. No rainbows arched overhead, no doves alighted, no olive branches were in sight, but the trio was at peace.

Abruptly, Tony broke free and began gathering stones into a pile. Hasan dashed about, adding to the collection. With a whoop of delight, Reg harvested some, and the makeshift altar rose waist-high.

From the ridge above, Muhammed Barzani, his men, and their Russian captives, looked on in silence. There was a commotion at the rear, a shout, and Nikolai Shkidchenko burst through the clot of men. As he ran down the slope, clutching an ancient rock to his chest, a rifle was leveled at his back. But no shot was fired. Barzani's upraised hand forbade it.

Lieutenant Cayan walked slowly into the clearing, wondering if she belonged. Reg smiled reassuringly, reached for her hand, and placed in it a stone.

Ibrahim Hasan riffled the pages of the old Bible, laughed aloud with exceeding joy, and read from Genesis:

"I will never again curse the ground for man's sake, although the imagination of man's heart is evil from his youth; nor will I again destroy every living thing as I have done.

> While the earth remains,
> Seedtime and harvest,
> Cold and heat, Winter and summer,
> And day and night
> Shall not cease."

Without warning, the ground beneath the Landing Place began to rock and roll.

HIGH atop the mountain of agony, up where man never stood, some three thousand feet above and beyond the rejoicers and altar builders, devil winds and demon cold awoke and rode the backs of foggy steeds down, down. Stampeding wildly off the ledges of unseen heights, they streamed and drained down the mountain's jagged back. Currents of ice and snow, whipped by merciless winter overseers, fled in screaming mayhem before the mindless beating.

And deep in the mountain, superheated molten rock from the earth's liquid center blasted to the surface with brute velocity.

VOLCANOLOGIST GEORGE LACEY was shaking. He had pulled every string he had to get President Pierce to leave the celebration at the White House, already six hours old, and talk to him. The president looked a little green around the gills, but one glance at Lacey's countenance and the commander in chief was all ears.

Lacey looked as if he were in the late stages of malarial fever. He was sweating profusely, he had a three-day growth of beard, and he smelled like a gymnasium. Seventy-two hours of coffee and donuts, no sleep, and no bath will do that to a man.

"Mr. President, Mount Ararat is going to blow its stack in the next twelve hours," he said in a cracked, hoarse voice. "She's at least two thousand feet taller today than she was when she emerged from the Flood. Over thousands of years, that means the cinder cone was built up by frequent—repeat, *frequent*—volcanic activity with a capital *A*."

Pierce started to protest, but Lacey's labored

breathing and general agitation stopped him. He waved the man to continue.

"I've just learned from my contacts at the volcanic monitoring station in Kars, Turkey, that you have a team of researchers half a mile from the summit of Ararat. Why they were not evacuated when the rest of the Anatolian populace was, I don't know, but, Mr. President, to leave them there a moment longer is mass murder. I can't say it any plainer than that."

Pierce got to his feet. "I'm afraid it would be impossible to abort the mission now, Mr.—what was the name, Macy?"

"Lacey, sir."

"Mr. Lacey. You've done your job. But I've taken full responsibility. Some missions are too important to stop."

"The Noah's Ark Expedition is not one of them," said Secretary of State Frederick Delaney, striding into the office with the vice president of the United States and several FBI officers. George Lacey sank to a chair, suddenly drained of his last ounce of strength. Pierce was so stunned to see Delaney alive that he collapsed speechlessly onto another chair.

"Sorry for the shock, Thirsty, but I didn't know any other way to do this," said Delaney as the FBI agents flanked the president. "I saw the handwriting on the wall long ago, and when you sent me to the Caribbean the other day for 'a little rest and relaxation,' I figured you meant to shut me up permanently. So I had the Coast Guard report a dummy plane missing with me aboard, and I went into hiding until the State Department could verify the Ark expedition had not been evacuated despite a Turkish Civil Defense Emergency declaration—by your direct orders."

"Uh, Freddy, lis—listen to me," stammered Pierce, a slight slur in the words.

"Not now, Mr. President, we haven't a moment to lose. We need to radio Reg Danson and tell him to prepare for evacuation."

THE expedition team heard the approaching tempest and felt the ground convulse beneath them. They ran for the Landing Place—they, Barzani's men, and their captives—and cried out to God. They begged God to spare their lives.

The sky grew dark, as if the rising sun held no power here. A seething, roiling mass of thunderclouds obliterated the day. The numbing cold turned bones brittle and fingers awkward and inflexible. Someone shouted, pointing at the peak. Smoke and ash belched from the crater, and brilliant orange veins of lava snaked down the mountain toward them. Without warning a torrent of melted snow and ice burst over the stone wall where Shkidchenko had taken aim on the Dansons, and rained down upon the Landing Place.

"Allah have mercy!" screamed Ahmed Kassem in terror. Guns dropped uselessly, all distinction gone between captor and captive. A frightened human wail ascended the cliffs of Ararat. Weeping, their faces in their hands, the people huddled around Reg Danson. He stood in their midst, holding Ibrahim Hasan's Bible to the sinister sky.

"Almighty Jehovah!" he shouted above the bedlam descending the mountain toward them. "You have told us through Your apostle Paul that *nothing* can separate us from Your love, neither death nor life nor demons—"

Two cataracts of hot sulfur water thundered over the stone wall; a third shot out over their heads as if from a fire hose. Voices raw with screams and pleadings, they shrank inside their parkas for protection from the rain of liquid fire.

Reg grabbed Tony's hand and held tight. "Neither the present nor the future, nor any powers can divide us from Your love!" The sky cracked in a thousand lightning-shattered shards. The ground heaved and rolled, but the tightly packed bodies held, and Reg did not fall.

Stinking, steaming water gurgled and swirled around their little knoll. The orange veins split and cracked and flared tongues of fire, so close now that molten death must soon pour over their skin and reduce them to cinders. The crying, moaning men looked imploringly at the hole in the Ark, willing the vessel to become seaworthy and save them from the horror to come.

A mass of fiery ash blew onto Danson's neck and burned deep into the flesh. He bellowed against the elements but did not release his hold on Tony's hand or drop the Bible. He gritted his teeth in defiance of the searing pain and cried louder, "Not *anything* else in all creation will be able to separate us from the love of God that is in Christ Jesus our Lord!"

They heard a new sound distinct and near, so different from the random shrieking of nature. The mechanical "shwoop! shwoop!" of helicopter blades chopped the air rhythmically. An enormous flying crane, half dragonfly, half praying mantis, materialized out of the darkness and hovered over the Landing Place. The thin white body and black numerals denoting Israeli aircraft reflected the oranges and yellows of lightning and lava. Men in aviator jumpsuits and white helmets maneuvered the craft into position. Though roughly buffeted by the hot winds, powerful on-board gyrostabilizers steadied the Sky Crane.

Slung from the monster machine's gaunt belly was a giant rectangular basket. "We will lower the rescue bin," said a clipped voice through a bullhorn. "When it touches ground, load thirty-five only from your party. Once inside the bin, sit around the walls. Engage the safety belts and use the hand grips for balance. Do not, I repeat *do not*, stand once you are airborne. Another aircraft will move into position when we have cleared the site."

Instantly, the rescue bin was lowered and Reg, Tony, Nilay, and Ibrahim supervised the loading as best they could. Men leapt frantically into the bin without regard for nationality, political persuasion, or religious conviction. The more disciplined among the Turkish and Russian soldiers held back and let others take the places they might have secured if they'd jumped first. The wriggling, momentarily confused ball of humanity on the bin floor quickly sorted itself out, and men snapped themselves into the safety belts and grabbed for the hand grips as if they would be safe if only they could squeeze hard enough.

In this dreadful life-and-death game of musical chairs, there were two men too many. For one awful moment, no one moved; then a Russian soldier unsnapped his belt and gave up his place. The second stranded man was one of the geologists, and he quickly bailed over the side as the basket was jerked heavenward. A few of the Russians crossed themselves furiously as the mountain fell away, and thousands of feet of empty space suddenly separated them from the ground below. The bin was winched within fifty feet of the Sky Crane, and the chopper veered off toward the military base at Karaköse.

As the second helicopter jockeyed for position, an explosion at the summit spun all heads in that direction. A geyser of molten lava sprayed the heavens, then fell back to earth in scarlet splashes. The second basket was quickly loaded, and the passengers were wrenched skyward without ceremony.

A third mutant chopper swung into view and hovered directly overhead the moment the second veered toward the safety of the plain. Short, severe blasts of hot wind slapped the craft like a giant cat batting at a catnip mouse. The basket rose and fell, rose and fell, knocking its fearful occupants into a jumble on the floor before they could secure the safety belts. A Turkish soldier managed to get just one leg over the side before he was flung doll-like into the outstretched arms of those remaining to be rescued.

The copilot of the fourth Sky Crane grabbed a bullhorn and shouted above the rising wind, "Is your radio damaged? We've tried raising you—nothing but dead silence. If you can, turn it to frequency nine, repeat, frequency nine."

Reg grabbed his pack, removed the radio, reinserted the batteries, and fumbled with the dial. The water steaming over the Landing Place reeked of brimstone, and the air sizzled with static electricity. A bloody orange fountain of lava gushed from Ararat's churning belly and spurted down the mountain with alarming speed. Most of the remaining team members shouted a needless warning—every eye was already riveted on the summit in hopeless fascination. The bowl of rock and ice surrounding them amplified the howls and roars of nature gone mad.

Reg forced himself to concentrate and fix on frequency nine, but before he could signal the men in the helicopter, the muzzle of a submachine gun pressed coldly against the back of his head. "I will take that, American fool!" Wild-eyed, face purple with a mindless excitement, Lieutenant General Shkidchenko ripped the transmitter from Danson's grip and pressed the switch.

"You will *not* abandon the Ark of Noah!" the Russian commander barked into the handset. "It is of far greater value than a few wasted lives, so listen to me carefully. Release the bin and lower the harness cable. Radio the other pilots to land their passengers and return with their portions of the Ark harness at maximum speed. We will make ready to attach the apparatus. Deviate from my instructions, and I will shoot everyone, including Reg Danson! Do what I say and do it *now!*" Shkidchenko switched off the radio and smashed it hard against the rocks. It lay in the rising water, shattered and silent.

The helicopter crew stalled five seconds too long. Shkidchenko turned on Tony and pulled the trigger. The muzzle spit fire. Tony tumbled backward into a pile of packs, the smoking sleeve of his parka soaked in blood. Reg jumped forward and met the submachine gun barrel as it swung in his direction. He kicked the barrel upward, and a yellow-white tracer of bullets rent the ugly sky. Ararat answered with a roar and a mighty shudder. Rock and ash fell in a fiery hailstorm. Screaming and clutching each other to keep from falling, expedition members bolted for the protection of the Ark.

Cevdet Demirkol darted from boulder to boulder in the rocky declension behind the armed Russian. He could not get to a gun without being seen, nor could he get close enough to use his scimitar without being heard. In his hand was one of Norman Leagues' stainless steel pans for sterilizing surgical instruments. A clap of thunder rattled the clearing, and Cevdet ran forward.

Shkidchenko turned at the sound of splashing from behind and received a panful of scalding water on his right cheek and ear. He screamed, whirled, and tore open Cevdet's left leg from knee to thigh with a stream of hot lead from the machine gun. The faithful Janissary fell back onto a table of rock and grabbed his leg in agony.

Before Danson could seize the advantage, the Russian commander leveled the barrel of the machine gun at Ibrahim Hasan, hatred for the betrayer twisting his mouth into an evil slit. Lieutenant

Cayan jumped in front of the priest and faced gun and gunman with a prayer for deliverance. Shkidchenko looked at her with surprise and a begrudging admiration. There was movement to his right and he fired upon Ahmed Kassem, stopping the munitions expert in his tracks unhurt, but shaking with fear. Shkidchenko looked back at Cayan and nodded once, lips in an mocking sneer.

A wide river of molten lava oozed over the rock face and raced for the ship. Eyes nearly bugging out of his head, Shkidchenko lunged and whipped the butt of the machine gun in a vicious upward arc, catching Danson a glancing blow on the chin. Reg crashed onto his back, stunned, and the wily lieutenant general grabbed Ahmed Kassem and rammed the barrel of the gun into his side. "Move!" he shouted savagely.

Kassem and Shkidchenko dodged falling debris and the released rescue basket cable, and reached the Ark a hundred feet ahead of the wave of lava. Prodding with the machine gun, Shkidchenko herded Kassem up a ladder to the roof of the Ark.

Lightning stabbed the ground in blinding streaks. Deafening bombs of thunder blasted the Landing Place. Shkidchenko held the gun on Kassem and shook a fist at heaven. "You will not destroy this holy boat!" he raged, the cords in his neck bulging from the strain. "Lieutenant General Nikolai Shkidchenko claims the Ark of Noah in the name of Mother Russia!"

Never had Allah seemed farther from Ahmed Kassem. He prepared to be devoured by the devils of Ararat.

Reg's senses cleared and he looked into the business end of a heavy steel shackle descending from the Sky Crane above. "Tony, you okay, son?" he called.

"Yeah, Dad. Just my arm, that's all."

Reg thanked God for Tony's stamina and called to Cevdet. "Demirkol, are you with us, friend?" A weak, gasping answer told Danson the man still had fight left in him.

Reg reached for the cable and jumped on. He was hoisted with wrenching speed into the air.

Sailing above the fantastic scene below, Reg prayed for a miracle. He did not know why but he wanted more than anything to save the morbid Iraqi. In some ways, Shkidchenko couldn't have seized a more unlikely hostage. Most of the expedition forces wouldn't have given a counterfeit bus token to redeem the pessimistic munitions expert. But that made it seem even more right, even urgent, that Reg do so. He and Ahmed had both bungled their faith, and Reg did not want Kassem to be cheated of another opportunity to see the light.

It was so dark now, would any of them ever see the light again?

The Sky Crane circled behind the Ark, out over the bottomless Ahora chasm. Reg felt his insides heave as the chopper turned and centrifugal force flung him outward like the parachute ride at the county fair. If he lost his grip now, his body would never be found.

Suddenly the turn was complete, and he accelerated at incredible speed toward the two men on the roof of the Ark. Danson zeroed in on the back of Nikolai Shkidchenko, still shaking a defiant fist at God.

The lava surged ever closer to the Ark, and Shkidchenko stared at it, mesmerized by the malevolent
flow that threatened to seal the Ark forever in a volcanic entombment. He waved the gun menacingly,
cursing the lava as if it could be halted by mere
threats.

Reg's gloved hands gripped the cable firmly. The
thunder crashed without pause, and just as they
sailed over the roof of the great boat, the pilot hit the
searchlight.

Shkidchenko jerked around and faced the blinding light, his mouth a feral snarl. Reg braced himself,
extended his legs and looked full into the demented
eyes of the military commander. He struck Shkidchenko square in the chest and felt the sudden drag
of Kassem leaping onto his back.

The gunman cartwheeled over the edge of the
roof, still clutching the machine gun, and disappeared beneath the surging lava.

Danson and Kassem glided to earth and hit the
ground running. Ararat roared and exploded its anger, orange rivers of lava cracking the unnatural
night created by the descending ash cloud. Reg
looked back, and the last he saw of Noah's Ark, it
was enveloped in a gray blanket of blinding ash. Like
the prop in some gigantic magic show, it was there
one minute and gone without trace the next.

Choking and retching from the hot, ashy air, Reg
joined the others racing for the rescue bin being lowered from one of the other Sky Cranes returned from
Karaköse. He grabbed Cevdet, pale and bloody, and
with the help of Tony's good arm dragged the

wounded man to the bin. They tumbled and pulled one another inside in a frantic rush to be free of the descending terror.

The last of the expedition cleared the mountain, great gusts of frigid air at last filling their lungs with sweet blessed oxygen. Behind them, the Mother of the Earth boomed her objections to their hasty retreat.

Reg Danson held his wounded son all the way to Karaköse.

Epilogue

NEWSPAPERS HEADLINED the narrow escape of scores of climbers from the heaving shoulders of Mount Ararat in eastern Turkey. The heroic airmen from Jerusalem received commendations for bravery.

Full-page color photographs of the Ark caused a brief international sensation, lengthy interviews with the explorers filling the media from Moscow to Washington, D.C. One long feature dealt with the refusal of the expedition's American leader to accept reinstatement at the Smithsonian Institution.

But with the failure to retrieve the Ark itself, debaters were soon explaining the phenomenon away. Perhaps what the expedition found was a replica of the original, built on the heights by zealous religionists who wanted the world to believe the story of the Flood. History was replete with examples of zealots going to great lengths for sanctified reasons.

Other news reported the rapid spread of Christianity in metropolitan Istanbul and how one particularly fiery ex-Muslim priest had ignited the hearts of his people to conversion with the aid of a former Turkish Janissary at his side. They were particularly effective in revival-style meetings held on military bases throughout the country. Turkey's Third Army spokesperson, the first woman ever promoted to the rank of general, said the energetic priest was planning to raise funds for a mosque in the poorest shanty town on the outskirts of Istanbul.

The men shot on Mount Ararat fully recovered from their wounds. Tony Danson returned to school but took to spending as much time as possible helping his dad prepare for a trip to Africa. Reports of mysterious, "prehistoric" creatures on the attack, demanded investigation.

The mountain Kurds, who along with their Armenian and Muslim fundamentalist allies had kept eastern Anatolia in a dangerous state of agitation, sued for peace. They found an unlikely coalition of Iranian, Iraqi, and Turkish representatives at long last amenable to establishment of a Kurdistani homeland.

In a stunning political turnabout, U.S. President Thurston Pierce resigned three months before the election, citing personal reasons including poor health. His running mate, Frederick Delaney, once secretary of state, went on to win the election. One of his first presidential acts was to turn the newest, but vacant, Smithsonian exhibit hall into a giant indoor theme park. "Disney D.C." became a living exhibit of American fun.

Presidential challenger Matthew Handford had lost momentum in September when the voters learned that family influence, not pacifistic ideals, had kept him out of the Persian Gulf War.

Mount Ararat never did experience a full-scale eruption, and the plains population was allowed to return home. Shifting weather patterns created a massive convergent zone over the mountain following the period of exceptional melt. Lowland shepherds below six thousand feet reported harrowing tales of bears and wolves descending from the heights to escape the severe cold and setting upon the flocks with a singular savagery. Many shepherds chose to flee, but not before several lost their lives. The military was ordered to move the upper nomads to safer pasture.

In the Year of the Great Freeze, Ararat's secrets were once again secure.

> He who forms mountains,
> And creates the wind,
> Who declares to man what his thought is,
> And makes the morning darkness,
> Who treads the high places of the earth—
> The LORD God of hosts is His name.
>
> Amos 4:13

The End